THE Q

THE Q

AMY TINTERA

CROWN

NEW YORK

Text copyright © 2022 by Amy Tintera
Jacket art copyright © 2022 by Robert Ball

Visit us on the Web! GetUnderlined.com

Educators and librarians, for a variety of teaching tools, visit us at RHTeachersLibrarians.com

Library of Congress Cataloging-in-Publication Data is available upon request.
ISBN 978-0-593-48617-7 (hardcover) — ISBN 978-0-593-48618-4 (lib. bdg.) — ISBN 978-0-593-48619-1 (ebook)

The text of this book is set in 11-point Plantin.
Interior design by Ken Crossland

Printed in the United States of America
10 9 8 7 6 5 4 3 2 1
First Edition

THE Q

RADIO QUARANTINE WITH HADLEY LOPEZ

Special Joint US/Quarantine Zone Broadcast

HI, KIDS, THIS is Maisie Rojas, coming to you live from the Q.

That's right, I'm inside the quarantine zone *right now*. I was born here, actually, eighteen years ago, when all of you were just a twinkle in your parents' eyes.

Hadley Lopez was kind enough to let me jump on her program today, so don't worry, all you Q listeners. Your girl will be back shortly.

I'm here today because schools in the good ol' US of A are trying a new thing this year, letting some of us inside the Q record a segment for you guys as part of your history lessons. Which is cool, I guess. I mean, I always thought school was boring as hell, but maybe I can spice things up a bit for you. And for those of you in the Q, we thought we'd broadcast this to you live, just for fun. If you don't like it, turn it off! I don't care.

So! They want me to tell you a little about the history of the Q, from my perspective. I told them it was probably a bad idea to let me do this, but here we are. No one can say I didn't warn you.

All right, they told me to start at the beginning, which I think you all already know, but whatever. They said they want to hear my version of events. So here we go.

There was a virus, and it was bad. Death, sadness, et cetera.

I'm probably supposed to tell you some science stuff here, but I slept through those classes. You have the internet out there, don't you? You can look it up.

Anyway, this virus started in Austin, Texas, which I hear was a pretty nice place back in the day. It quickly spread to Houston and Dallas and some other places I forgot. The US government, which had dealt with two major pandemics in the past twenty years, was like, "Yo, we got this, we got this."

They built a massive quarantine zone around Austin and started shuttling all the sick people over there. Everyone without symptoms went to a separate quarantine zone.

Problem was, a lot of people couldn't get out of the Austin quarantine zone, even if they weren't sick yet. Some people, like my parents, didn't have a car and couldn't catch one of the buses because there weren't nearly enough. You had to, like, fight to the death to get on one of those buses, and my parents weren't about that life.

Your history classes will probably teach you that it was just the unlucky people or the stupid ones who stuck around and caught the virus, but that's a load of shit. It was mostly just the poor people.

Wait, Hadley is holding up a piece of paper telling me I can't say "shit." Well, fu . . . dge. I'll try to clean up the language, kids.

Right, so we have this quarantine zone with all the sick people, and it's a real bummer in there, because it turns out that the virus has a 40 percent mortality rate.

On the upside, the president of the United States has become a damn hero for containing the virus before it spread outside of Texas and killed half the world's population. Good for him, I guess.

Meanwhile, the 60 percent who lived and were still in the Q were like, "Hey, are we getting out of here or what?"

Spoiler alert: they did not get out.

Because, bad news—this virus does not provide long-term immunity to people who get infected with it. Which meant everyone inside the Q kept getting sick, over and over, and no one could develop an effective vaccine because the virus kept mutating. On the plus side, the mortality rate kept getting better, so people weren't dropping dead left and right anymore.

People started to try to escape the Q, which did not go great for them. President Howard was like, "Yo, that's not cool," and built a huge-ass wall around the whole Q to keep us all in.

He said it made people feel safer while they worked on a vaccine. Dude had to do something—it was an election year!

He won, by the way.

Inside, everything went to hell. Laws didn't apply anymore. All the military and law enforcement we had in here peaced out and stopped showing up for work. Which, fair enough, considering they hadn't been paid for like a year.

Eventually, the Q seceded from the US and we figured things out ourselves. Now the Q is ruled by two gangs—or families, as we usually refer to ourselves—the Spencers up north and the Lopez family down south. The Spencers are jerks and the Lopezes are geniuses who figured out the artificial organs that are keeping all our asses alive.

Oh wait, now Hadley is telling me to stop because she thinks I've broken too many of their arbitrary rules.

Well, for all of you still listening up here in the Q, I will end this history lesson because history is boring as shit.

Let's get to the good stuff.

LENNON

THIS WAS NOT the first time Lennon Pierce had been kidnapped.

The first time was fifteen years earlier. He had no memory of it, but when he was four years old, he apparently wandered away from his parents at the farmers market. A woman had given him a cookie, scooped him up, and made a beeline for the parking lot.

His mom saw the kidnapper just in time, started screaming, and chased the woman down. According to his parents, he'd been completely unfazed by the whole thing. He was happily eating his cookie when his mom snatched him back from the stranger.

Later, the would-be kidnapper claimed she didn't know that the young boy was the son of a congressman. She'd just thought he was cute.

She never gave much more of an explanation than that, which had always baffled Lennon. Impulse-kidnapping a small child just because you liked his chubby cheeks didn't make a whole lot of sense.

This was not an impulse kidnapping. He'd glimpsed the bodies of his two secret service agents before the kidnappers had tied a blindfold over his eyes.

He was in some deep shit this time.

He'd lost track of how long he'd been in the van. For a while, he'd been able to see hints of sun from the bottom edge of his blindfold, if he tilted his head up. It had been a relief, because there'd been nothing but darkness since they grabbed him from a gas station.

But now it was dark again, and he could have sworn he'd been on this bumpy ride for at least two days. But that couldn't be right.

His hands were cuffed behind his back. Everything ached. His wrists, where the cuffs dug in; his back; his ass, from sitting on the hard floor. They could have at least let him sit on a seat. Maybe this vehicle didn't have them.

His stomach rumbled. They'd given him a few sips of water but no food, and he felt weak. He'd considered running, the first day. Or fighting back, when he got the chance. Now he was pretty sure that would not go so well.

The vehicle screeched to a stop so suddenly that he toppled over onto his side. He stayed there, listening to the sounds of two doors slamming shut.

Another door opened. Someone grabbed his ankle. He heard a *snap* as they cut off the plastic tie.

"Get out," a male voice said. Southern accent. They'd taken him from Georgia, but Lennon had no way to know if the accent was local to the area. He was from Los Angeles. Everyone down here sounded the same to him.

Fucking Georgia. He'd told his dad that his time was better spent in one of the Rust Belt states, but the senator had insisted.

Georgia's going to turn our way, I just know it, his dad had said, overly optimistic as usual.

Actually, maybe it would now. Nothing drummed up sympathy for a candidate like having their only son kidnapped.

Lennon briefly wondered—hopefully—if maybe his dad's campaign had done this. A sympathy kidnapping! Not a bad idea, come to think of it.

No, his dad's campaign manager would have come up with a much posher kidnapping. They would have locked him up in a nice apartment. There would have been food, at least. Cal Franklin would *absolutely* kidnap someone to win an election, but he'd do so with a smile and a bottle of champagne.

"Out! Now!" the Southern accent yelled.

Lennon struggled to sit up and then scooted forward until his legs hit air. He planted them on the ground and stood, slowly.

"Can I have some more water?" he asked. They hadn't gagged him. There probably wasn't anyone around to hear him scream.

"No. We're almost there."

Where? He wasn't stupid enough to actually expect an answer, so he didn't ask.

The blindfold was yanked off, and he blinked and squinted in the sudden light. It was morning, the sun rising directly in front of him.

They were at an airplane hangar. A small plane sat not far away.

Screw his hunger and weak limbs. He was not getting on a plane to be dropped off in some foreign country.

He took off running.

He made it three whole steps before one of the men dropped him flat on his ass.

He gasped as he hit the ground. The bearded face of a man appeared above him as he rolled over.

"Don't be a pain in my ass and make me drag you to the plane," he said. No Southern accent. This one could have been from anywhere in America.

It seemed like a bad sign that they weren't wearing masks. Lennon tried to memorize their faces.

The other man roughly dragged Lennon to his feet. He screamed, and his voice cracked. If there were manliness awards for kidnap victims, he wasn't getting one.

He made the men drag him. He was nothing if not a pain in the ass.

They wrestled him up the steps and into the small plane. There were only four seats, facing each other on either side. The bearded guy shoved him into one and strapped him in.

"I'm not flying this thing until you put his blindfold back on," a new male voice said.

Well, at least someone had hope that he was going to get out of this situation one day.

They tied the fabric around his eyes. Everything was dark again.

They were up in the air. Lennon was trying to think how much fuel a plane like this could hold. How far could they make it?

Did they have a way to get out of the country? The FAA didn't just let people fly wherever they pleased.

"Now," the Southern accent said. He sounded nervous, for the first time. "He needs to get out now."

Get *out*? Of the plane? They were still in the air.

Someone grabbed him and yanked him out of the seat. His handcuffs snapped off. His wrists screamed in relief.

"You've skydived before, right?" another man asked. "I read in an article that you skydived. Real daredevil type."

His mouth was too dry to speak. "Uh . . ." He had skydived, once. Strapped to an instructor.

They were attaching something to his back.

"You just pull to open the parachute," the Southern accent said. "Before you get too close to the ground."

There had been a lot more instructions than "before you get too close to the ground" when he had gone skydiving. He suddenly couldn't remember a single one of them.

Several hands pushed him forward.

Wait. They hadn't been in the air that long. At all.

Wind whipped through his hair.

Someone ripped off his blindfold again. He squinted against the wind. He was at the door of the plane, and he braced both hands on either side. He looked down at the world beneath him. They were flying pretty low to the ground.

He'd seen an aerial view of this place before. The buildings, the homes clustered together.

The quarantine zone in the middle of Texas.

"No, no, no, no." He tried desperately to move back into the plane. The men held him in place.

"He needs to go now!" a voice shouted.

"No!" he yelled again, frantic. He'd rather go to a foreign country. Literally any country in the world. Throw a dart at a map and he'd go there.

Hands roughly shoved him forward. His grip on the plane began to slip.

"Don't forget to pull the cord!" a voice yelled.

They pushed him out.

MAISIE

JUST ONCE, MAISIE Rojas wanted people to run away in fear when they saw her coming.

She'd yell after them, "Yeah, you better run!" and they'd cast a terrified glance over their shoulder and, of course, keep running. Because she was so terrifying.

Instead, the two men standing in the empty loading dock smiled as she approached them.

Joe spread his skinny arms wide like she might want to hug him. "Maisie!"

For fuck's sake.

"I liked your broadcast yesterday," he continued. "Very informative."

"Where is the truck?" She'd meant for the words to come out angry, but she just sounded worried. She'd never been very good at masking that particular emotion.

Nathan scratched at his black-gray beard. "Well, it's not here."

"Obviously," she snapped.

Hadley's voice crackled from a radio in the corner. *"Why do you think they didn't want us to say* fuck *to the American children? Do the kids over there not know that word? Or are we not supposed to know about* fuck? *So many questions."* Maisie might have laughed, if not for the empty loading dock in front of her.

"Did you call Declan?" she asked.

Joe blanched at the mention of the name. *That* was how people looked when they were terrified of you.

"Not yet," he said. "We thought maybe it was just late."

Maisie sighed. It wasn't late. The shipment hadn't come for weeks. Someone up north kept stopping them. Declan said he was working on tracking them down, so she'd hoped that this one would make it, but no such luck.

"I'll tell him." She pulled out her phone and sent a quick text to Declan.

"Thanks, Maisie." Nathan grinned at her. Several of his teeth were still missing.

"I thought you were getting new teeth," she said, sliding her phone back into her pocket.

"I'm saving up for a new kidney first."

"He's ugly as sin with or without teeth." Joe laughed heartily at his own joke.

"Why do you need a new kidney?" she asked. "Lopez fixes them for free."

"I still have my original kidney."

Her eyebrows shot up. "No shit! How'd you manage that?"

He looked proud. "Got tough kidneys, I guess."

"I guess so." She pulled a small tablet from her pocket and held it out to Joe. "What do you have for me?"

"Ah, come on, Maisie." Joe gestured dramatically with his arms. "No shipment! No shipment means no booze, which means no money."

"You still have local stuff. I saw people in the bar last night." She tapped her fingers impatiently against the tablet.

He took it, grumbling. He pressed his finger to the screen and then swiped a few times as he transferred credits. "I've only got five hundred right now."

"You owe us a thousand."

"I'll get you the last five hundred next week. Assuming Lopez can actually get the shipment through this time."

She cocked an eyebrow. Joe shrugged.

Most days, she would press harder. Declan would threaten to replace her again if she didn't collect. Tell her to go work at the garbage plant if she couldn't get the business owners to respect (he meant *fear*) her.

But not today. Joe had a point about the shipment. Lopez needed to fix it, fast.

She tucked the tablet back into her pocket. "You better hope they get us the medical shipment first, not liquor, or Nathan's shit out of luck for that new kidney."

Both men looked startled. She turned and walked away from the loading dock.

"It's that bad?" Nathan asked.

"Yes!" she called over her shoulder.

The streets of the Q were crowded, as usual. Maisie slipped into the crowd, keeping a hand on the tablet in her pocket. Most people would never be dumb enough to rob her, but if there was one thing you could count on in life, it was that there was always a stupid asshole around every corner.

A bicycle sped past, nearly clipping her arm.

"Watch it!" she yelled.

The rider flipped her off without turning around, like him almost hitting her had been *her* fault. There was one of the stupid assholes right there.

She looked left for more bikes, and then right, but there were only people on foot crowding the sidewalks and street. Out beyond the wall, people spent most of their time in cars, but not in the Q. No gasoline inside the walls. There were a few solar-electric cars and buses around, but they were mostly for Lopez business. Everyone else traveled by foot or bike and stuck to their own neighborhoods.

Maisie slipped into the tall building on River Street. It was cool inside, thanks to the low temperatures today. She took the elevator to the tenth floor. It smelled like popcorn as she stepped into the hallway, and beer as she approached the door.

The studio was an even bigger disaster than it had been yesterday. A long desk took up one whole wall, covered in laptops and radio equipment. A trash can in the corner was overflowing with beer bottles and chip bags. A song that was released before her parents were born played softly from the speakers.

Hadley Lopez sat in a chair in the middle of the mess, black boots propped up on the desk. Her long dark hair was pulled into a ponytail, and she wore a pair of ripped jeans and a neon-green shirt. A bowl of popcorn sat in her lap.

She tilted her head back, her upside-down face breaking into a grin. "Hey, Maisie. Welcome back."

Maisie flopped down in the chair in the corner.

Hadley spun around in her seat and held out the popcorn. "Want some?"

"I'm good, thanks."

"Lopez liked your broadcast, by the way."

Maisie lifted a skeptical eyebrow.

"He did!" Hadley exclaimed. "He said you were relatable."

Maisie leaned her head back and made an annoyed noise.

"Only you would think that being *relatable* is a bad thing," Hadley said with a laugh. "It's why he picked you to do it."

"I should have been . . ." Serious. Slightly scary. Like her dad, basically. Instead, she got nervous and just blurted everything out as it came to her.

"We sent them the recording anyway," Hadley said. "But Lopez won't blame you if they don't use any of it. You know how they are over there."

"Yeah."

"Did the medical shipment come?"

Maisie shook her head.

"Shit."

"Yeah."

"What'd Declan say?"

Maisie pulled her phone out of her pocket and checked. "He hasn't replied yet."

"He's probably pounding someone's face in."

"That does sound like him."

"Are you guys broken up for real this time?" Hadley looked hopeful.

"Yes."

"For *real*, for real?"

"Yes!"

"Thank god. Don't tell him I said that."

"I try not to talk about anything but work with Declan these days." Maisie preferred not to dwell on her relationship with Declan. Mistakes were made.

"You know that the Reapers are getting restless," Hadley said. "Talking about how it might be time for a leadership change."

Maisie sighed. "I know." The Reapers—the only gang in the south that Lopez hadn't managed to quash—had been threatening to seize control for years. They didn't have the numbers, but if Lopez couldn't deliver the shipments soon, they might have better luck recruiting.

"Hey, did you know Nathan Fredrick still has his original kidney?" Maisie asked.

"What!"

"I was impressed too. He should keep it. Put it in a box and show it off."

"Only you would think that's a good idea." Hadley spun around in her chair again to face her desk. "Hold on." She slipped her headphones over her ears and leaned into the mic in front of her. The music faded out.

"I've got a few news updates for you this morning—first, we've got a garbage pileup happening at the plant right now, so everyone's going to have to keep their garbage to themselves for the next week. Regular schedule resumes next week, supposedly."

She looked at the laptop screen to her left. "Some news from beyond the wall today—Lennon Pierce, the son of Senator Camden Pierce, has been kidnapped. Camden Pierce is the

Democratic nominee for president of the United States and has suspended all campaign activities since his son's kidnapping a few days ago. The election is tomorrow.

"And in news you actually give a shit about, Rosa's Bakery has started making those blueberry scones again. Run, don't walk." She clicked off the mic, music filling the room once more.

Maisie leaned forward. "Who sent you that news about the senator?"

"The State Department. They're always sending me election updates. They're relentless this time, insisting I update the Q on everything. They think we're actually going to care about this Pierce dude because he's campaigning on a platform about finding a cure and tearing down the walls."

"They always say that."

"They sure do. Apparently, they think he actually means it." She put her feet up on the table, crossing one boot over the other.

"Does it even matter? Hasn't the same family won every year since before the Q?"

"Yeah, always the Howards, just a different one every time they run into term limits. I think they like to pretend it's a fair election, though. Makes them feel better, I guess." Hadley shrugged. "Never voted, couldn't say."

"Eh, doesn't sound that great anyway."

Elise appeared at the door, dragging her oxygen tank with her. Her curly blond hair was tied in a messy bun, and she pulled her mask down to her neck and smiled at them. Her pale skin was almost translucent these days, and the skin beneath her eyes was a deep purple. She held up a white paper bag.

"Blueberry scones," she said.

"Yesss," Hadley said.

Elise offered Maisie one, and she shook her head as she stood. "I'm good."

"Any word on the shipment?" Elise asked.

"It's . . . in progress." Maisie tried to sound more confident than she felt. "We're working on it."

Elise didn't seem convinced as she pulled her mask back up to cover her mouth and took a breath. Her one remaining lung wasn't really up to the task of breathing anymore, and if they didn't get the medical parts shipment in, there was no way for her to get a new set. Without the medical supplies in that shipment, most of the people in the Q couldn't get the surgeries they needed.

Elise was getting a new set of lungs, even if Maisie had to go get the shipment herself. Elise, Maisie, and Hadley were First Five—babies born in the first five years after the Q was established. Most of the First Five died as infants. Many more as children.

Only eight First Five babies remained in Lopez territory. Maisie wasn't about to see it become seven.

"What the—" Hadley sat up in her chair, dropping her boots off the table. Her eyes were on the window. "Is that *a plane*?"

Maisie moved forward to look. It couldn't be. Airspace over the Q was restricted. She'd only ever seen a plane in pictures.

But there it was, flying north over the Q.

Something—a large object, maybe—fell out of the plane, and Maisie squinted as she moved closer to the window.

"Is that . . . ?"

An orange parachute opened.

"Holy shit, that's a *person*," Hadley breathed.

Maisie turned around and bolted out of the studio and across the hall, to the security room. Elise was already there, sitting down in front of the computers. The rest were blinking to life, showing camera footage from around the Q.

"Lopez is going to want to know exactly where they land," Maisie said.

Elise didn't look up. "I know. Give me a minute."

Hadley rushed in, leaning down behind Elise to peer at her screen.

"Do you see them?" Maisie asked.

"Camera eight," Elise said. The image on the computers all changed to the view from camera eight.

The skydiver was still in the air but getting closer to the ground. Elise zoomed in.

"It's a man," Hadley said.

"You know you have dead air right now," Elise said.

"Shit." Hadley darted out of the room. Her voice filtered through the speakers a moment later.

"Well, folks, don't know if you've noticed, but we've got some weird shit happening right now. A dude just jumped out of a plane over the Q. It is literally *raining men out there this morning. Hallelujah."*

LENNON

LENNON FELL FOR several seconds before his brain clicked into place.

He opened his chute. He had no idea if it was the right time—he didn't know how far up they'd been—but earlier seemed better than too late.

He grabbed his toggles. Maybe, if he steered east or west, he could land outside the quarantine zone. It was fifty miles north to south, but only about fifteen east to west.

Which way was west? Fuck.

The sun. Right. It was rising in the east.

Problem was, the wind was pushing him south.

And he was pretty sure the kidnappers dropped him directly in the middle of the quarantine zone, which meant that his odds of moving several miles east or west were very slim.

He looked down at the ground below him.

It was coming at him too quickly. He needed a plan. He needed time to think. He was desperately trying to remember what those CDC people had said to him about vaccines and a cure for the virus. Vaccines had been impossible so far because of how the virus kept mutating, but they had said some hopeful shit about possible cures and progress with short-term vaccines.

He should have listened closer to that hopeful shit.

If he was being honest, he hadn't really bought into his dad's whole "I'm going to save the quarantine zone!" shtick. A lot of people thought it was only a matter of time before the whole zone revolted and tore down the walls. It was a miracle it hadn't happened already. They'd been in here for over twenty years.

President Howard had made it clear that he would destroy everyone inside the walls before he let the people inside infect them all.

So. Lennon was going to get sick or he was going to get blown up. Or both!

The ground was approaching faster now. The quarantine zone didn't care that he hadn't made a plan or made peace with his terrible options.

There was grass, at least. This would be his first solo landing, and he had a feeling it was not going to go great. At least he wasn't landing on concrete.

He put his feet together and prayed. He wasn't religious, but it couldn't hurt.

His feet touched the ground, and for a hot second he thought he might nail the landing. Then he was rolling and grunting and there was grass in his mouth. He was tangled in his parachute. He had not nailed anything, and for a moment, he was glad that his friends weren't there to capture it on video.

He finally stopped. He couldn't see anything but the orange parachute. His body felt numb, panicked, and he didn't want to move for fear of discovering he'd broken several limbs. It took him a moment to realize that his mouth was still wide-open from screaming. He snapped it shut.

He shifted his arms. They felt fine. He moved his legs. One knee ached, but it was probably just bruised.

Slowly, he crawled out of the parachute.

He stopped with just his head peeking out, bracing both hands on the ground.

Grass and rolling hills. In the distance, he could see an old boarded-up gas station and a two-lane road.

He shrugged off the parachute and stood, turning in a circle. There was no one.

He had no idea if he was in the north or the south. The quarantine zone didn't have a formal government, just rival gangs that controlled the two halves—the Spencer family in the north and the Lopez family in the south.

He had no idea which to hope for.

It occurred to him suddenly that if there was no one nearby, there was no way for him to catch whatever form of the virus was floating around this place. Maybe if he just stood right here and waited, the military would send a helicopter. There was plenty of space for it to land.

His heart lifted. It wasn't totally unreasonable. Surely people had seen the plane over the quarantine zone. And the people in here had ways of communicating with the US government. They just chose not to, for the most part.

But they'd loosened up a bit lately. They'd even agreed to some audio recordings, which Lennon had lobbied hard for.

The airspace above the quarantine zone had been re-stricted for years, but they could make an exception. It was an emergency.

Of course, he would need to talk to someone in here about this plan, which was a problem. But he could try to maintain enough distance not to catch anything and just yell for help.

It was a solid plan. It could work.

"RUNNER!"

Lennon whirled around at the sound of the voice.

"RUNNER FROM THE NORTH!"

He spotted the source of the voice—a man stood on the roof of the gas station, holding a megaphone.

A rumbling noise sounded from behind him, and he turned to see three people on motorcycles zooming his way.

He stumbled backward, holding his hands up in the air. He wasn't sure why. It just seemed like the right thing to do.

The motorcycles all stopped about twenty yards away. Lennon slowly lowered his hands. None of the riders wore helmets, but they all had on black masks that covered the bottom half of their faces.

He tried to think of what his dad would do in this situation. His unflappable father, who could cheerfully converse with people who were screaming at him. He'd once waved at a person who'd thrown an egg in his face at a campaign stop and quipped, "I prefer them scrambled!"

His father would say to be polite and friendly. *No one ever regretted being too nice, son.*

Lennon doubted that was true, but he begrudgingly had to admit that it was good advice. He took a deep breath to steady himself.

"Uh . . . hi?" he yelled. "I—"

He cut himself off at the sound of footsteps behind him. He turned.

Four men were charging straight toward him.

"No, no, no!" he yelled, putting his hands out in front of him. "Stop! Please! Just stay there!"

The men did not stop.

They came at him faster.

He turned and ran.

MAISIE

"WHERE DID HE go?" Maisie asked. Camera eight showed nothing but blue sky.

"Hold on," Elise said. "He veered north, and he was already pretty close to the neutral zone. If he crossed into Spencer territory, we've lost him."

Maisie waited while Elise clicked her keyboard. Over the speakers, "It's Raining Men" played. Hadley ran back into the room.

Maisie's phone rang, and she looked down at the screen. *Declan.* She tapped to answer.

"Hey. I'm already in the comms tower. Elise is pulling him up on the cameras."

"Where is he?" Declan asked. He was panting, like he was running.

"Last saw him near the neutral zone."

"I'm headed that way now. I need an exact location."

"We're getting it." Maisie gave Elise a pleading look. The

image on the screens changed. The man hit the ground hard, the parachute covering his body as he rolled.

"Got him!" Maisie said. "Just landed outside Neutral Zone Station One."

"That's going to leave a mark," Hadley said with a wince.

"He's down?"

"Yeah, he's down," Maisie said. "Might be hurt. Rough landing."

"Okay. Stay there and keep an eye on the cameras. We're going after him."

The line went dead, and she slipped her phone back into her pocket.

"Has anyone ever tried to get *in*to the Q before?" Maisie asked, her eyes on the motionless orange blob on the screen.

Hadley leaned closer to the screen. "Yeah, those people who tried to tear down the walls like fifteen years ago."

"Oh yeah. That didn't go so well for them," Maisie said. "You think he's dead? Oh, there he goes!"

The orange blob moved. A hand emerged from beneath the parachute, and then the top of a head. He paused for several seconds before crawling out from underneath the fabric and standing.

He had dark hair, and looked to be fairly young, though it was hard to tell from this distance.

"Elise, can you zoom in?" Maisie asked.

"Yeah."

The image shifted. The guy's face was clear on the screen now. He *was* young, maybe late teens or early twenties. He wore a rumpled button-down shirt, his tie loose around his neck.

"Holy shit," Hadley said. "That's Lennon fucking Pierce."

"Who is Lennon fucking Pierce?" Elise asked.

"Lennon Pierce! The guy—the kidnapped guy!"

"The senator's son?" Maisie asked.

Elise's eyebrows shot up. "The one who's running for president?"

"Yes!" Hadley exclaimed. "They sent me a picture with the news report. I remember that face. And that hair."

He did have wild hair. It was thick and sticking up in every direction.

"Hold on," Hadley said, and ran out of the room.

"That senator is the one who's been talking big about tearing down the Q walls, right?" Elise said.

"Yeah."

Hadley ran back into the room and handed Maisie a piece of paper.

"See? That's totally him."

It was, indeed, totally him. This version of Lennon Pierce was smiling, all straight teeth and glowing skin. His wavy hair was impressively coiffed, with one tendril lazily grazing his eyebrow. She wondered if they'd had to take the picture several times to make him look so effortlessly douchey.

She passed the picture to Elise and returned her attention to the screen. Lennon was still just standing there. A frozen dumbass.

"Do you think they dropped him in here against his will?" Hadley asked.

"Yes," Maisie said. "Look at him. He has nothing on him." She turned to Hadley. "Is Lopez reachable?"

"Oh. Right." Hadley grabbed the phone and dialed. "Hey. Where's Uncle Franco right now?" She listened. "I know you said not to—" She cut herself off, taking a deep breath. "It's an emergency. Tell Uncle Franco that we know who just dropped out of the sky and he needs to call the comms tower right now." She hung up.

Maisie dialed Declan.

On the screen, Lennon scrambled backward, his hands in the air. He whirled around. Elise zoomed out. Four men ran toward Lennon. Behind him, Maisie could see the black masks on the faces of the men on the motorcycles.

"Shit," she said.

"Maisie," Declan snapped over the phone, not for the first time. *"What is it?"*

"It's Lennon Pierce," she said hurriedly. On the screen, Lennon took off running. "The son of the US presidential candidate. And the border patrol just spotted him."

Hadley did a double-take at the screen, alarm on her face.

There was a long pause. *"Where is he now?"*

"He's running. He—" She stopped talking as the four men swarmed Lennon, tackling him to the ground. "They've got him."

Her phone beeped, and she looked to see who was calling. *Franco Lopez.*

"Declan, it's Lopez on the other line."

"Go."

She switched to the other call. "Lopez? I'm here."

"Get down to my lab. As fast as you can." He hung up.

She raced toward the door, glancing back at Hadley. "Can I take your scooter?"

"Yes, take it!"

"Thank you!"

Hadley's scooter took Maisie through the streets of the Q so quickly that people had to jump out of the way when they saw her coming. She used the annoying horn that she'd often teased Hadley about.

She practically fell off the scooter when she arrived at the lab and lurched for the door.

A direct request from Lopez was unusual. She could only remember it happening once or twice before. Everything went through Declan now, and her dad before that.

Paul, one of Lopez's bodyguards, stood just inside the building, and he nodded at her and pointed down the hallway. She ran for the door. It opened automatically.

Lopez was at his desk in the lab, his brow furrowed as he wrote something in a notebook. He looked up at her briefly.

"One second, Maisie."

"Sure." She tried to breathe quietly.

He finished writing and stood. He was a heavyset man with dark hair, now streaked with gray. He wore square-framed glasses, and he rubbed his hand over the stubble on his chin. His smile was friendly, and she was surprised to see him give her one.

She shouldn't have been. Lopez was always calm. Eerily so. It was probably why he'd gotten along so well with her father. The two had been lifelong friends until her dad's death a year ago. Isaac Rojas would punch a guy in the face for looking at him wrong. Franco Lopez would jump in and immediately smooth things over.

"I would like some options for when I speak to the CDC and the FBI about our newest arrival," he said.

"The F-B-I?" she repeated, searching her brain for the words that went with the familiar letters.

"The Federal Bureau of Investigation," he said patiently. "Cops."

"Right."

"I need for you to give Mr. Pierce this in the next hour." He passed her a small black pouch. She opened it to see a plastic needle loaded with a clear liquid. "It will provide immunity from the virus for a short period of time."

She looked down at the needle. "Seriously?"

"Yes, seriously. That's what you've been helping me with."

"How short a period of time?"

"In our tests we got up to four days," he said. "I may be able to convince the CDC to let us do a little experiment. Get him out of here before those four days are up."

"You think they would actually let someone leave the Q?"

"I think his father will be highly motivated to get him out, and that could work to our advantage."

"How would he even do that? Where would he exit?"

"We'll figure it out. I'll probably ask for permission to scale one of the walls. But for today, I need you to get him that now, or none of this matters." He touched her upper arm. "Inject him there. Whether he wants it or not. It is not optional."

She nodded.

"Declan and his team are closing in on the area. They'll cover you while you grab Pierce. I'm trusting you with this because I know I can count on you not to kill him."

"Of course."

"And I need someone who Pierce will at least let close to him. He'll be less likely to try to punch you."

She bit back a laugh. "Sure. Let's hope, anyway."

"After you've injected him, you and Declan's team will bring him back here immediately."

"Got it."

"Good. Go."

Lopez pulled a bus out of service for her, and it whipped down the street at a pace that made Maisie's teeth rattle in her head. The driver laid on the horn every twenty seconds, maybe to alert people to get out of the road. Maybe just to annoy her.

Hadley's voice came crackling out of the speaker on the roof.

"Bus four is out of service, folks, and you're going to want to steer clear of the roads until further notice. And please keep an eye out for any other men falling from the sky."

The bus screeched to a stop and Maisie darted out.

Declan stood on the side of the road. He had a man by the neck, his fingers digging into his skin. Blood poured out of the man's nose, one of his eyes already swollen.

Declan looked up at Maisie. He released his grip, and the man crumpled to the ground with a moan.

"Pierce is in there," he said, pointing to the shack down the road. He took a step back, gesturing to the field that stretched out beyond it. Three motorcycles and several men on foot raced toward the shack.

"I'm going to go help my boys ward them off," he said, and turned to go.

She took off running. She pumped her arms as fast as she could, her shoes crunching against gravel as she raced toward the shack. The pouch Lopez had given her was tucked in her pocket, the needle heavy against her thigh.

She skidded to a stop at the door and threw it open.

A man stood on the other side, a machete aimed at her face.

She ducked just in time. The blade sailed over her head.

She popped up, launching her foot into the man's chest. He wheezed and dropped his weapon as he stumbled back. She caught a glimpse of his face as he fell to the ground.

Grady Ruben. A constant pain in her ass.

She looked quickly around the shack. Lennon Pierce was tied to a beam. He pulled desperately at the zip tie binding his hands around it, to no avail. A red handkerchief was tied around his mouth.

His clothes were dusty and wrinkled, his ridiculous hair falling in his eyes. He squinted at her through it and froze. He had a bruise forming on one cheek and blood drying under his nose.

Grady struggled to his feet, reaching for his machete. She kicked it away, jumping forward and grabbing him by the collar. She pulled her left hand back and made a fist.

"Dammit, Grady, what did I say last time?"

He looked at her fist nervously. "He's a runner from the north! Runners from the north are fair game!"

"What did I say?" she repeated, louder.

He licked his lips. "That if you heard about us capturing and eating any more people, you'd cut off my balls."

Lennon made a horrified noise from behind his gag.

She threw a punch straight into Grady's face. He hit the

ground hard, his nose and mouth bloody, and went still. Pain radiated through her hand, and she resisted the urge to wince.

She turned back to Lennon. He looked from her to the man on the ground.

She pulled the needle from the pouch. His eyes widened. He shook his head.

"Calm down." She held both her hands up, holding the needle in between two fingers. "I'm here to help you, okay?"

Outside, someone fired a gun. Lennon jumped, turning his attention to the one small, dirty window. It didn't show much.

He turned back to Maisie, gaze bouncing from her to Grady, who was still motionless on the floor.

She took a tentative step forward. Calm and friendly was probably the way to go here. He looked like a scared dog.

"Don't worry." She tilted her head down toward Grady. "I would never actually touch his balls. For any reason."

Lennon's eyebrows drew together in an expression of horrified bewilderment.

"Anyway, welcome to the Q." She smiled. "We're not a bunch of cannibals in here, by the way."

Grady moaned. She kicked him in the ribs.

"These guys are just a little . . . eccentric."

Lennon looked unconvinced.

She took another step closer, lifting the hand with the needle. "This will provide temporary immunity from the virus. I'm just going to stick it in your arm, and then we're going to get out of here."

He violently shook his head back and forth. He tried to talk, but it just came out as muttered nonsense.

She reached for him. He darted away, swinging around to the other side of the beam.

She made a frustrated noise. "Dude, I'm seriously trying to help you here."

She reached for him again. He swung around to the other side again.

Maisie sprang forward, using her body to smash his into the beam. He made a muffled screaming noise.

"Dumbass. I understand that you've had a bad couple of days, but if I don't stick this needle in your arm and get you to Lopez, we're both going to be in a shitload of trouble. So hold still."

She jammed the needle into his arm. He whimpered.

"Calm down, you're fine. You're welcome, by the way." She pushed in the liquid and pulled the needle out.

He was breathing heavily, and he turned his head slightly, looking down at where she'd stuck him.

"I need to untie you so I can get you out of here, but I'm not doing it if you're going to run. So, listen. I'm Maisie Rojas."

His eyes went wide, like he recognized the name.

"I'm supposed to get you back to Lopez, who is trying to work out a deal with the CDC to get you out of here."

He took in a sharp breath.

"There are some guys outside taking care of the rest of these jackasses, and *trust me,* you do not want to see what they will do to you if you make them chase you down. So, I'm going to untie you, and you're not going to be a pain in my ass. Agreed?"

He slowly nodded.

"Okay." She stepped back and pulled out her knife. She walked around the beam and cut Lennon loose.

LENNON

LENNON DROPPED HIS arms as the zip tie fell to the ground and stared at the girl in front of him.

He'd seen a picture of Isaac Rojas once—Dr. Lopez's right-hand man who had killed a lot of people to secure the southern part of the quarantine zone for the Lopez family. Dark hair, six foot three, broad as shit, scary-looking dude.

His daughter was not that.

She was at least a foot shorter than her dad, with long dark hair pulled back in a ponytail, a bright pink streak running through it. Pushed-up sleeves revealed tattoos on both her arms. Blood dripped from her knuckles, a result of the truly impressive punch she'd delivered to the man still moaning on the ground.

"Are you going to take that off?"

Right. The gag. He yanked it off, tossed it on the ground, and resisted the urge to spit. That handkerchief tasted like it had been to a lot of other places before it was shoved in his mouth.

"You . . . What was . . . ?" He had too many questions to settle on just one.

"Come on." She strode to the door. "You can ask Lopez the questions. I'm just your ride."

"Fr-Franco Lopez?" he stammered.

"Of course Franco Lopez." She stood at the doorway impatiently. She started to wrap her fingers around the frame, but quickly lowered her hand, the slightest hint of pain crossing her features. "Would you hurry your ass up?"

He blinked, and the girl stepped forward and grabbed his arm with her uninjured hand, pulling him through the door.

She broke into a run as they stepped outside. It was sunny, and warmer than it had been in Georgia. He squinted and nearly stumbled.

She held on to his arm harder, and Lennon realized he was unsteady on his feet. He was swooning. He was literally the least-manly kidnapping victim ever. People would tell stories about his lack of manliness for generations to come.

They were headed for a bus. It was covered in graffiti—or art? Hard to say.

She practically shoved him inside. He collapsed onto the first seat he saw.

Her face appeared in front of him, eyebrows knitted in concern. "Did they give you anything?"

He shook his head. "You gave me something."

Now her eyebrows thought he was a dumbass. He searched his memory for the first name she'd given him.

"Mary?"

"Maisie."

"What?"

"My name is Maisie."

"Maisie." His vision began to tunnel. "I feel weird." His body slumped. He fell onto his side.

Maisie put her hands on her hips, peering down at him. She was becoming a tiny spot in his vision. When she spoke, she sounded far away.

"I think this dude just fainted."

He was on the bumpy bus, and then someone was dragging him to his feet.

"I didn't hit him!" Maisie said. He couldn't see her. It was too bright. "He just fainted out of nowhere. He's very delicate."

He tried to mumble that he was *not* delicate, but no words came out. Besides, there were two men on either side of him, supporting nearly all of his weight, so maybe she had a point.

It suddenly wasn't so bright, and then he was on a soft surface. A man stared down at him. Olive skin. Dark beard. Glasses.

"Holy shit," he said, and sat up so quickly that he got dizzy and promptly ended up on his back again. Jesus Christ. He *was* delicate.

"Nice to meet you too," Dr. Franco Lopez said with a hint of amusement.

"Is this a reaction to that stuff we injected him with?" Maisie asked. She was sitting in a chair across the room, one black boot propped up, an arm slung across her knee. He could see her tattoos more clearly now—a black butterfly on her arm, one wing detailed, the other destroyed, a wispy mess of lines. She had her left hand, the one that she'd used to punch his captor, tucked into her body like she didn't want anyone to see it.

"Could be," Dr. Lopez said. A younger man appeared beside him. He was probably in his early twenties, but with the same olive skin and black hair as Dr. Lopez. He regarded Lennon suspiciously.

Dr. Lopez looked down at Lennon. "They didn't give you anything, did they? Those boys who grabbed you?"

He shook his head, which felt foggy. "But I haven't eaten in, like . . . What day is it? I haven't eaten since Georgia."

"Who is Georgia?" Maisie asked.

"He means the state," Dr. Lopez said. "They grabbed him in Georgia, two days ago."

"Two days does make you weak," Maisie said, like she'd gone two days without food before. The younger guy nodded in agreement.

"Beto, go make him a sandwich. There's some meat and cheese in the fridge. Maisie, get him some water."

They both immediately obeyed the order, leaving him alone with the doctor.

"Listen," Dr. Lopez said, pulling over a chair and sitting down in it. "I know that you've had a hell of a time. But you're safe here, okay?"

He was having trouble thinking straight through the brain fog, but *safe* seemed like the entirely wrong word to use in these circumstances.

"Maisie said . . ." He sat up very slowly, blinking. "She said that she gave me temporary immunity from the virus."

Dr. Lopez nodded.

"That's not possible, is it?" Lennon asked. "There isn't a vaccine. If there was, you'd all be out of here."

Dr. Lopez laughed. Lennon wasn't sure which part was funny.

"There is no vaccine that provides long-term protection from the virus, no," Dr. Lopez said. "The virus mutates quickly, so that has been a challenge. But you've heard of passive immunity?"

"Yes? Uh, something about antibodies?" His head still felt too fuzzy to put thoughts together.

"Right. I have had some success using antibodies to provide immediate, short-term protection from the virus. I've actually been talking to the CDC about letting some volunteers from beyond the wall visit us in here, using what I just gave you as protection."

He blinked. "Seriously?"

"Still early talks. But now you're here, so we're giving it a go after all."

"Are you sure it actually works?"

"I'm sure. It would have been better if you'd been given it before arriving in the Q, but we got it to you very quickly. You can thank Maisie for that."

She had just walked back into the room with a glass of water, and Dr. Lopez smiled at her. She handed it to Lennon.

"Thank you." He took several long gulps. It tasted off, but he knew for a fact that the water in the quarantine zone was safe to drink. They'd all have died years ago otherwise.

He wiped water from his chin as he lowered the glass. "And thank you for . . ." He gestured at his arm.

"Sticking a needle in your arm against your will?" she guessed.

"Yes. Sorry I was difficult, it's just that you're very . . . scary." The last word slipped out before he could stop it. Shit. He still couldn't think.

But the expression that crossed her face was absolute delight. She grinned, lightly swatting Dr. Lopez's shoulder.

"Did you hear that? He thinks I'm scary!"

Beto walked in, holding a plate with a sandwich on it. "Maisie, he's from the other side of the wall. He's probably terrified of all of us." He handed the plate to Lennon.

"Well, he only said that *I* was scary," Maisie countered.

Lennon took the plate and inhaled the sandwich in only a few bites. The bread was fresh, and the sandwich was made with a thick slab of chicken and cheese.

He already felt steadier. He could sort of think again, though the exhaustion was still making things hazy.

He swallowed the last bite, a thought suddenly occurring to him.

"The antibodies . . ." He glanced from Maisie to Dr. Lopez. "The antibodies that people get, they're not, uh, what's the word? Protective. They don't protect people from getting the virus again. Or from, uh . . ."

"Reactivating," Dr. Lopez finished for him.

"Right. Reactivating." The scariest part of the TARV virus was the fact that it didn't leave the body once someone recovered from it. It lay dormant, only to reactivate when the immune system was weakened by another illness. A simple cold—or even stress—could bring the virus back. It was why no one inside the quarantine zone could leave.

"It's true that for most people, the antibodies they produce do not protect them from getting the virus again."

Lennon's eyebrows shot up. "For *most* people?"

Dr. Lopez just smiled, and then stood, clapping his hands together. "All right. My guys are sweeping the area, and once they're done, we'll head over to the comms tower to call my contacts at the CDC."

Lennon glanced around. Were there no phones here?

"You need a satellite phone to call outside the Q, and they're only in the comms tower," Maisie explained, clearly noticing his confusion.

"Right."

"Do you want to shower while we wait?" Dr. Lopez asked.

"God, I really do."

He pointed at the hallway behind Lennon. "Down there, to the right. There should be towels in there already. Beto, grab him some clothes, would you? Go next door, they should have something that fits him."

Beto nodded and strode out of the room. Lennon got slowly to his feet. He felt much better with food in his stomach.

"How long does this work for?" Lennon asked, putting a hand on his arm.

"We've gotten up to four days, but the CDC will probably want to play it safe and get you out right away."

He tried not to look too relieved. Maybe he wouldn't even have to spend a full day in the quarantine zone. He'd definitely have to spend some time in isolation once he got out, but he could probably arrange some remote interviews. A story about how nice and welcoming everyone was inside would do wonders for the senator's campaign.

He'd leave out the part about the cannibals.

"Five minutes max in the shower," Dr. Lopez said. "Our water supply isn't what you're used to."

"Got it," he said. Even a five-minute shower sounded amazing at this point. He smelled like hot garbage. Probably looked it, too.

He paused at the edge of the hallway. "Thank you. For all of this."

Dr. Lopez glanced up at him with one raised eyebrow. "I'm not doing this out of the kindness of my heart, son."

Lennon hesitated, but couldn't help but ask. "What do you want in return?"

Dr. Lopez just chuckled.

Beto brought him pants that were a little too baggy and a soft gray shirt. He even brought him a pair of boxer briefs, which looked clean and Lennon sincerely hoped were brand-new. They were better than the ones he'd been wearing the past two days, anyway.

The shirt, oddly, had a mask sewn into the inside, just below the collar. It covered his face from the nose down and hooked behind the ears.

He tucked it back inside. Maybe all their shirts had those attached. Not a bad idea.

He finger-combed his hair and leaned forward to examine his face in the mirror. Could be worse. He'd expected worse, actually. He had a bruise on one cheekbone, but otherwise his face was the same as always. He ran his hand over the stubble across his jaw. He'd been clean-shaven every day for weeks on the campaign trail.

Maisie and Beto were gone when he walked back out into the lab, but Dr. Lopez sat at his desk.

Lennon gestured to the dirty clothes he held in his arm. "I didn't know what to do with these."

"Just put them in there," the doctor said, pointing to a basket in the corner. "You won't get those back, though."

"I am totally fine with that." He dropped the clothes in the basket, watching as the bright blue tie disappeared beneath his grimy white shirt. His dad had picked out that tie. He'd say "Nice tie" to Lennon every time he wore it, and then chuckle. It was annoying, and sort of endearing.

He considered grabbing the tie and stuffing it in his pocket. But he'd never actually liked it that much. He only wore it on the campaign trail.

He turned and walked back to Dr. Lopez, who was getting up from his desk. "I've been wondering . . ."

Dr. Lopez looked at him expectantly.

Lennon took a breath, wondering if he was making a mistake by bringing this up. But it seemed wrong not to.

"There are rumors that you guys have some access to American news in here?"

"No."

"I mean, a select few of you have access to news, when you want it." He didn't expect a reply to that, and didn't get one. He didn't think Dr. Lopez was going to cop to the quarantine zone's draconian media laws. "I'm just wondering if you understand what people are saying about the quarantine zone out there. If you're aware of . . . certain solutions that have been proposed for dealing with the zone."

Lennon couldn't actually bring himself to say, *Are you aware that a significant portion of the population wants to blow you all up?*

"I am aware that there are plenty of people out there who would prefer that the Q be gone entirely. They've been advocating for that for years."

"But do you understand that the idea has become more mainstream lately? And that my being dropped in here has probably caused a significant uproar with that group now?"

Dr. Lopez nodded once, curtly. "I understand. It's one of the reasons I think it's best that we get you out of here as soon as possible."

"Right. Yes." He blew out a breath, relieved. "Maybe you could let me communicate with some outside journalists? And let them record the call? It could really help if people knew that I was okay in—"

"No," Dr. Lopez cut in. "They'll know you're fine when you leave." He picked up his phone from his desk and slipped it into his pocket. "I need you to keep this to yourself. No one in here needs to know how they talk about the people in the Q."

Lennon hesitated, because he didn't agree. He thought the residents of the quarantine zone had every right to know that a growing, vocal portion of Americans wanted to destroy the zone, along with everyone inside. They deserved access to information about the rest of the world, if they wanted it.

"It would cause chaos," the doctor continued. "And there's nothing they can do about it. Keeping people calm has always been the best course of action, in my opinion." He clapped Lennon on the shoulder. "Can I count on you?"

Lennon smiled. "Of course." He may have been lying. But Dr. Lopez wasn't exactly being straightforward with him, so he was happy to return the favor.

He followed the doctor outside to a waiting van. It was old and dented, with a large solar panel attached to the roof. It was also windowless in back, and Lennon's stomach clenched as he climbed inside. He was avoiding vans after this. Nothing good came from getting in a van.

Curiosity had begun to poke through a bit of his panic, and he leaned over to try to look out the front windshield as the van lurched forward. But there was a plastic partition between the front seats and back, and it was dirty and covered in scratches. Everything past it was just a smudgy blur.

"Do you . . . use this van often?" he asked carefully. Dr. Lopez sat beside him.

"Occasionally."

"It's solar and electric, right?"

"Yes."

"I was just wondering. I'd heard that not many vehicles operated in the southern portion of the quarantine zone, except for . . ." Except for public transport and the ones used by the gangs. It seemed impolite to say.

Dr. Lopez didn't appear interested in what he'd been about to say. He stared straight ahead.

"How long can they operate, when fully charged?" Lennon asked.

"Three to four hours."

"That's pretty good."

"It's enough for the area we travel."

Lennon nodded, trying not to let his face betray his

emotions. He'd gotten good at that the past few months. He didn't need Dr. Lopez to know that he was horrified at the prospect of living a life contained to such a tiny area.

They came to a stop outside a tall building. Lennon craned his neck to try to see past Dr. Lopez and onto the street as he climbed out of the van, but the doctor clapped a firm hand on his shoulder and steered him inside. Lennon got the feeling that they were making an effort to keep him from seeing much.

They took an old elevator up to the tenth floor. A song from the late twentieth century played over the speakers.

Lennon spotted her right away when they stepped into the hallway—standing in a doorway, arms crossed over her chest, hair up in a ponytail, and a flower tattoo peeking out from the back collar of her shirt. Maisie looked over her shoulder as they approached, and then moved away from the door.

"Watch him for me, will ya, Maisie?" Dr. Lopez said pleasantly.

She smiled. " 'Course."

He was vaguely insulted that he had to be watched, but on the growing list of his kidnappers, these were certainly the nicest ones.

Dr. Lopez disappeared into a room across the hall.

Maisie gave him a quick once-over. "You look less disgusting."

"Thank you."

A girl appeared from inside the room where Maisie had been hovering, a delighted expression on her face.

"It's you! In the flesh!" Her black hair was pulled into an

alarmingly large bun on top of her head, and it wobbled when she spoke. Large headphones, like the old kind that covered the entire ear, hung around her neck. She wore bright red lipstick and thick black eyeliner that made her eyes look huge.

"Uh, yeah. It's me."

"I'm Hadley. Hadley Lopez."

"Oh, shit," he said, before he could stop himself.

She let out a loud cackle. Maisie gave him an amused look.

Hadley Lopez was not what he had pictured. He'd known that she was a couple of years younger than him, but he realized he'd always pictured her as older. He'd only heard snatches of her radio programs—the ones they could get their hands on after they were declassified—and she'd always sounded so confident. *The voice of the Q,* his dad had called her.

Also, an *actual* member of the Lopez family. Everyone in the gang called themselves *family* (from what he'd heard), but she was actually the niece of Dr. Lopez.

"I take it you've heard of me," she said.

"Sorry. Yes. It's nice to meet you." He extended his hand.

She stared at it. "You guys still do that out there?"

He quickly pulled it back. "Sorry. Yes. We do." He'd heard that they didn't shake hands in the quarantine zone.

"Gross." She glanced over her shoulder. "Oh crap, hold on a sec."

She darted back inside the room. Lennon edged in a few steps as well, glancing over to see if Maisie was going to stop him. She just followed him inside.

It was a radio studio. Hadley dropped into the chair, pulling her headphones over her ears. She leaned into the mic.

"And next up, folks, we have what was once considered by many to be one of the worst songs ever recorded, and a personal favorite of mine, 'We Built This City' by Starship. You're welcome."

The music began playing, and she pulled her headphones down, swiveling around in her chair to face them. Maisie leaned against the doorframe. Blocking his exit, he noted.

"My parents like twentieth-century music too," he said to Hadley.

"I'd never have guessed."

"I think there are a lot of songs worse than this."

Her lips twitched into a smile.

"Oh, wow, it really is you."

He turned at the sound of the new voice to see a young woman standing in the doorway. Leaning, really. She was thin and pale, and looked like she might topple over at the smallest breeze. She had breathing tubes in her nostrils, and an oxygen tank at her feet.

"Lennon, Elise," Maisie said. "Elise, Lennon."

"Hi," he said.

She studied him for a moment before turning to Maisie. "So he's *not* going to get the virus?"

"Apparently not. Lopez gave me this temporary vaccine," Maisie disclosed. "It's not like a real vaccine. They're not sure exactly how long it will last."

"Right. I heard something about that once. Lucky you." She pulled her mask up and took a breath.

"So you met the border patrol, huh?" Hadley asked, propping her boots up on her desk.

Lennon looked questioningly at Maisie.

"They're not actually the border patrol," she said. "They're just a bunch of inbred idiots."

"I mean, they're inbred idiots who have volunteered to patrol the border, so." Hadley lifted her arms.

"Did someone tell them they could eat runners from the north?" Maisie asked.

Hadley made a so-so motion with her hand. "I think maybe it was implied that no one would be that upset about it if they did."

"For fuck's sake," Maisie said, exasperated. "I do not think we should be encouraging that."

"Take it up with Declan," Hadley said. "Apparently he thinks they keep people from the north from trying to come here."

Elise pushed her mask down. "He's not wrong."

Lennon was almost afraid to ask. "They're really . . . cannibals?"

"Yes," Maisie said with an eye-roll. "They're a bunch of idiots who think that eating human flesh protects against all illnesses."

"We tried telling them that they get sick less often because they never leave the border and interact with other people, but there's no arguing with stupid," Hadley said.

"Sure." Lennon was still thinking about how someone named Declan had implied they wouldn't be that upset about eating people from the north. He'd heard that the Spencer/Lopez rivalry was intense, but that was next level.

"Listen, fancy-pants," Hadley said, and he could only assume she was speaking to him. "Once you get out of here, tell everyone how smart and cool we were, okay? Me, specifically. Tell them how cute I am."

"I . . . uh . . ." It would not be a lie to tell people that Hadley was cute, but he'd also undergone extensive media training with a serious man named Trevor who had threatened to punch him in the nuts if he ever discussed a woman's appearance. Or anyone's appearance, actually. But especially women.

His father was above all that. They were projecting an image. He would need to go back and say Hadley was "polite and friendly and professional."

"I'd prefer you tell no one how cute I am," Maisie said dryly.

"Maisie, shut up," Hadley said pleasantly.

"I think that maybe he'll have more important things to discuss," Elise said, and coughed.

"I doubt it." Hadley waved a hand and they all laughed. He didn't quite get the joke.

He glanced from Elise to Maisie to Hadley. He'd heard about them—not them, specifically, but the generation born inside the Q. Generation Q, people called them. He'd seen a show once exploring what it must be like to have grown up in a confined area, under constant threat of illness or death. It had been a grim hour of television.

And they'd gotten it completely wrong. These three girls seemed fine. Happy, even. Well, not Elise, but she seemed in good spirits despite the obvious lung problems. He wondered if she was going to get a new one. Surely it helped to be friends with Dr. Lopez's niece and the daughter of Isaac Rojas.

He heard footsteps in the hall, and turned to see Dr. Lopez approaching the door. His expression was tight, annoyed.

"Mr. Pierce? Seems like we're going to have more trouble getting you home than I expected."

MAISIE

MAISIE WATCHED AS Lennon's carefully arranged expression gave way to horror. He'd been doing a pretty good job of pretending not to be absolutely appalled at ending up in the Q, but his bravado faded at Lopez's words.

He straightened and put the blank expression back on his face. Given how quickly he'd recovered, she guessed that he was used to pretending everything was fine when it actually wasn't.

"Why?" Lennon asked. "What did they say?"

Lopez turned. "Come with me. Maisie, you too."

She followed them across the hall. Lopez gestured for her to close the door. He leaned against one of the tables, crossing his arms over his chest.

"I've talked to my contact at the CDC," he said. "They're only giving us seventy-two hours to get you out. Said that the tests we did don't prove that the vaccine will work any longer than that. And that's seventy-two hours from when you were dropped, so technically . . ." He looked at his watch. "About seventy hours from now."

"Is that . . . not enough time?" Lennon asked.

"It would be plenty of time, if they'd let us scale a wall. But they said it's out of the question."

"Why?"

"They think that if we do it, everyone else in the Q will get ideas and start trying to hop over. Absolutely no scaling walls. They'll shoot us if we try."

"Can they send a helicopter?" Lennon asked. "There was plenty of room for them to land out where I was before."

"They definitely won't do that," Lopez said.

Lennon appeared confused.

"Last time they sent a helicopter in, people mobbed it," Maisie explained. "Pilot was killed. Not to mention that people used to shoot down planes."

"Mostly in the north," Lopez added hastily. "They developed some impressive antiaircraft technology in order to make the gate the only option for supplies."

"But that incident with the helicopter was, what? Fifteen years ago?" Lennon asked. "And we're in the south. You're not going to shoot down any planes, are you?"

"They're not a forgiving bunch out there," Lopez said. "They said no helicopter. They insisted that there is only one legal way in and out of the Q. Through the northern gate."

Maisie laughed.

Lennon looked at her sharply. "What's wrong with the northern gate?"

"It's on the other side of Spencer territory."

Lopez nodded grimly. "Northgate—the territory where

the gate is—is at the northwest tip of the Q, deep in Spencer territory. Which we do not enter."

Lennon appeared alarmed suddenly. "So . . . ?"

"So, I think you're stuck here, Fancy-pants," Maisie said. Lennon turned quickly to Lopez.

"No," Lopez said. "I'm going to put a team together and we're going to try."

Maisie's mouth fell open. "Are you serious?"

"Yes."

"Why would you do that?"

"Because I'm not scared of going into Spencer territory. We'll be fine." He said it with so much confidence that Maisie knew immediately he was lying. Maybe he was reluctant to tell the Americans that relations with the north were so bad he couldn't transport Lennon fifty miles to the gate.

"Maisie, why don't you go find Declan and get him up to speed?" Lopez asked. "Tell him to start thinking about who he wants to send. We'll leave tonight or tomorrow."

"Sure." Declan was *not* going to be interested in transporting this dude anywhere, which Lopez must have known. She moved toward the door.

"We have a call scheduled with the FBI," Lopez said to Lennon as Maisie opened the door. "They want proof you're alive. And they have a few questions about your kidnapping."

"Yeah, do you know who did this to you?" Maisie asked, pausing halfway into the hallway.

"I'm sure it was Howard or someone from his campaign," he said.

"What? Isn't that dude your president?"

He nodded. "We get a lot of threats. Everyone who runs

against a Howard does, and I'm the quarantine zone point person for the campaign. They hate me a lot." He said it like he was almost proud of it.

"Huh." Maisie glanced at Lopez, who was focused on his phone. "Sounds like a real shitshow out there."

"Well, Senator Pierce is ready to change all that. He's running an honest, straightforward campaign that will—"

"Mr. Pierce, we can't vote in here," Lopez said, glancing up from his phone with an amused expression.

"Right. Sorry. Habit." He smiled sheepishly.

Maisie lifted a hand in goodbye and walked out the door, closing it behind her. If Lennon was smart, he wouldn't get his hopes up. The chances of a team making it to the northern border—alive—were incredibly slim.

Declan took the news about Lennon about as well as she'd expected.

"I am not transporting that little shithead anywhere," he said, tossing a wrench across the garage with impressive force. Declan loved throwing things across rooms. It was his main hobby.

"I figured you'd say that." She leaned against the side of the truck while one of the guys fished the wrench out of the corner and delivered it back to the toolbox.

Declan pushed his hands into his hair. He had great, thick hair. She used to run her fingers through it all the time.

The urge was very much gone now. In fact, if she got her hands on that hair, she might rip out a few strands.

"He didn't say why he wants to get Pierce out of here?" he asked.

"Not really. He just said he wasn't scared to go across Spencer territory."

"It doesn't matter whether he's scared or not. He's giving up leverage. I'd keep the son of a US senator, if it were me."

"Possibly the son of the next president," she pointed out.

"I doubt it. The Howard family hasn't lost an election since before the Q was formed."

"Who are you going to send?"

"Not you, if that's what you're thinking." He gave her a look that she knew very well—he had zero faith in her abilities.

She considered arguing, but she actually didn't want to transport the dude anywhere either.

"Maybe whoever you send can figure out why our shipments keep getting held up," she said.

"Maybe." He braced his hand against the side of the truck as he peered under the hood. "This wouldn't be a problem if Lopez would just let me put a team together and take the north."

Maisie rolled her eyes. Declan was convinced that he could take the north from the Spencer family, if just given the opportunity.

Lopez pointed out—correctly—that trying to take the whole Q for themselves meant a bloody battle, with lots of lives lost.

Declan said it was worth it, to stop having to deal with the Spencers to get shipments from the US. They desperately needed the medical supplies in those shipments, and relying on the north to deliver them was risky. And Declan thought it was only a matter of time until the north invaded them anyway. He'd always been the type to shoot first, just in case, and ask no questions later.

Maisie thought that was a dumb strategy, but no one had asked her opinion.

"Are you done collecting for the day?" Declan asked.

"No."

"Then get to it." He gestured to her bloody knuckles. "Did you break your hand again?"

"No," she lied. The hand ached. She'd almost certainly broken her knuckle for the third—or was it fourth?—time. Her last break had barely fully healed. But Declan didn't need another reason to think she was weak. "You know you have a problem, right? If people aren't getting their stuff, they're not going to pay. The Reapers are increasing their numbers. We might have a problem there."

"I got your text."

"Are you going to do something about it?" she asked impatiently.

"The Reapers have been whining about something or other for as long as I can remember."

"Yeah, but people may think they have a point this time. They deliver a pretty great pitch about the benefits of their stupid 'no leader, we all do what we want' lifestyle."

"If it's stupid, then we don't need to worry about it."

"Not everyone is as smart as me."

Declan just squinted at her. He never had appreciated her sense of humor.

She sighed. "If we can't deliver what they need, we should give people a break from rent for a week."

"They still get plenty."

"They're getting angry. We can smooth things over, make people feel better about—"

"Make people *feel* better?" He straightened, cocking an eyebrow. "I'm not a fucking shrink. People are going to pay because I'm going to go knock their heads together if they don't. I don't give a shit about their feelings. Now, can you collect or not? Because you can go—"

"Work at the garbage plant, I know." She turned away, resisting the urge to flip him off as she went. She might have done it if they were still together. But he probably wouldn't let her get away with it anymore.

She walked out of the garage and down the street. If her father were still alive, he probably would have said the same thing. *No one will ever respect you if they don't fear you.* He said it all the time when she was younger. Not so much as she got older, though. Not after it became obvious that Declan was going to be the next second-in-command, not Maisie.

Maybe she'd volunteer to go north with Lennon after all. Just as a *screw you* to Declan.

LENNON

LENNON SNUCK OVER to a window when no one was looking.

They were on the tenth floor of the comms tower, and he could see a large expanse of the quarantine zone from up here.

There were buildings he recognized from pictures of Austin before the virus. The capitol, and a couple of skyscrapers. Others were long gone. Aerial shots had shown the change in the area in the twenty years since they were all put in here. He'd spent time poring over them with the rest of the quarantine zone team.

The people inside had left Austin mostly untouched until the walls went up. But after the walls were erected, the people inside stopped thinking of themselves as Americans and the area around them as Austin. It was just the Q, and they were allowed to do whatever they wanted with it.

They'd torn down some buildings—no one wanted a huge football stadium—and built others. All law-enforcement buildings were demolished. They kept the libraries. Ransacked all the homes in the suburbs, then bulldozed them down and built farms. They picked a few important roads to maintain, and let the rest fill with potholes and weeds. From the satellite images, it looked like the north had demolished more of the old Austin than the south had. The north had been suburbs and large shopping centers before the quarantine zone was established. Now, the satellite images showed fields, open space, and new, smaller buildings.

The comms tower was at the edge of what had once been downtown Austin. He was facing north, so he couldn't see most of the old downtown. He could see the big highway leading out to buildings and homes. An apartment building on the side of the highway had a big flag on the side of it that said KEEP THE Q WEIRD.

"Mr. Pierce."

Lennon turned. Dr. Lopez gestured for Lennon to join him at the table.

"Lennon is fine," he said as he walked to him.

"Let's call the FBI, Lennon."

"Right." He sat down next to the doctor. "Did they say what was going to happen to me after I get to the northern gate?"

Dr. Lopez was reaching for the phone, but he pulled his hand back and turned his attention to Lennon. "You've seen the northern gate? From the other side, I mean?"

Lennon nodded. He'd visited once, with his dad.

"They'll let you through the gate that takes you to the other side of the wall. There, they'll administer a test to see if you're positive for the virus."

Lennon's stomach clenched. "And if I am? Will they make me go back in?"

"They didn't say. They did say that there will be a hazmat suit waiting, and you'll need to put it on before they let you through the next gate. But there will be someone there to do the test and help you. Then you'll be quarantined, though they didn't tell me how long. I imagine at least a month, to be on the safe side. Okay?"

He tried not to look nervous as he nodded. "Okay." He could picture the place that the doctor was talking about. There was a chain-link fence around the northern gate, a secondary precaution in case anyone ever escaped through during shipment deliveries. It was about twenty feet from the wall, with signs that said DO NOT APPROACH—YOU WILL BE SHOT. It was not an empty threat.

Dr. Lopez reached for the phone. "I think they're going to patch your father in as well. He asked to speak with you." He seemed to think that Lennon would be pleased to talk to his father.

In reality, Lennon would have preferred to just stick with the FBI.

He'd had numerous conversations with his father about the threats against the family. The senator had suggested more extreme security measures for Lennon, as most of the vitriol being spewed at them was aimed at him. He delighted in pissing off the Howard family, and he was really, really good at it.

He already had a security team that didn't even let him go to the bathroom by himself. He'd declined more, and told his father that scaling back his public events—or showing up under heavy guard—was the wrong move this late in the campaign.

It'll look like we're scared, Lennon had argued.

We should *be scared,* his father had countered.

So. Lennon had been wrong, and his father was right. As usual.

He shouldn't have joined the campaign at all. His parents had been hesitant about it, happy to let his sisters—his cheerful, perfect sisters—take on that role instead. The son who had set a family record for arrests wasn't the type of guy you wanted on your presidential campaign.

Of course, the family arrest record had been zero before Lennon, so it wasn't much of an accomplishment. He'd set the bar high for future generations, though.

But their hesitance had made him want to do it even more. He was sure he would be good at campaigning, and it wasn't like he had anything pressing to do, anyway. It had been strongly suggested that he should take a hiatus from Yale (*Perhaps you should reconsider whether this is the best choice for you,* the dean had said wearily), so it was the perfect opportunity.

They'd agreed, and Lennon had been so smug when he became the star of the campaign. All the papers said he'd follow in his father's footsteps and run for president one day. Yale was going to be begging for him to come back next year.

Now look at him. Kidnapped three times, currently held hostage in the most dangerous place in the world. Absolutely distracting from the campaign at the most crucial point. He should have stayed in New Haven and ignored that little voice that said he had to prove his parents wrong, in the most public way possible. His girlfriend at the time had told him that he would never find happiness through their approval, and he should grow up.

She was annoyingly right all the time. Everyone was right,

and Lennon was wrong. He should have it tattooed on his forehead, since they'd all never let him live this down.

Dr. Lopez dialed on the clunky phone and pressed it to his ear. He listened for a moment. "Yes, this is Dr. Lopez. I have Lennon Pierce here." He passed the phone to him.

Lennon raised the phone to his ear. "Hello?"

"*Mr. Pierce? This is Agent Johnson. Are you in a safe location right now?*"

"Yes? Yes." *Define "safe,"* he wanted to say.

"*We have footage from the gas station of two men grabbing you. Is that correct?*"

"Yeah, there were two."

"*And when they took you to the airport? How many there?*"

"Three. The two who took me and the pilot."

"*That's all? No others?*"

"Not that I saw. Did you get them?"

"*The plane was shot down right outside the quarantine zone. All three men aboard are dead.*"

"Oh." He barely stopped himself from saying, *Good.* "Do you know who they were?"

"*We're still working on that. I have Senator Pierce on the line. He'd like to speak with you briefly.*"

"Sure."

"*Lennon.*" His dad said his name with an exhalation of air. "*Are you okay?*"

"I'm fine. I'm good."

"*Are you sure? Are they . . . Are you . . . comfortable?*"

"Yes. Dr. Lopez has been very hospitable. They gave me some food and clothes and they've promised to help get me out of here."

His dad blew out a breath. *"Christ. Okay."*

"How is, um . . ." He glanced at Dr. Lopez. "How is the news framing this?"

There was a brief silence. *"There is significant concern. Your face is on every news station in the country right now."*

Lennon could read between the lines of *that* statement. He could only imagine the media hysteria. "There's no need for significant concern, for the record. I'm doing great. Really."

"I know that everyone will be very relieved to hear that. You can tell them yourself as soon as you get out."

"I will."

"Agent Johnson would like me to wrap this up. He has some questions for Dr. Lopez."

"Okay. Tell Mom I'm fine. And Stella and Caroline. Tell them I'm actually excited to see the quarantine zone first-hand." He could just imagine the reaction to that from Caroline, his older sister. She would put her hands on her hips and say something like, "Tell Lennon to stop being ridiculous."

Stella, however, would probably be a little jealous. His sixteen-year-old sister was just as obsessed as he was with the quarantine zone. She was going to relentlessly hound him for information when he got back.

Dr. Lopez peered at him skeptically.

His dad chuckled. *"I'll do that."*

"Bye, Dad."

Agent Johnson's voice returned to the line. *"May I speak with Dr. Lopez, please?"*

"Sure." Lennon handed the phone back to the doctor. "Agent Johnson."

He took it, pressing it to his ear. "Agent Johnson, we expect to have Mr. Pierce to the northern gate in twenty-four hours. There shouldn't be any—"

Boom.

Dr. Lopez stopped talking. Lennon stiffened.

Boom.

Was that . . . a bomb?

Surely not.

"Let me just check on something and call you back," Dr. Lopez said hurriedly, and then hung up the phone. He jumped to his feet and ran to the door, yanking it open. "Hadley! Emergency alert! Now!"

MAISIE

A LOUD BOOM sounded from behind Maisie. She turned.

Boom.

Louder.

Gunshots.

Around her, people began running.

She spun in a circle, trying to find the source of the gunfire.

The building next to her exploded.

Maisie flew backward, hitting the ground hard. She squeezed her body into a tight ball as debris rained down around her.

"Take cover. I repeat—TAKE COVER. The Q is under attack."

Hadley's voice rang out from somewhere as the debris stopped.

Maisie slowly lifted her head. Burning chunks of building were scattered all around her. She sat back on her heels.

The building in front of her was half gone. A charred, blackened body was strewn across the grass.

"Take cover," Hadley's voice repeated from nearby speakers. *"Follow instructions from Lopez family members. Do not—"*

Hadley's voice cut off with a scream. Over the speakers, gunfire sounded.

She heard the rush of footsteps, and quickly stood and turned to see Nathan rounding the corner. He was panting, his nearly-toothless mouth open wide.

"Maisie, what the hell is going on?" he yelled.

She shook her head. Gunfire rang out again, and she turned to look. It was maybe two blocks over.

Behind her, Nathan yelled something.

"What?" She glanced back at him. He was already turned to go, but he paused, cupping his hands around his mouth.

"I said, your arm is on FIRE!"

She looked down. Flames licked up the shirtsleeve of her left arm. Her brain clicked into place, and she could suddenly feel the heat on her skin.

"Oh, shit." She hit the ground, smothering the fire in the grass. She straightened, and quickly pushed the blackened sleeve up. Her arm was red and slightly singed, and it burned a little, but the damage wasn't too bad. Her hand, though, ached even worse. Not a great day for her entire left arm.

She got to her feet and did a quick inventory of the rest of her body. Nothing else was broken.

She reached back, pulling out the gun tucked into the waistband of her pants. She ran down the street toward the comms tower, keeping her weapon pointed at the ground and pumping her arms as fast as she could.

A blast erupted from her left. She skidded away from it, using her arm to shield her face, and then took off again, her boots pounding the pavement.

The comms tower loomed in front of her, still standing. No signs of bombing.

She threw open the door and lifted her gun. She took the stairs two at a time. More gunfire from above.

She stopped at the door to the tenth floor and took in a deep breath. She slowly turned the knob, opening the door just a crack.

Silence greeted her. She cautiously peered around the corner.

Two men lay dead on the floor, blood seeping out of bullet wounds in their chests. They'd been wearing masks, and both were pushed up to reveal their faces. Maisie moved a little closer. Two white dudes, in their thirties or forties. Vaguely familiar, but she couldn't remember their names. She had a sinking feeling that she knew why.

She edged closer to the studio. It was empty, bullet holes in the wall.

The door across the hall was closed, and she raised her gun as she walked to it and turned the knob. She nudged the door open.

A gun was pointed in her face.

Hadley let out a breath, lowering the gun. "Jesus. I almost shot you."

Maisie lowered her own weapon, glancing into the room behind Hadley. Lennon stood several feet back, also holding a gun. He gingerly set it on the table.

"You gave him a gun?" Maisie asked.

"He said he knows how to use one."

Maisie looked at him skeptically.

"Why do you both look at me like that?" Lennon asked. "I've been to a shooting range before."

"Where is Lopez?" Maisie asked.

"He left with his guys," Hadley said. "He told me to stay here with Lennon."

"These guys . . ." Maisie gestured at them.

"Reapers? Yeah." Hadley nodded grimly.

"Shit. I thought so." She would have known anyone else in the south. But the Reapers weren't exactly friendly with a collector from the Lopez family.

"Is it bad out there?" Hadley asked. "What are they bombing?"

Maisie looked over her shoulder, taking a step back. "I'm going to go find—"

The stairwell door banged open. Three men wearing black masks streamed into the hallway.

"Oh, shi—" Hadley's voice cut off as Maisie shoved her inside the room.

She stuck her gun out of the doorway and leaned forward just enough to see the men heading for them. She fired.

Bullets ricocheted off the wall. One of the men collapsed, blood spurting from his neck.

She squeezed the trigger again, but nothing happened. She was out of bullets.

A hand yanked her into the hallway suddenly, and she ducked just in time to miss the bullet aimed at her head. She dropped her gun and slammed her fist into the attacker's stomach, ignoring the flash of pain across her injured knuckles. He wheezed and dropped to his knees.

She grabbed for his gun, but he rolled over, holding it tight against his chest. Behind her, she heard Hadley yell, followed by more gunfire. She launched onto the man's back, yanking his mask off and then grabbing a fistful of his hair. He yelled in protest. She almost screamed too as pain shot through her hand.

"Hey." The voice was oddly calm, and she took a quick glance to the side to see a hand holding a gun out to her.

She grabbed it, aimed it at the man's head, and fired. He stilled beneath her.

She climbed off his body. It was Lennon who had handed her the gun, and he stood there, eyes wide.

"Thanks," she said, glancing into the room. Hadley stood over the other dead man.

"Sure," Lennon said. "I figured you had a better shot of hitting the target than I did."

She cocked an eyebrow.

"I said I knew how to use a gun, not that I was good with it."

"I have a question," Hadley said, stepping over the man she'd killed to join them in the hallway. "Why do all these assholes keep coming up here with guns? To the tenth floor? I'm usually the only one up here."

Maisie rolled the man in front of her onto his back and grabbed the gun that fell out of his hand. Another Reaper. She recognized this one. He worked security at one of their bars.

"Let's go." She clicked the safety on the gun and handed it to Lennon. "You two are sitting ducks up here."

"Does this happen a lot?" Lennon asked as they jogged to the stairwell. Maisie pushed open the door and started down the steps.

"No," Hadley said. "There haven't been bombings since . . ."

"Since we fought the Spencers and divided into north and south." Maisie threw a glance over her shoulder and saw her feelings mirrored on Hadley's face. This attack felt very similar to that one, and they'd barely defeated the Spencers to keep the south. She wondered if the Reapers had increased their numbers more than anyone had realized, and were taking a page from the Spencers' book.

Maisie pushed open the door at the bottom of the stairwell and jogged across the lobby. She stopped at the door, holding her arm out to indicate Lennon and Hadley should wait.

"Jesus, are you okay?" Lennon asked. He stared at her arm, horrified.

She glanced over at it. The cut on her knuckles had opened up again, spilling blood down her hand.

"I'm fine. It looks worse than it is." She peered out the smudged glass door. The street was empty, an overturned garbage can rolling to a stop at the curb.

"Are you sure? It—"

"Do you usually ask so many questions during a gun fight?" she interrupted, cocking an eyebrow.

"Sorry," he said sheepishly.

"Come on. Lennon, walk behind me. Hadley, walk behind him and keep an eye on our backs."

She opened the door, and the two lined up behind her as ordered. She stepped out of the building and onto the street.

"Where are we going?" Hadley asked.

"We're going to drop off Lennon at my apartment, and

then go find Lopez or Declan and figure out what the hell is going on."

They walked in silence to the end of the block, and then for several more. They turned a corner onto a street lined with small houses. Maisie stopped short.

Lopez was on his knees in the middle of the street. A truck sat not far away, two men standing in the bed, guns in hand. Another masked man stood over Lopez, a gun pointed at his head.

"Go back, go back," she whispered, turning and gesturing for Lennon and Hadley to move. They ran back around the corner.

"What?" Hadley whispered.

"They have Lopez. We need to—" She cut herself off, glancing at their surroundings. They'd see her coming a mile away if she just waltzed down the street. She needed to get inside one of the homes. Maybe then she could surprise them.

She ran to the back gate of the closest house, opening it and sprinting across the lawn. She hopped the chain-link fence, glancing behind her to see Hadley and Lennon climbing over as well.

They jumped the next two fences, until they hit a small red house near the middle of the block. She ran to the back door and peered in the windows. An empty kitchen table, and beyond that, a living room. Seemed deserted.

She tried the door. It opened easily.

Her shoes squeaked faintly as she stepped inside. Behind her, she heard Lennon's and Hadley's footsteps following.

She checked her left, and then right.

An older man and a woman were huddled together on the kitchen floor. They were clutching hands, eyes wide. They looked vaguely familiar, though she couldn't remember their names.

She lifted one finger to her lips. They both nodded. The woman actually appeared a little relieved, like the sight of Maisie in her kitchen was a welcome one.

Maisie darted to the front window and just barely nudged the curtain to the side so she could see to the street. Lopez was still on the ground. The guy above him had his phone pressed to his ear, gun still aimed at Lopez.

"I need to distract the guys in the truck," she whispered. She glanced back at the couple on the floor. "Do you have any explosives?"

Lennon looked at her with a baffled expression, like this was the weirdest question he'd ever heard.

"No," the man said, with genuine disappointment. His eyes lit up. "I've got lighter fluid, though." He stood up and dashed out the back door.

The woman jumped to her feet and opened the cabinet under the sink. She began pulling glass bottles from her recycling bin.

"Yesss, great idea," Hadley said. She grabbed a dish rag off the sink and tore it in half.

"Are you making . . ." Lennon watched as the man brought the lighter fluid back inside and began pouring it into the bottle. He didn't finish his question. He'd clearly figured out the answer.

"I need someone to throw it," Maisie said. "And I'll go for

the guy with Lopez. Hadley, how's your arm? Think you can throw it accurately from the porch?"

"Uh . . ." She winced. "Probably not. And you know I can't aim a gun for shit at that distance. I'd probably hit Uncle Franco."

"I can do it," Lennon said. "Throw it, I mean. My shooting skills also leave something to be desired."

Maisie shook her head. "Forget it. I'll do it myself."

"You can't do both," Hadley said.

"Sure I can." She reached her left hand out for the bottle. Pain seared up her arm as she tried to close her fingers around it. She gasped and pulled her hand back.

"Did you break your hand *again*?" Hadley asked. "Don't you still have a metal plate in there from last time?"

"It might just be bruised." She moved her fingers and winced. "Shit."

"I can do it," Lennon repeated. "Seriously. I have a good arm."

Maisie sighed. It was her only option, unfortunately.

She stepped closer to him. "You can't wuss out at the last minute, okay? You're going to throw that and light those assholes on fire, and I don't want you getting a sudden attack of conscience when we step out there."

He nodded.

"Because if you do that, all three of them will fire on us, and we're both dead. Okay?"

"Okay."

The man carefully handed the bottle to Lennon, along with a lighter.

Maisie moved closer to the door. He followed her, his eyes on the bottle in his hand.

"You light that the *second* I open this door. I'm going to move to the left immediately, and you're going to come out, throw it, and hit the deck. Hadley, stay right behind us, just in case we need backup."

Lennon nodded. Hadley pulled out her gun and took off the safety.

Maisie put her hand on the doorknob. She met Lennon's gaze. He looked calm, strangely enough. Maybe later she'd ask him if this was his first time throwing a Molotov cocktail. She got the impression that it was not.

"On three," she said. "One . . . two . . . three!"

She pulled the door open and darted onto the porch. The men in the truck both turned. She aimed her gun at the man on the street.

Lennon ran out the door, arm poised to throw. He took two quick steps and let the bottle fly.

It sailed through the air with surprising speed. He had not been kidding about having a good arm.

It crashed into the truck bed. Flames engulfed the men.

Out of the corner of her eye, she saw Lennon hit the deck, as ordered. A bullet sailed past her ear.

She fired her gun. Lopez jumped to his feet.

The man jerked as her bullet hit him in the shoulder, but he didn't go down. She fired again.

He turned, aiming his gun at Lopez instead of at her.

Shit.

She fired again, but so did he. Lopez collapsed.

She darted off the porch as she squeezed the trigger again.

The man took off, weaving so that her bullets sailed just past him. He raced for the truck and threw open the driver's door.

One of the men in the truck rolled out and onto the ground, desperately trying to extinguish the fire on his pants.

"Hadley, take care of them!" she yelled, pointing at the truck as she ran for Lopez. She heard shots a moment later, and then tires squealing. She glanced over to see the truck flying around the corner and out of sight.

She sprinted to Lopez, who was still on the ground. He'd rolled over onto his back. Blood pooled on the concrete beneath him. His eyes fluttered and then shut. His body went still.

"Oh god," she said, kneeling down beside him. She fumbled for her phone, and then shakily dialed and pressed it to her ear.

"This is Maisie Rojas. I need you to send someone right now. Dr. Lopez has been shot."

LENNON

had been pushed from an airplane,

was captured by cannibals,

had gotten injected with an experimental vaccine
against his will,

had participated in (okay, mostly watched) several
gun fights, and

had lit two men on fire.

It had been quite a day, to say the least.

An ambulance had appeared to take Dr. Lopez away,
and Lennon had been ushered inside with Hadley and

Maisie. They took him to a hospital, and Lennon was deposited in the hallway, where he'd been waiting for the past two hours.

Apparently, they were no longer worried about him running away.

He'd actually considered going outside. He still hadn't had much of an opportunity to explore, but he didn't know what he'd do if he lost track of Maisie and Hadley. He had no phone—the kidnappers had taken it in Georgia—and even if he had, he didn't think it would connect to the network in the quarantine zone.

People rushed by in the hallways, but rarely paid much attention to him, sitting on the floor with his back to the wall.

It was remarkably like a regular hospital. He wasn't sure what he expected—chaos, maybe—but it all looked the same. Nurses and doctors in scrubs and masks, everyone holding a tablet that probably had patient charts on it. He wondered how they were trained. Schooling in the quarantine zone was a mystery, though everyone he'd talked to so far clearly had some kind of education. He was ashamed to admit that he'd sort of imagined them all as those cannibals at the border—dirty idiots with no common sense.

The door at the end of the hallway opened, and Maisie walked out. Her shirt had blood splattered across it—Lopez's—and she'd haphazardly wrapped a piece of white bandage around her left hand.

"Sorry," Maisie said as he got to his feet. "We wanted to stay until he got out of surgery, but turns out it's going to be a while."

"Is he doing okay?" Lennon asked.

"They think he's going to pull through."

"That's good."

"Listen, I don't really know what to do with you, so you're just going to come home with me. Hadley's going to meet us there later."

"Do you guys live together?"

"No, one of the bombs destroyed her place." She sighed, pushing a hand over her ponytail. "You okay to walk? It's a couple miles, but buses aren't running. We walk a lot here."

"Yeah, that's fine."

She strode past him, leading him down the hallway, through the lobby, and outside. The sun had just gone down, streetlights clicking on as darkness fell.

He glanced at her. She was peering at her phone, her eyebrows drawn together. She noticed his gaze as she slipped it back into her pocket.

"A lot of people haven't checked in yet," she explained.

"Do you know who did this?"

She shook her head. "Nothing for sure."

He wanted to ask about the plan to get him out of here, but it seemed callous under the circumstances. Besides, there was still plenty of time. Last time he'd checked a clock it was just after eight p.m., meaning he still had sixty hours to meet the CDC deadline. He could spare a few hours for sleep.

And thank god for that. His steps were heavy, exhaustion starting to creep into his body. He'd nodded off a couple times in the van with the Georgia kidnappers, but other than that, he'd barely slept the past two nights. He didn't even care if he had to sleep on the floor—he just wanted somewhere to collapse for a few hours.

He looked over at Maisie to see her watching him.

"What do people think of us out there?" she asked.

"In the US?"

"And everywhere."

He hesitated. He'd told Dr. Lopez he wouldn't tell anyone the truth of what a lot of Americans thought of them, but he still wasn't sure that lying was the right choice. In his opinion, the people of the quarantine zone should have access to the same internet as every other free nation. They should be able to watch the news themselves.

On the other hand, Dr. Lopez was right about the panic. And maybe his dad was about to win the election, and it didn't matter what a bunch of very loud idiots thought. His dad would never bomb the quarantine zone. He'd made that promise publicly, and Lennon knew him well enough to be sure that it wasn't just politician talk.

Besides, now that he was actually faced with having to explain what people thought of the inhabitants of the quarantine zone, the prospect was uncomfortable.

"*We can't just keep hoping this problem will go away,*" a congressman had argued once, on cable news. "*When a group of lawless thugs have taken over a part of our country, drastic action is necessary.*"

He was not going to repeat the term *lawless thugs* to her.

Also, he thought that most people in the quarantine zone would take issue with the phrase "taken over a part of our country," considering that every single one of them was trapped in the zone against their will.

"It's a mix of emotions," he said carefully. "Some people are sympathetic. Some are scared. Mostly, people are fascinated and want to know how you guys are doing in here."

Her lips twitched, and she looked away from him. "You're a good liar, Lennon."

He wasn't that good, if she was calling him out on it.

"It's not a lie," he said. It was a half-truth. Close enough. "I do think that people would be more understanding if you communicated with the outside world occasionally, though. People are scared of what they don't understand."

She tilted her head and said nothing.

"I think it will be helpful for me to tell the story when I get out of here," he said. "People will be interested to know what it was like in here."

"They'll probably be more scared of us than ever."

"I can always find the good parts of a story."

She gave him an amused look. "I have no doubt."

He heard the murmured sound of voices and music up ahead. The glow of lights was brighter.

They turned a corner. He stopped.

Maisie, a few steps ahead of him, turned to see him frozen. "What?" He kept gaping. She followed his gaze.

The street was crowded with people. They milled around, some of them carrying cups in their hands. Two women played guitar on the corner, and a few people were helping to sweep up glass and debris from a bombed building.

Giant bright billboards flashed over the buildings. An old music video played on one. An advertisement for a local brewery was on the other.

A man whizzed by on a scooter, wearing a pair of goggles and a bright pink mask.

"What?" Maisie asked again.

"I just . . ." He was trying to remember what he'd read about the quarantine zone. *Unreliable electricity, mostly powered by solar and wind. Crumbling infrastructure, left over from pre-virus era. Strict curfew. Gangs rule with an iron fist. Executions in the street.*

"Is there a curfew?" he finally managed.

She looked at him strangely. "No. Does the US have a curfew?"

"No, I'd just read that you did."

"Spencer territory has done that in the past. Not sure if they still do."

"Oh."

A group of men were helping put together a broken picnic table outside a bar, and Lennon watched them, still trying to process this version of the quarantine zone.

"You thought it was a real shithole in here, didn't you?"

His gaze snapped back to Maisie. "I, uh . . ."

She rolled her eyes, a spark of amusement on her face. "Come on. My apartment's not far."

Lennon followed Maisie to a five-story apartment building. It appeared the entire street had gone untouched from the bombings. It was quiet and dark, most of the streetlights out.

Her apartment was on the top floor, a one-bedroom with huge windows that showed off part of the city. He eyed the plush brown couch in the living room, hoping that would be his for the night.

Maisie walked into the kitchen, flipping on the light. She

had a small table that was covered in clutter—papers, a few empty bottles, books, and a laptop.

Something fell to the floor with a *plop,* and his eyes followed the sound. It was a piece of bloody bandage from her arm. It had fallen off and landed on the kitchen floor.

He almost laughed. He was getting punchy.

"Well, that's gross," she said. She unwrapped the rest of the bandage with a wince. Her hand looked bruised and dirty, like she hadn't had it cleaned at the hospital. Too busy dealing with Lopez, maybe.

She stretched her fingers and sucked in a breath.

"That does not look great," he offered unhelpfully.

"Just a little . . . broken." She made a sound that was both a moan and a laugh.

"You've broken it before? More than once?"

"Who's counting?" She made a face as she walked into the kitchen. She turned on the water and stuck her hand under it. "Shit, that hurts."

"Was it always from punching people?"

"What?"

"Breaking your hand. Always from punching someone?"

"Oh. Yeah. I tend to get a little too . . . enthusiastic in the moment."

He let out a short, completely inappropriate laugh. She cocked an eyebrow.

He cleared his throat. "I'm sorry."

"That's fine, I'm just in a ton of pain here."

He blanched, shifting uncomfortably. "I, uh, I didn't mean—"

Maisie threw her head back with a laugh. "I'm just messing with you."

He let out a relieved sigh and laughed weakly.

"This entire situation is too fucked-up not to be funny," she said.

His thoughts exactly.

"Are you hungry?" she asked as she carefully dried her arm with a cloth. "I don't have a lot, but there's some bread and . . ." She walked to the refrigerator. "Some dry sausage. Oh, and I should eat these apples before they go bad. We had a good batch this year."

"Sure," he said, his hunger overtaking his exhaustion at the mention of food. That sandwich from earlier hadn't stayed with him for long.

She pulled the food out as he sat down at one of the bar-stools. She put a plate in front of him with a hunk of bread, some sausage, cheese, and half an apple.

He tore off a piece of the bread, glancing at the half loaf left on the counter, wrapped in a kitchen towel. "Did you make this bread?"

"Yes."

He wondered if he was asking too many questions, if she could tell he was equal parts fascinated and horrified by it all. He was trying very hard not to imagine himself sitting across from every major journalist in the country, telling them everything he'd learned during his time here, but it was hard. He was already rehearsing.

"Does everyone make their own bread?" he asked, unable to help himself.

"No, you can get some at a bakery, if you want. Kind of a waste of money, though."

"It's really good."

"Thank you."

Her phone beeped, and she pulled it out of her pocket, a smile crossing her face. "Lopez is out of surgery. He's not awake yet, but the surgery went well."

"That's great," he said, with genuine relief. He'd been very worried that whoever made decisions after Lopez wouldn't be so interested in getting him out of here.

"We'll go see him tomorrow, find out what the plan is for you." She said the words while typing on her phone. She frowned at whatever reply she got, but didn't share it with Lennon.

After they'd finished eating, she fished a blanket and pillow out of the closet for him and pointed him to the couch.

"Hadley will come in later, but she can sleep with me. Tell her that if she tries to cuddle with you."

He tossed the pillow onto the couch. "Honestly, I'm so tired I'm not sure I'll wake up if she comes in and starts jumping up and down on top of me."

"I'm not going to tell her you said that, because she will definitely test it out." Maisie headed toward her bedroom.

"Maisie?"

She turned.

"Thank you. Really. For everything."

She stared at him for a moment, her expression guarded. She opened her mouth, and then seemed to think better of whatever she was going to say.

"Good night, Lennon."

MAISIE

"GOOOOOD MORNING TO all of you out there in the Q who didn't get blown up yesterday. That was some shit, wasn't it?"

Hadley's voice floated out of the speakers in the living room, too perky. She was always overly perky when she was scared.

On the couch, Lennon stirred. Maisie poured coffee into her cup, watching as he rolled over and blinked several times.

"Good morning," she said.

He sat up slowly, a confused look on his face as he glanced around the room.

"The hospital has asked that only one person per family waits in the waiting room, as they're getting a little crowded down there," Hadley was saying.

"Oh." Lennon ran a hand through his hair with a laugh. "I thought I heard Hadley."

"She slept at the studio." If she slept at all. Maisie doubted it. She hadn't wanted to fill Lennon in on everything that had happened, but it was obvious that yesterday was a coordinated attack on the Lopez family, and there were a lot of people injured, and even a few dead.

The entire Q was on edge, and Maisie had wanted to stay at the hospital, but she knew Lopez would be disappointed if she let anything happen to Lennon. She didn't care whether or not he made it out of the Q, and she doubted that Lopez still planned to try, considering yesterday's chaos. But she was going to keep him safe until someone broke the bad news to him.

Lennon pushed off the blanket and stood. He'd slept in the clothes Lopez had given him. She should probably find him something else.

"What time is it?" He searched for a clock.

"About seven."

She could see him doing the math in his head. Forty-nine hours left for him to get out.

"Do you want coffee?" she asked quickly, before he could inquire about a plan.

"Yes, please."

She reached for a mug with her left hand, sighing when pain seared through her fingers. Part of her had hoped that her hand would magically reveal itself to just be bruised the next day. No such luck, apparently.

She grabbed the mug with her other hand, poured Lennon a cup, and then disappeared into her bedroom to rummage around in the drawers. She walked out with pants, a slightly threadbare black T-shirt, and a lightweight gray jacket.

"You can wear these," she said, tossing them on the couch. "Declan might get pissed, but I told him three times to come get his stuff, so it's his own fault."

He walked across the living room, touching the shirt. "Declan?"

"Ex."

"Ah."

"Shower's through my room. Be quick."

The hospital was buzzing with an angry energy when they arrived. Maisie searched the crowd for Declan, but she didn't see him. She hadn't heard from him since before the bombings yesterday, and no one had seen him. She was starting to think he was dead.

She walked down the hallway, Lennon following. There was a crowd around Lopez's room. Beto stepped forward when he saw her.

"Hey, can I go in and talk to Lopez?" she asked.

He shook his head, his expression grim. "Not right now. Only my mom, my sister, and I are allowed for now."

"Can you ask him about Lennon, then? I need to know what the plan is."

"I, uh . . ." Beto shifted from foot to foot.

She frowned. "What's wrong?"

"Nothing."

"Have you heard from Declan?"

"No. Why does everyone keep asking me that? I don't take orders from Declan."

Julio turned, clearly annoyed. "If we're not taking orders from Declan, who the hell are we taking orders from?"

"Would you be quiet?" Beto snapped at Julio.

"No!" Julio's face went red. "You cannot keep this fucking

quiet! Declan is MIA, and Uncle Franco is unconscious! We need to figure out what to do!"

Maisie gaped at Julio. "What do you mean, he's not conscious?"

"He never woke up from surgery," Julio said. "Beto and Jasmine were trying to keep it a secret."

Maisie glanced around for Lopez's daughter, but Jasmine was nowhere to be seen. She was a doctor in this hospital—maybe she was in the room with her dad.

"*Goddammit,* Julio." Beto glared at him. "I was trying to keep people calm!"

"You were trying to run shit while your dad is unconscious."

She glanced at the men around her. Julio, Beto, all the various Lopez cousins—they were all ready to come to blows. There was no plan in place—as far as she knew—for who would take over after Lopez's death. Declan ran things, but the orders came from Lopez. Without him, there was no one to call the shots.

Not until one of these guys decided to take charge. She watched as Beto put a hand on the gun at his waist. He'd never seemed particularly interested in taking over for his dad, but maybe he was about to get interested.

Maisie discreetly reached out and wrapped her fingers around Lennon's wrist. He jumped, just barely, but recovered quickly.

She slowly stepped away from Julio and Beto. Lennon moved with her.

Beto's eyes slid briefly to her, but Julio stepped forward, getting in his face. He lost interest in Maisie.

Well, at least there were some benefits to everyone thinking she was harmless.

She maintained an even pace until they were outside the hospital doors. She let go of Lennon's wrist. He fell into step beside her.

"Is this bad?" he asked.

"Could be fine."

"You're practically running."

"I have short legs."

"Are those guys about to fight for control of the Lopez family?"

"I'm sure they'll cool down in a minute," she lied. She glanced over her shoulder. No one was following them. She let out a breath and pulled her phone out of her pocket. She texted Hadley.

> Are you alone?

> Yes. Why?

> We're coming to you.

"I don't mean to sound, uh, selfish, but are we still going to be able to get to the northern gate in"—he looked down at his bare wrist, seeming to forget that there was nothing there—"uh, however long we have left? Less than forty-eight hours?"

"Not now, Lennon."

—

"What do you mean, *unconscious*?" Hadley blinked, wide-eyed.

"That's what they said," Maisie said.

Hadley slowly sat down in her chair. They were in the studio, an old song playing softly from the speakers. Lennon stood in the doorway. He kept fidgeting with his shirt—pulling on the collar, tugging a piece at the bottom around his finger—and then suddenly stopping, like he didn't want anyone to notice he was nervous.

"They really didn't tell you?" Maisie tried to keep the suspicion out of her voice, but Hadley looked at her sharply.

"No. I wouldn't have kept that from you."

"You know your cousins are about to start knifing each other. Julio, especially."

"What else is new?" Hadley tried to sound flippant, but she chewed on her lower lip.

"Can I ask a question?" Lennon asked.

Maisie sighed. "Why not?"

"On the outside, I heard that Lopez was technically the head of the family, but he wasn't really in charge. That was your dad, wasn't it?" he asked Maisie.

"He was the enforcer, but Lopez made the decisions," Maisie said carefully.

"It's fine," Hadley said, rolling her eyes. "Yes, Isaac Rojas was technically second-in-command, but everyone knew he was the one calling most of the shots."

"They were a team," Maisie said. "They'd been best friends since they were kids. My dad said that he'd always known that Lopez was a genius, and he was going to do everything in his power to make sure that the guy who could save us all was protected."

"And he had a few guys that were like his second-in-command," Hadley said. "They helped him keep everything in order. But they all died in the bus accident, and we've been winging it since."

"Bus accident?" Lennon repeated.

"Bus flipped over during heavy rain last year, killed everyone on board," Hadley said.

"Oh." Lennon cast a sympathetic glance at Maisie. She looked away.

"Our intelligence said that you were being groomed to take over for your father," Lennon said. "Was that wrong?"

"It wasn't wrong," she said bitterly. "They decided I couldn't cut it."

"That's not it," Hadley protested. "It's because she was only seventeen when he died."

Maisie shrugged. She'd doubted it would have mattered if her dad had lived until she was fifty. Declan was only twenty-two. But she didn't command respect the way Declan did. The way her dad had.

There's nothing wrong with sticking with what you're good at, Declan had said to her, in that gentle voice he only used with her. He hadn't specified what exactly she was good at. Following orders, maybe.

"Who took over for your dad, then?" Lennon asked.

"Declan," she replied.

"Your ex-boyfriend, Declan? The one . . . ?" He tugged at the bottom of his shirt.

Hadley looked from Lennon to Maisie with a start. "Did you give him a rundown on your dating history?"

"No. I just gave him Declan's clothes."

"Did you guys have a heart-to-heart last night?" Hadley's lips twitched. "Now I'm sad I didn't come over."

"We did not have a heart-to-heart," Maisie said. She looked at Lennon. "Declan took over for my dad, though it's not quite the same."

"Lopez calls all the shots," Hadley said. "Declan just takes orders and yells at everyone."

"So with Lopez out of commission, there's no clear leader? Even if Declan is fine?"

Maisie and Hadley exchanged a glance.

"I mean, it's complicated," Hadley said.

"No, you're right," Maisie said. "Most of the Lopezes wouldn't just line up behind Declan and let him take charge. A bunch of them trained under him as doctors, and the rest all run things. Like how Hadley controls all the information that goes out." She gestured at her. "Ceding that power to Declan is unlikely."

"There are better choices," Hadley grumbled. Her phone beeped, and she lifted it to read the message. "They're calling a meeting."

Maisie looked down at her own phone.

> Family meeting, 10 a.m. Beto's.

Maisie deposited Lennon at her apartment before heading to the meeting. She didn't entirely trust him to stay put, but she also couldn't bring him to a family meeting. Outsiders weren't allowed. And a dude from beyond the wall *really* wasn't allowed.

Beto Lopez lived in a giant house on the west side of town.

Maisie had never understood why people liked being in those houses. She liked her small apartment, with a view of the city. It was easy to keep clean.

And it felt safe. Two doors, one with a dead bolt and the other five stories up. She didn't worry for her safety much these days, but she had vivid memories of the years right after the walls went up. Her dad once killed two men in one night, after they both tried to break in, hours apart.

Things were fine now, but she was always preparing for when they wouldn't be.

Hector, one of Lopez's nephews, greeted her at the door, gun in hand.

It was going to be *that* kind of meeting.

Hadley was already there, sitting on one of the giant couches in the living room. The back windows showed off views of the massive backyard. Beto's boyfriend, Owen, sat outside in the grass with a few of the younger Lopez cousins.

Her phone buzzed. A text from Declan.

I'm fine. Had to dig some of my guys out of rubble. Where are you?

She rolled her eyes and slipped her phone back into her pocket. It was just like Declan to not bother texting her back for twelve hours, even though her last text had literally read: text me so I know you're not dead.

Maisie sat down next to Hadley. The room was starting to fill up, but Declan wasn't there. She wondered if he'd been invited.

Maisie leaned closer to Hadley, speaking softly. "You know I'm on your side, right?"

Hadley turned to her, clearly surprised.

"I'm on your side. I don't know if this is going to turn into a Declan-versus-Lopez-supporter thing, but I'm with you guys. I just want you to know that."

Hadley smiled, then bumped her shoulder against Maisie's. "I know."

"Good."

"I think Declan's going to be very disappointed to hear that, though."

Maisie just shrugged. She couldn't argue. Declan always had been oblivious—or indifferent—to her feelings about most everything.

"I told you not to date him," Hadley said, barely suppressing a smile.

"Are you ever going to stop reminding me of that?"

"Nope."

Maisie watched as more people streamed in. Alan and Leticia, also Hadley's cousins, walked into the room. Leticia's arm was in a cast, her face bruised. She'd had a close call yesterday.

Alan nodded at Hadley before glancing down at Maisie.

"Your arm looks weird," he said.

"Your face looks weird," she retorted. Hadley snorted.

Beto walked to the center of the room, his face grim. Silence fell over the crowd.

"It's true that my dad is still unconscious," he said. "But it's because he's in a medically induced coma. The doctors expect to bring him out of it within the next few hours."

Maisie released a slow breath. That was better news than she'd been expecting.

"I've heard from Declan, and he's fine," Beto continued.

A few people looked around the room, like they were expecting Declan to be there.

"Why would you lie about Uncle Franco?" Hadley asked. She was slumped down on the couch, arms crossed over her chest.

"I was trying to keep everyone calm," Beto said. "The doctors told me they were optimistic. People hear the word *coma* and think the worst."

"Half of us are doctors, jackass," Hector said.

Beto reddened. "Well, the other half aren't. Not to mention all the people we're trying to keep safe."

"Speaking of, are we going to go after the fucking Reapers?" Leticia asked. "They executed a coordinated hit on the family."

"Yes. We should do that now," Beto said. "Julio, take some guys and—"

"Wait, wait," Maisie interrupted. "You can't just roll over to the Reapers now. They did serious damage, and they'll be expecting us. You need to do some recon, coordinate the attack so you don't lose even more people."

Beto shifted from foot to foot. He was trying to appear confident, but Maisie knew him too well. He kept lifting his hand to his mouth to bite his fingernails, and then quickly stopping himself.

"She's right," Julio said. "Do you have a plan? Or do you just want us to roll in there, guns blazing?"

"We need to start assessing damage, too," Leticia said before Beto could respond. "You realize that they hit the warehouse where we had grain shipments? Most of our stock was destroyed. And they burned a bunch of our greenhouses. We don't have new shipments coming in, and our supplies are dwindling to the point that people are starting to notice."

"Was there ever a plan to find out what was happening with the shipments?" Hector asked. "What was Declan doing about that?" He looked at Maisie when he asked, like she'd ever been able to convince Declan to do anything.

She lifted her hands. "You'd have to ask him. I just collect rent."

"Let's all just calm down," Beto said. "Julio, send people out to do some recon. See what the Reapers are up to right now. Hadley, put out an announcement that everyone who is missing friends or family needs to go to the hospital to identify bodies. We need to let people know exactly how much damage the Reapers did. They need to know that they're not safe with them."

"That'll be a cheerful announcement." Hadley made a face.

"And the shipment problems?" Hector asked. "We can live without the food shipment, but we need the medical one."

"No one is dying today, are they?" Beto asked.

"No," Hector muttered.

"Then let's just table that for a day. Find out what Declan's plan was."

"And what about Lennon?" Maisie asked.

Beto stared at her. "Damn. I forgot all about that guy."

"Where is he, even?" Leticia asked.

"I let him stay with me last night," she said. "He's still expecting that we'll transport him to the northern gate. Are we doing that?"

"Hell no, we're not doing that," Hector said.

"Uncle Franco had his reasons for wanting to get him out of here," Hadley said.

"Well, he never told me what those reasons were, so that's too bad," Beto said. "Unless you want to take him up there yourself, we can't spare a team."

Maisie let out a short, humorless laugh. "No, thanks."

"That's what I thought," Beto said.

"What are we going to do with him?" Hadley asked.

"Maisie, go see Betsy about vacancies. I think there are a few apartments open."

"You do realize that his father is a US senator?" Hadley said. "Maybe the next president? We're just going to keep him here against his will? You don't think that might end badly for us?"

Beto made an annoyed sound. "Listen, if the dude wants to go to the northern gate, he can be my guest. Give him a map and tell him to have at it."

Maisie glanced at Hadley. They both knew how that would end. Lennon probably wouldn't make it a mile into Spencer territory.

"I'll let him know," Maisie said.

The sound of the door opening made them all turn.

"Oh, shit," Hadley said.

Two men in black masks stood in the doorway.

Holding machine guns.

LENNON

MAISIE TOLD LENNON to stay in her apartment.

But, honestly, the way she'd said it gave him the impression that she didn't actually think he would listen.

She was right.

He spent about ten minutes staring out the window before leaving, pulling the door shut behind him. He heard the lock click into place.

He jogged down the stairs and to the street. It was a clear, slightly cool day. Really nice weather for November. He'd rarely been to Texas, but he'd heard that the quarantine zone was unbearably hot about six months out of the year. He desperately hoped he wouldn't be around to experience that for himself.

Maisie lived in the center of what was once downtown Austin, and he spotted a few things that advertised the zone's roots. A sign for the Austin library. *ATX* carved into a sidewalk. People still talked about rebuilding Austin.

Of course, that would require a cure for everyone inside, which hadn't happened.

Or a bombing.

Some of the old storefronts on the street were boarded up, and he kept walking, turning a corner until he was in a more crowded area. There were some street vendors here—a small group of people selling fruits and vegetables, and a man selling some "healing balms" that looked suspiciously like plain lotion to Lennon.

A woman was standing at a cart advertising churros, and he slowed as he walked by. She clamped her tongs together a few times, gesturing at the churros.

"*¿Quieres un churro?*" she asked, then shook her head and said, "Do you want one?"

"No, thank you." He spoke some Spanish, but he nearly always felt too self-conscious to speak it around people unless he absolutely had to. He was pretty sure that his accent was terrible.

She sighed.

"I mean, I would, but I don't have any money. Or, uh, credits. You call them credits, right?"

The wrinkles at the sides of her eyes became more pronounced as she peered at him. "Huh?"

"Nothing. Sorry. Ignore me." He flashed her a smile.

"Put that away." She wagged the tongs at him.

"What?" he asked, confused.

"That smile. You're trying to get a free churro, aren't you? It won't work on me."

"I wasn't!"

"Sure you weren't."

"This is just how I smile." He showed her again.

She snorted, dug the tongs into the cart, and produced

a churro. She slipped it into a paper sleeve and held it out to him.

"No, no, that's okay," he protested. "I really don't have any way to pay you."

"Take it. They're not selling well today anyway. I'll have to throw half of them out tonight."

"Thank you." He took the churro. "That's very kind of you."

"You're that guy who fell from the sky, aren't you?" she asked.

"Is it obvious?" He took a bite of the warm churro and brushed sugar from his lips.

"Yes."

He looked down at himself. He hadn't realized he looked so out of place.

"Thank you for the churro," he said again. "I appreciate it."

She waved her hand. "That's all right."

He kept walking, wandering down a street full of theaters advertising their latest plays and musicals. He'd had no idea that live theater was such a draw in the Q. He made a note to share that later. People would love it.

His dad would love it the most, actually. His father used to take him and his sisters to the theater all the time when they were younger. Lennon would always get in trouble for making too much noise while eating his candy, or for falling asleep.

He paused in front of a sign for *Mamma Mia!* It should have been his dad who was dropped in here for seventy-two hours. He would have already started brokering peace between north and south, and earned the devotion of a good chunk of the population.

Lennon, as usual, was just the crappy substitute. The son who looked like his father but could never compare.

He sighed as he turned away.

He eventually made it back to Maisie's apartment, and went around to the side of the building, where there was a shaded stoop. As he sat, stretching his legs out in front of him, he overheard a man talking.

"Is Maisie in there?"

Lennon leaned forward, peering around to the front of the building. Two men stood at the bottom of the stairs, and a third man stalked up to them. He was in his early twenties, broad and muscular, with thick dark hair. He looked like the kind of guy who talked about protein powders and had very firm opinions about proper dead lift form.

"No one answered when I knocked," one of the others said. He had tattoos covering both arms. "She must still be down at the family meeting."

The broad man cursed. Lennon started to get to his feet.

"Don't worry, Declan, the guys know not to hurt her," the tattooed man said. "They know Maisie is your girl."

Lennon stopped, glancing back at the men again. Declan was the name of the ex-boyfriend whose clothes he was wearing. Why was he worried about Maisie getting hurt at the family meeting?

Also, it suddenly made sense why this shirt was a little baggy on him. He tried not to feel self-conscious about his pecs, which he'd always been quite proud of up until about thirty seconds ago.

"What's the word on Lopez?" the man with a mustache asked.

"Still unconscious." Declan leaned back, taking a look around, like he wanted to make sure no one was listening. Lennon quickly sat back down, hidden from sight. "I really didn't want Maisie anywhere near that meeting. I don't want her getting caught in the cross fire."

Lennon stiffened. *The cross fire?*

"You know Maisie," the tattooed man said. "She can take care of herself."

"Go down to the end of Cypress," Declan said. "Catch the stragglers. I'm going to wait for Maisie at the garage."

"Sure thing." The tattooed guy began to walk away, but he stopped, turning back to Declan. "What do you want to do about that guy? The one who got dropped from an airplane? I think Maisie was put in charge of babysitting him."

"I really don't care." Declan crossed his arms over his wide chest. "No, actually, grab him for me when you see him. Put him in lockup until I can decide what to do with him. I don't need him running around right now."

"You got it."

Lennon didn't release a breath until the men's footsteps had completely faded.

He stood and walked to the corner of the apartment building. He paused, making sure the coast was clear, then stepped out into the street.

He wasn't sure where he was going. He didn't know where the family meeting was. He wasn't even entirely sure what Declan had been talking about.

But he suspected that here, *the cross fire* meant literal gunfire. Declan wasn't worried about Maisie getting caught in the middle of a screaming match.

He tried to remember what she'd said before leaving.

Stay put or I'll kick your ass when I get back.

No, not that part.

Before that. *I'm going to a family meeting not far from here. I won't be long.*

Not far from here didn't exactly narrow it down. The entire quarantine zone wasn't far from here, by his standards.

He couldn't just stand here and do nothing, though. Not if he had time to get to Maisie and tell her that it sounded like her ex-boyfriend was about to kill a lot of people.

He jogged down the street and back to the churro lady. "Hey," he said breathlessly.

"Come for another one?" She snapped her tongs together.

"No. Thank you. I mean, it was amazing, but—" He cut himself off with a shake of his head. "Do you have any idea where a Lopez family meeting would be?"

"At one of the Lopez houses, I imagine."

"Is there one close to here?"

"Yeah, Jasmine lives about a mile down that way, and Beto is . . ." She turned in a circle. "He's not even half a mile down Eighth Street."

Beto. It had to be Beto. He'd been the one angling to take over for his father.

"Down that street?" He pointed. "Do you know the number?"

She frowned, considering. "Sure don't. Big brown house. Roof goes like this." She lifted her elbow, letting her arm hang down in a slant.

"Thank you," he said, taking a step back. "Really, thank you!" He turned and took off running.

MAISIE

MAISIE DOVE OFF the couch, pulling Hadley with her. Bullets sprayed across the living room.

Someone fell on top of her, and she grunted, collapsing beneath the weight.

"Shit shit shit." Hadley yanked her hand out of Maisie's. She got up on her knees, covering her head with her hands as more bullets flew through the air. Beto and the other Lopezes returned fire.

Hadley shoved the body off of Maisie, who gasped as the pressure left her lungs. She rolled over, bracing her hands against the carpet.

The room went quiet suddenly. Maisie cautiously got to her knees, peeking over the couch.

The two men at the doorway were on the ground, blood pooling around their bodies. Maisie counted two of their own dead, motionless on the living room floor. Beto had a hand pressed to a hole in his shoulder.

"Get out," Beto panted. "Everyone. Now. They're targeting us." He darted toward his back door.

Maisie sprang to her feet and ran to the door with Hadley. They sprinted outside and onto the street.

"What in the hell is happening?" Hadley yelled as they ran.

A figure appeared at the end of the street, running toward them. Maisie put her hand on the gun at her waist.

"Is that Lennon?" Hadley asked.

He spotted them, waving both arms in the air, like they hadn't noticed the dude running straight at them.

He pointed suddenly, frantically, and Maisie stopped. She turned.

A truck was barreling toward them, a gun sticking out the window.

Maisie grabbed her gun, flipping the safety off as she raised it. Beside her, Hadley did the same.

The truck slowed as it drew closer to them.

It took a sharp turn and left them in its dust.

Maisie slowly lowered her gun.

"Maybe those were Beto's guys," Hadley said.

"Maybe." Maisie slid her gun back into its holster. Behind her, she heard Lennon's footsteps, and turned to see him coming to a stop in front of them.

"What are you doing here?" Maisie snapped. "I told you to stay in my apartment."

"Yeah, I . . . didn't . . . do that." Lennon took a deep breath.

"You should not be—"

"Just listen, listen," he interrupted. "When I was coming back to your place, I saw these three guys outside. Declan was one of them. And I heard them talking about something going down at the family meeting."

Hadley's eyebrows drew together. "But it just happened, like, a minute ago."

"Did someone attack you guys?" Lennon asked. "It sounded like that's what they were talking about."

Hadley shot Maisie a concerned look. "A couple guys came in shooting."

"Yeah." Lennon nodded. "Exactly. Declan was talking about cross fire and not wanting Maisie to get hurt. One of the guys said that everyone knew not to hurt you."

Hadley's eyes widened and she pointed to where the truck had disappeared. "Oh, shit."

"Wait." Maisie shook her head. "No. How do you even know it was Declan?"

"Because one of the guys called him *Declan.*"

"That's a pretty solid clue," Hadley said.

"There's more than one Declan in the Q," Maisie argued, even though she knew it was stupid.

"Tall guy? At least six foot two?" Lennon held a hand up level with his own head. "Looks like he works out a lot? Early twenties?"

Shit.

"That's him," Hadley said.

"Maybe you misunderstood," Maisie said. "What did he say *exactly*?"

"He was upset you weren't home. He didn't want you anywhere near that meeting. He said, 'I don't want her getting caught in the cross fire.'"

"That asshole," Hadley said forcefully.

"He also told them to put me in lockup when they found me. He doesn't want me running around."

"And yet, here you are, running around," Hadley said.

"I'm notoriously difficult." A smile twitched at his lips.

"Guys." Maisie put a hand to her head.

"Sorry." Hadley looked at Lennon. "It annoys her how I make jokes in tense situations."

"I actually find it kind of comforting."

"Thank you."

Maisie closed her eyes and took a breath. If Declan had staged this whole attack, it could only mean one thing.

He was moving to overthrow Lopez.

"Was he still at my apartment when you left?" Maisie asked. "He didn't see you, did he?"

"No, I was around the corner. He said he'd wait for you at the garage."

Right. She was supposed to do her daily check-in soon.

"Okay," she said. "You two, go hide at my apartment."

Hadley nodded her agreement.

"Where are you going?" Lennon asked.

"To check in with Declan."

Declan was pretending to work on a car when she arrived. She knew that he could see through to the street from a small window at the back of the garage, so he would have noticed her coming.

He stood over the open hood, frowning like he was trying

to figure something out. She'd learned quickly what actual concentration looked like on Declan—it was a more subtle, less self-aware expression.

This expression, with the deep frown and the intense gaze, was for show. It was what he did when he wanted to get out of going somewhere with her.

"Hey, Maisie." He straightened and smiled. "How's it going?"

She took a beat before answering. She had to play this right. "There was a shoot-out at the family meeting."

His face turned into a mask of surprise. This expression could have been real or genuine. She really didn't know. Declan was actually a pretty good liar, and she'd only learned a few of his tells over the course of their relationship.

"Was anyone hurt? Are you okay?" He did a quick sweep of her body.

"Lots of people were hurt. Several are dead."

He held her gaze.

"They were Reaper guys."

"Christ. What a fucking mess."

"Yeah."

"Okay." He sighed, running a hand across the stubble on his jaw. "Let's get an official tally of everyone who died so we can let their families know. I'll go over to the hospital to visit the injured ones."

"Why weren't you there?" she asked. "At the family meeting?"

"I had some things to take care of. And I knew it was just going to be Beto posturing, trying to act like Lopez would want him to take over."

"Do you know who Lopez actually wants to take over?"

"No." Declan looked down at the car. "Listen, do you still have that guy? Pierce?"

She hesitated, considering. "No."

"Weren't you keeping an eye on him?"

"I had to leave him alone while I went to the meeting. He took off."

"Find him for me, will ya? Throw him in lockup. None of us have time to babysit him right now. He'll be safe in there."

"Sure." She eyed him, wondering if maybe Declan had reconsidered whether letting an outsider leave the Q was a good idea. *Safe* might have been the entirely wrong word for his experience once he got to lockup.

Her stomach clenched. It was obvious that Declan was responsible for the attack. It had been obvious since Lennon told them what he'd heard.

And she had a terrible feeling that she knew exactly who had shot Lopez.

She took another step toward him, and he turned his attention from the car to her.

She had to admit, she was a little surprised that he'd wanted her protected at the family meeting. Their breakup hadn't been nasty, but she would have thought he was kind of ambivalent about her.

Apparently not. And she could use that to her advantage.

She put a hand on his left arm and smiled. His lips began to turn up as well.

Then she drew back and hit him in the left shoulder.

He yelled in pain and stumbled back. "Maisie, what the fu—"

She yanked the collar of his shirt down to reveal the bandage on his shoulder. "I shot the guy who tried to kill Lopez. In that shoulder."

Declan went still. She could see him debating, trying to decide if it would benefit him to lie.

He sighed and twisted his shirt out of her grasp. "I didn't mean for it to go down like that."

She gaped at him. "You were executing him in the street!"

"I was trying to get him to listen to reason. He won't listen—hasn't listened, for years—and I thought it might finally get through if he had a gun to his face. I didn't want to hurt him, but sometimes you just have to get shit done."

Maisie swallowed back the urge to scream at him. Declan wouldn't listen to her if she got emotional—he barely listened to her as it was.

"What did you want to say to him?" she asked.

"We have to take the whole Q. The north holds all the power, since they get all the shipments from beyond the wall. It was different back when supplies were still dropped by plane, but for the past ten years or so . . ." He shook his head. "This can't go on. The north is holding our shipments right now because they can. Because they know we're weak, and we won't fight back. There are some people inside the Lopez family who understand that, but there are a *lot* of other folks in the south who get that."

"Which folks? Reapers?"

"Some of them, yeah." He stared at her like he was daring her to challenge him.

"Reapers don't have loyalty, Declan. If you're looking to

rule the entire Q—or even just the south—they won't help you do that. They don't follow leaders."

"Well." A smug grin crossed his face. "Some Reapers have started to come around to the idea of a more organized leadership. They've been getting screwed by a few guys holding all the power for years."

"So they might as well get screwed by you instead?"

He laughed like he thought she was joking.

He stepped forward, putting both hands gently on her arms. She resisted the urge to smack him away. Using his feelings to her advantage. She needed to remember that.

"You should know that I never wanted you to get hurt in any of this. In fact, I told them—"

A yell from outside cut him off. They both turned at the sound.

One of Declan's guys sprinted up the shop driveway and skidded to a stop.

"He's dead," he said breathlessly. "Lopez is dead."

LENNON

LENNON WENT WITH Hadley to Maisie's apartment. He sat on the couch while Hadley paced back and forth in front of the door.

Hadley's phone dinged, and he watched her expression change as she read something there. It was bad news.

"We're fucked," she breathed.

Very bad news.

"Is . . . everything okay?" he asked hesitantly.

"Uncle Franco is dead." She covered her mouth with her hand, turning her face away from him.

Dr. Lopez was dead. The leader of the south, the genius who was responsible for keeping so many people in the Q alive. Dead.

This was bad on so many levels.

"I'm sorry," he said quietly.

She sniffed, then checked her phone again. "Maisie's on her way over. Wait here, okay? We'll be right outside."

He nodded and watched as she hurried out the door. She

was gone for a long time, and when she walked back in, her eyes were red and she had Maisie in tow. Maisie pushed the door shut and locked it behind her. Lennon stood.

"You were right," Maisie said to him. "It was Declan. All of it. He's the one who shot Lopez."

"Bastard," Hadley muttered, even though she clearly already knew this information.

"He told you?" Lennon asked Maisie, surprised.

"Yeah, he told me." Maisie crossed the room and leaned against the wall near the kitchen, chewing her lip.

"You think he'd at least be ashamed," Hadley spat. "He must know you're going to tell everyone. He just let you leave?"

"You know what Declan thinks of me."

Hadley rolled her eyes, but Lennon just looked at her in confusion.

"He thinks I'm harmless," Maisie explained. "It doesn't matter if I know, because there's nothing I can do about it anyway." She scrunched up her face. "Also, I think he may be under the impression I still have feelings for him."

"Ew," Hadley said.

"So, what now?" Lennon asked.

"Now I need to find out who Declan has brought over to his side, because there is no way that he did this without recruiting some of the family in addition to the Reapers. He'd need both." Maisie looked at Hadley. "Everyone at the family meeting couldn't have been in on it. Or else they wouldn't have come."

"Or at least they would have stepped out before people started firing. Did anyone step out?" Hadley asked.

Maisie considered, and then made a face. "Shit. I don't know. I was focused on Beto."

"Well, at least we know he's not in on it."

Lennon pushed a hand nervously through his hair. There hadn't been any talk about him, and the clock was ticking. It was too rude to ask, when Dr. Lopez had just died.

But he really needed to get out of here. He'd thought the situation was bad before, but it was downright *dire* now. He did not want to be here if Dr. Lopez was dead and Mr. Musclehead was ready to start a turf war.

"If he goes up there and takes the shipments by force, even more Lopezes might want to join him," Hadley said. "They're pissed about the situation."

"I know." Maisie turned her attention to Lennon. "Declan asked about you. I told him you took off and I didn't know where you were."

"What'd he say?" Lennon asked.

"To lock you up when I found you. Listen." She sighed. "You're not going to make it to the northern gate."

His stomach fell to his feet. He'd been expecting it, but still, the words hit him like a smack to the face.

"There's no one who can take you. We actually talked about it at the meeting—"

"Before the shooting," Hadley added.

"—and Beto said there was no team to send. You're welcome to go by yourself, but I don't recommend it."

Relief coursed through his veins. At least she wasn't going to lock him up, like Declan wanted. He still had a chance. "I can go by myself."

"When Maisie says she doesn't recommend it, she means you will definitely die if you go by yourself," Hadley clarified.

He gave Hadley an exasperated look. "Contrary to what

you both seem to think, I am fully capable of taking care of myself."

"Yeah, you haven't even fainted once today," Maisie said dryly.

"You're never going to let me live that down, are you?"

"Nope. And seems like you're going to be here for the next several decades, so I have plenty of time to give you shit about it."

"One, I'm going to that gate, so, no, you don't; and two, if I stay, isn't it certain that I'll get sick? And possibly die?"

"Don't be so dramatic," Maisie said. "You're not going to die. Do you have any serious health conditions?"

"No."

"You are probably going to get sick, yes," she said. "The virus will likely shut down an organ or two, and you'll get new ones like the rest of us. Half of my organs are artificial, and look at me. I'm doing great."

"Same," Hadley said.

He swallowed. He couldn't really argue with that. It was common knowledge that the residents of the quarantine zone had adapted to live with the virus. Their technology kept them alive. But they couldn't be released into the general population because they were still contagious and millions of people would die when exposed to the virus for the first time. And there was no way to know how the virus would mutate again once it had the chance to infect millions of new people.

But he was young and healthy, and Maisie was right.

"We actually don't know how long your immunity will last," Maisie said. "Maybe you won't catch it at all. I have badass antibodies."

"Those were your antibodies that they gave me?" he asked, surprised. She nodded.

"Of course they were." Hadley said it like he should have already known this. She opened her mouth to say more, but Maisie shot her a look and she closed it.

"Anyway, my point is, you may be helpful in developing a vaccine," Maisie continued. "You're the first person to receive temporary immunity. There's a possibility that your immunity could last even longer than a few days. Maybe Lo—the medical teams—can use you to finally make some progress on a real vaccine."

"There are people in the US working on vaccines. I'd be happy to help them."

"Wow, you really don't want to stay in here," Hadley said.

"I didn't mean—" He took a deep breath. "I don't belong here. My family is on the other side of the wall. My parents. My sisters. All my friends. My entire life. I'm just going to never see any of them again?"

Hadley gave him a baffled look. "Isn't your dad running on a platform that advocates for finding a vaccine and tearing down the walls in the next ten years?"

Shit.

"Do you not believe him, or is that just a load of crap?" she continued. Maisie seemed amused suddenly.

"It's not a load of crap. . . ." He'd never really considered whether he believed it could be done. Democrats always ran on a platform of liberating the quarantine zone. It was just a given.

He'd listened to a host of doctors and scientists on the issue, and they'd certainly been hopeful, but also cautious.

There wasn't enough funding. There wasn't enough help from inside the zone.

It's become a war zone in there, one had said to him. *They rarely send out samples anymore. They rarely communicate with us at all, and when they do, we're not sure if they're even telling us the truth. It's hard to fix a situation that we can't even fully understand.*

"I believe that he wants to," he finally said. Maisie cocked an eyebrow. "But there are challenges. Most of all that you guys don't communicate with us."

Hadley and Maisie glanced at each other.

"What?" Lennon asked.

"Well, all the communication has to go through Lopez. We can't talk to anyone out there now, even if we wanted to."

"I know," Lennon said. "But you have to understand, people are scared of you guys in here."

"We understand that fine," Maisie said with a frown.

"We can fix that, though. If I get out, then this isn't just some terrifying place that no one's seen. I will have been in here and come out the other side. I can tell people what you're like. How you helped me. People won't be as likely to—" He cut himself off abruptly.

"As likely to what?" Hadley asked.

He hesitated. Lopez had told him not to say anything, but Lopez was dead now.

He took a breath. "I just want to apologize in advance."

"Well, that sounds bad," Maisie said.

"There are some . . . people who . . . think we should just bomb the whole quarantine zone."

They both stared at him. Hadley's lips parted.

"They want to *bomb* us?" Maisie repeated.

"What did we ever do to them?" Hadley exclaimed.

"It's a fringe idea. Or it was." He winced. "It's starting to go mainstream lately. There are some people who think that if the Howard family gets elected again, they may be able to get Congress to support it."

"Can they just do that?" Maisie asked. "Just kill us all?"

"I mean, we do have US history books in here," Hadley said. "They've bombed a lot of people throughout the years."

"Crap, that's a good point," Maisie said.

"My dad would never, if he won the election," Lennon said quickly.

"Oh, his dad would never," Maisie said dryly. "I feel so much better about everyone wanting to murder us now."

"But, listen. Here's the thing. They're going to have satellite photos of what just happened in here. The US government, I mean. They will know that someone just bombed the south."

"So?" Maisie asked.

"So it will strengthen their argument that this is a dangerous war zone that needs to be controlled. Especially now that Dr. Lopez has died. They don't usually release information to the general public about what goes on in here, but if President Howard wants support to bomb you guys, he will do it this time. I need you to understand how truly screwed you might be now."

He saw Maisie draw in a slow breath.

"I get dropped in here, then there's a bloody turf war, *and* the world-famous doctor everyone is counting on for the cure is killed? The people who want to bomb the zone have worked themselves into a frenzy out there, I can guarantee it, and they only know about the first thing so far."

"I mean . . ." Maisie threw her hands up. "Frankly, Lennon, we have no idea if you're full of shit or just exaggerating to get us to help you. We have no way to confirm this."

"Actually . . ." Hadley bit her lip. "I think maybe we do."

MAISIE

"YOU WANT ME to *what*?" Elise gaped at them through Maisie's laptop screen.

"I want you to bring up an American news station," Maisie repeated. They were all sitting around her kitchen table, talking to Elise on her screen. "You can do it, right? And stream it to my laptop?"

"I *can,* but I won't. Do you know what happened to the last person who accessed American internet without permission?" Elise coughed. "Only Lopez can authorize that."

"Well, he's dead," Hadley said flatly.

Elise flushed. "I'm sorry, I just . . ."

Hadley sighed, pushing a hand through her hair. "No, I'm sorry. It's been a really bad twenty-four hours."

"What happened to the last person?" Lennon asked.

"Lopez sent some guys to kick his ass," Maisie said. "Then they threw him out of his house, seized everything he owned, and sent him to do a five-year stint cleaning up after the border patrol. It's a job with a high turnover rate."

"Because they usually get murdered," Hadley added.

"Oh." Lennon swallowed.

"We can easily communicate with the outside world from the comms tower," Elise said. "But I have this job because Lopez knows that I never would, unless he approves it first."

"But Lopez is gone, and no one knows who's calling the shots now, so I say we take advantage of this window," Hadley said. "No leader, no rules."

"You have a point." Elise put her mask up for a moment to take a breath, and then poised her fingers over the keyboard. "We all should be taking orders from Maisie right now anyway."

Lennon looked at Maisie curiously. She pretended not to notice.

Elise punched a few keys. "Okay, should be up in a few seconds. . . ."

A second screen appeared next to Elise's face. It was a woman, enjoying yogurt more than anyone had a right to.

"What is this?" Hadley asked.

"A commercial," Lennon said.

Another woman replaced her, this one sitting behind a desk. "Welcome back. The situation in Spain has grown more serious today, and officials—"

"Try a different livestream," Lennon said.

Elise frowned but did as he said. Lennon's face filled the screen before it returned to a woman sitting at a brightly lit desk.

"Day three of the Lennon Pierce kidnapping, and we've yet to hear any word about his condition inside the quarantine zone. Supporters are keeping vigil outside the fence, the closest point that people can get to the zone."

The image changed to a video of hundreds of people lining a fence. Flowers and cards were stuck to it. Beyond the wire, armed men stood in front of a huge concrete wall with signs that read NO TRESPASSING. YOU WILL BE SHOT.

"Oh, shit, is that the other side of the wall?" Hadley asked.

"Yes," Lennon replied.

"Looks like people like you," Maisie said, pointing to a crying woman.

"Yeah, I'm great from a distance."

She blinked, glancing over at him, but he was staring at the screen. What a tragic thing for him to think about himself.

The image onscreen changed to a young boy, maybe four or five years old.

"Lennon Pierce, now nineteen, is the middle child of Camden and Melinda Pierce."

The image switched to child Lennon with two girls on either side of him.

"Change it, we don't need to hear about me," Lennon said.

"No, no, I want to see," Hadley said.

"Lennon showed great promise as a student, and his parents enrolled him in an exclusive private school. It turned out to be the first of many schools, as the young Pierce had a knack for getting into trouble. He became a favorite target for the tabloids."

The image changed to a picture of four naked people on a tennis court. All the good bits were blurred out, including Lennon's butt. The headline above the picture said: LETTING THE BALLS FLY—LENNON PIERCE ARRESTED FOR PLAYING NAKED TENNIS WITH THREE FRIENDS.

"Oh my god," Hadley said. She clapped a hand over her mouth to stifle a giggle. Lennon sighed.

"Lennon was arrested four times before turning seventeen, but he cleaned up his act after joining his father's campaign—"

"You were arrested four times?" Maisie asked, cocking an eyebrow.

"I like how you sound impressed by that," he said.

She was a little impressed, actually. She tried not to let it show.

"Was it always for playing tennis naked?" Hadley asked. "Is that, like, your thing?"

"No," Lennon said, but didn't elaborate.

"Is it against the law to be naked on the other side of the wall?" Elise asked. "My neighbor would get arrested, like, every week."

"Can we please change the channel?" Lennon asked.

"So demanding," Elise muttered. But she punched a few keys, and a man replaced the woman. There were two boxes next to his face, a man and a woman apparently calling in from a different location.

"It's not a matter of if this happens again, it's when," the man at the desk said. *"Lennon Pierce will not be the last person dropped into the quarantine zone against his will. Are we just going to ignore the fact that this situation has become untenable?"*

"I disagree," the woman said. *"This was a terrible, isolated incident, and everyone is taking precautions to make sure it never happens again."*

"But how did it even happen in the first place?" the man behind the desk asked. *"How did they even get the plane above the quarantine zone? It's restricted airspace. How can we trust that there won't be more breakdowns in security? If we're able to just drop people in now, who's to say that people can't start getting out?*

How long until they start trying to scale the walls again? You do know that there have been rumors that they've been biding their time inside, developing a way to break down the walls and escape."

"I agree," the man in the box said. *"We can't keep pretending that this isn't happening within our borders. It's no longer just a public health issue, it's a defense issue. They are a lawless, violent society in there, and Lennon Pierce will not be the last one to suffer for our inaction."*

"Jesus," Hadley said.

"We're not lawless," Elise said. "There are some laws."

"They're more like guidelines," Hadley said.

Lennon turned to Maisie. "You see what I mean, right? Listen to them. They hate you."

"Let's not forget that Lennon argued for the liberation of the quarantine zone," the woman said, and Maisie returned her attention to the screen. *"Repeatedly. He spoke often about his father's plans for the future of the zone."*

"What was the plan for the future?" Maisie asked.

"A cure, a vaccine, and a reintroduction to society for all of you," he said.

"Dream big, my dude," Hadley said.

"Senator Pierce's policies are radical!" the man in the box said. *"He's arguing for forgiveness for all crimes committed inside quarantine, plus money and housing for all of them once they're on the outside. I don't know why we would reward criminals with a free house, but I bet that if Lennon could weigh in now, he would have very different advice for his father."*

Maisie looked at Lennon expectantly.

"No," he said. "I don't have different advice. If anything,

being here has confirmed that I was right. And you need to let me tell them that."

"What, now?" Elise asked.

"You can broadcast outside the zone, right?" Lennon asked. "You just did that joint broadcast, didn't you? I missed it while I was kidnapped."

"Yeah, we did it. But the US has to approve it," Hadley said. "We can't just do it on our own."

"What about video? Can you get video out? The US government doesn't have to approve anything I send to a news station."

"I mean, we could, but . . ." Hadley chewed on her lip. "That's never been done. Not since the walls went up, anyway."

"Exactly," Lennon said. "People are scared of what they don't understand, and they don't understand any of you, since you cut off all contact years ago. But we can make them understand. We can make them root for us."

"Root for us?" Maisie asked skeptically.

"Yes. We make a video letting everyone know that I'm fine, and tell them about the progress on the temporary vaccine. We tell them that you're helping me get out." He pointed to the computer screen. "You saw them out there. They're acting like I'm dead. Let me tell them that I'm not."

Maisie ran a hand down her neck, considering. Lennon had a point about people hating them. It was obvious from the way the newscasters talked. And she'd heard some of the older residents of the quarantine zone speculating about the US government possibly taking drastic action. It hadn't been out of the realm of possibility, in their opinions.

Hadley was staring at her, eyebrows raised. She could obviously tell that Maisie was considering it.

Pop-pop-pop.

Maisie whirled around at the sound. Gunfire.

She rushed over to the window.

Outside, a man with a gun stepped over a dead body in the street. He said something into his phone, looking both ways with the gun still in his hand. He was clearly searching for someone.

Maisie cursed. "We need to get out of here."

"Where are we going to go?" Hadley asked.

"Let's find Beto. He was at his house last we heard, right?"

Hadley pulled out her phone. "Yeah. I'll text him to see if he's still there."

"We're sitting ducks here by ourselves. We need to find them and regroup."

Gunfire sounded from outside again, cutting her off. It was distant this time.

"He's not responding," Hadley said, eyes on her screen.

"Let's just go. It sounds like they moved to the next street anyway." Maisie strode to the door.

"What about—" Lennon began.

"Just give me a few minutes, okay? I'm thinking about it, I just need . . ." She trailed off, gesturing to the window, where she could hear more guns being fired. "I need to take one thing at a time."

He nodded, but she could see the nervousness on his face. He wanted out of here, and he was going to risk going north by himself, if he had to.

A plan was beginning to take shape in her head. A plan

that was either brilliant or the stupidest idea she'd ever had. She needed a minute to figure out which it was. She needed to talk to Beto.

She opened the door, pulling her gun out. "Let's go."

They stayed on the side streets as they made their way across town. Maisie and Hadley kept their guns out, but they managed to avoid the men combing the streets.

Maisie had rarely seen the streets of the Q so deserted. It was a ghost town, with everyone's doors and windows shut tight, despite the nice weather. She wanted to ask Declan how he could have ever thought that causing this type of fear was a good idea.

Beto's gate was closed when they approached, and Maisie typed in the code on the screen. It slid open.

They were halfway up the driveway when Beto charged out with a gun.

"Beto, what the hell?" Hadley yelled. Maisie raised her own gun, but she didn't take the safety off.

"No one is coming inside until I figure out what's going on!" Beto yelled.

"What's going on is Declan betrayed all of us," Hadley said.

"And how do I know you two aren't with him?" He pointed at Maisie. "You're his girlfriend!"

"Ex-girlfriend!" Maisie yelled, and then muttered, softer, "Jesus Christ, I make one bad dating decision and it blows up in my face."

Beside her, Lennon made a sound like he was stifling a laugh.

"I hear he's been running around, bragging about how he's got you on his side!" Beto yelled.

"You really think I would betray you like that? Betray the *family* like that?" She tried to keep the hurt out of her voice. But she'd known him her whole life—had been friends with him since she knew what a friend was—and he was pointing a gun at her.

Beto's face softened slightly, but he didn't lower his gun. "Some of the family has decided to jump ship and join him, so—"

"Wait, what?" Hadley looked stunned.

"They want to take the shipments by force. They want to attack the north and I . . ." He lowered his gun with a sigh. Maisie lowered hers as well.

"They'll die," she said. "Regardless of who wins, a lot of people will die if we attack the north."

"Some people think that's the price we have to pay." Beto took a step back. "I'm sorry. Go somewhere else."

"Beto!" Hadley exclaimed. "You have to do something!"

"I am doing something! I'm getting some people I trust together and we're . . . going to figure something out."

"Oh Christ," Hadley muttered. Beto turned and stomped inside, slamming the door behind him.

"What are we going to do?" Hadley asked.

Maisie put her gun back in its holster. "I don't know. They're right that we need the shipments. People will start dying without the medical supplies in them."

"So we just let them start a war with the north?"

Tempting. She considered, for a moment, just going home and hiding under the covers. Let Declan get himself killed. Let all the Lopez family members who were siding with him die up north in some stupid war.

But she couldn't do it. She couldn't let Elise die. Or everyone else in the Q who needed the medical supplies on those shipments as soon as possible.

She was getting that shipment, even if she had to go herself.

"Beto!" she yelled.

"I think he's done with us," Hadley said.

"I have an idea." She lifted her chin, yelling Beto's name again, louder this time.

The door swung open and he stepped out, arms lifted in annoyance. "Maisie, go home!"

"Let's go get the shipment," she said.

He frowned. "What?"

"You and me. Let's go get it. We'll steal it, or we'll negotiate. I don't know. But if we found a way to get the shipment peacefully, don't you think that would bring the Lopez family back together?"

"I don't know. Maybe."

"At the very least, it would make Declan look like an idiot and show people in the south that we still have their backs," Hadley said. "They're going to need support from the whole south to attack the north."

"Yeah," Beto said.

"So let's go get it," Maisie said.

"Just the two of us? Are you out of your mind?"

"Doesn't have to be just the two of us. We could gather up a few more. Should probably be a small group, though. Easier to travel that way."

"Maisie, I am not charging up north with you. At least

Declan has a plan. And weapons. *You* are just going to get yourself killed."

"Wow. Thanks for the faith."

He shrugged. He had so little faith in her he wasn't even going to pretend otherwise.

"I'll go with you," Lennon said.

She turned to look at him. "What?"

"I'm going north anyway, to get out of here. Help me get to the gate, and I'll help you get the shipment."

"How exactly are you going to help me get the shipment?"

"I don't know. But I'm not completely useless, you know." He gestured at Beto. "And it doesn't sound like you have any other options."

He had a point. She glanced over at Beto, who was regarding them skeptically.

"You can apologize to me later," she said to Beto, and then turned to Lennon. "You have a deal."

LENNON

"YOU ARE A terrible influence."

Lennon laughed and took the phone from Elise. "Believe it or not, that's not the first time I've heard that."

"Oh, I believe it." She walked across the room and plunked down in a chair. "But I'd just like to state again, for the record, that sending a video outside the Q is a very bad idea."

"Noted," he said.

They'd gone back to the comms tower, and he'd found the room with the best lighting for their video. It was mostly empty, with just a long table against one wall, and big windows that let the sun shine through.

He attached the phone to the tripod he'd set up on a table. Hadley and Maisie watched him from the doorway.

"You seriously have to make a video?" Maisie asked.

"It'll help," he said, with a confidence he didn't feel. He had no idea what would help. He'd never been in this situation before.

"The election is tonight, isn't it?" Hadley asked. "You just want to help your dad's campaign. They won't know whether or not you've gotten out when they vote."

"It's probably too late to help my dad's campaign. Most people have already voted."

Hadley looked at him skeptically.

"Fine, yes, it occurred to me that it could help. Early voting isn't really allowed in most places anymore, so there's a chance that . . ." He took a deep breath, shaking his head like he was getting off track. "It doesn't matter. Just, trust me. I'm really good at this. I change the narrative. Let me change this one."

Elise scrunched up her face and mouthed *the narrative* at Hadley. They both laughed. He pretended he hadn't noticed.

"What are you going to say?" Maisie asked.

"What are *we* going to say?" Lennon corrected.

"We?"

"Yes. They need to see someone from inside the zone, and you're perfect."

"Why am I perfect?"

"Because you—uh, because you're the one who is going to get me out. People will want to root for someone. And because you saved me. Which I'll tell them. Leaving out the part about the cannibals."

She hesitated, and then shrugged. "Yeah, all right."

He turned away. He'd barely stopped himself from saying, *Because you're very pretty, and confident, and you have this way about you that makes people like you and want to listen to you.* He got the feeling that Maisie would not appreciate being told that she was pretty. Or the suggestion that people might like her, come to think of it.

"We're just going to be casual," he said. "Sort of have a conversation. And I'm going to mention Dr. Lopez, but not that he's passed away." He glanced at Hadley, silently asking if that was okay.

"Yeah, that's best," she said softly.

"Good. Mind making sure we're framed okay?" he asked. She nodded and strode to the tripod.

He walked around in front of the phone and Maisie did the same. "Let's just lean against this table." He braced his hands against it as he leaned back casually. "It gives off the impression that we're relaxed. No one here is scared."

Maisie sighed but did as she was ordered.

He put his hand up, hovering over her ponytail. "May I?"

"Sure, why not?"

He pulled the hair forward, so it fell over her shoulder.

"Oh yes, that looks cute," Hadley said.

"Fix women's hair a lot for photo shoots, do you?" Maisie asked.

"Making people appear relaxed when they actually want to punch me is one of my strong suits."

She snort-laughed, a grin spreading across her face.

"See?" He smiled.

"Impressive," Hadley said. "Okay, are you guys ready?"

"Yes," Lennon said. Making a video pretending that he was happy and everything was going great was the most normal thing he'd done in days. Felt like returning to real life.

"Aaaand go," Hadley said.

"Hey, guys, I'm Lennon Pierce, and I'm here with Maisie Rojas inside the quarantine zone. We just wanted to give you a quick update on how I'm doing, since I know that everyone out there is curious." He tilted his head toward Maisie. "Maisie here came and got me as soon as I was dropped into the quarantine zone, and she helped make sure I was safe and fed."

"You left out the part where you fainted," Maisie said.

He gave her an amused look. "In my defense, my kidnappers didn't feed me."

"I'm just saying. You glossed over that part." A smile twitched at her lips.

"*Anyway,*" Lennon said, turning back to the camera. "Maisie and Dr. Lopez made sure to immediately get me a temporary vaccine that Dr. Lopez developed recently. You probably read about it. The antibodies in the vaccine will protect me, temporarily. The CDC isn't sure for exactly how long, so they've given me seventy-two hours to leave the zone. Actually, we're down to less than forty-eight hours now. But Maisie here has kindly offered to help me get to the designated area where I can exit."

"Anything I can do to help," she said, with a hint of sarcasm that would probably go undetected by anyone who didn't know her.

"The CDC has told me that I'll need to be quarantined in one of their facilities for a month after I leave, to make sure I didn't pick up the virus in here. Trust me, they will not let me out if there's even the slightest chance that I might infect anyone."

"They're very good about that," Maisie said.

"I've seen video of you guys out there supporting me, and I just wanted to take a minute to let you know how much I appreciate it, and to assure you that I am in very good hands. I'm excited to tell you about all the wonderful people I met in here. But in the meantime, keep an eye on your clocks, because I will be getting out in less than forty-eight hours. I can't wait to see all of you when I step out from behind the wall."

He nodded at Hadley. "Okay, that's it." He smiled at Maisie. "Thanks for bringing up the fainting."

"Anytime."

"No, seriously, it makes me more relatable. People will love it."

She squinted like she wasn't sure if he was being sarcastic. He smiled, which only seemed to confuse her more. She gave him a deeply suspicious look. "Do you need to do something before we send it?"

"Give me five minutes to edit the beginning and end, and we're good."

Lennon took the satellite phone from Hadley. "I have to call."

"Why?"

They were in the room across from Hadley's studio, where Elise worked. They'd just sent the video to a news station, and Lennon was trying to convince them to let him call out.

"Because they're not going to air it unless I confirm it," he said. "Someone could easily manipulate old video of me to make something like this. They may want to talk to you too, Maisie."

She was sitting a few computers down, boots propped up on the table. "Sure, why not? Let's call everyone."

"There's still no one to stop us, right?" Lennon said.

"Technically, I should stop you," Hadley said. "But Uncle Franco is gone, and so are his rules. So, sure, go ahead."

She waved a hand like she'd given up. Wearing people down was one of his many terrible talents.

Lennon dialed the number and pressed the phone to his ear.

"It went through, right?" he asked Elise. "The video?"

She kept her eyes on her screen. "It looks like it, from what I can tell."

"Hello?" the voice on the other end said.

"Hey, Zoe, is Constance around? This is Lennon Pierce."

There was a long pause. *"I'm—wait, what? Who is this?"*

"It's me, Zoe. Lennon."

Silence on the other end.

"When I visited the studio, I brought you doughnuts, and we talked about how no one else likes apple fritters, but how they're our favorite."

"Oh my god. Lennon?"

"Hi."

"Hold on. Holy shit. Hold on."

The line went silent as she put him on hold.

Constance picked up a moment later, sounded annoyed. *"Who is this?"*

"Constance, are you being mean to your assistant again? I'm sure she told you it was me on the phone."

"Lennon?"

"Yes, it's Lennon, I already proved it to your assistant, let's move on."

"Jesus. Are you okay? Are you safe? Wait, did you get out of the quarantine zone?"

"Not yet. Listen, there should be an email in your inbox with a video file. Do you see it?"

Short pause. *"Yes."*

"Open it. It's from me."

He heard the sound of his own voice playing on the other end of the line.

"Are you kidding me?" she said as it finished. *"Is this for real? You're getting out of there?"*

"Yes. And you have to run it, okay? I've seen what the other networks are saying about my disappearance."

"They watch the news in there? I thought they were totally cut off from the rest of the world."

"Uh, I struck a deal."

"Is that girl there with you? Maisie Rojas?"

"Yeah, she's here."

"Were you forced to record this video under duress?"

"No."

There was a pause. *"If you're in trouble, can you give me some kind of sign?"*

"I'm not in trouble, Constance. What I said on the video is true. Everyone has been nice to me, and Maisie is going to help me get out of here."

"Can I talk to her?"

"Sure." Lennon held the phone out to Maisie. "She wants to talk to you."

Maisie sighed, standing and taking the phone from him. She held it to her ear. "Hey. Yeah, this is Maisie." She listened for a moment. "I figured it was time to do my good deed for the year."

Lennon bit back a laugh.

"Yeah, I was born here. Eighteen. Is this an interview?" Maisie listened for a moment, and then handed the phone back to Lennon.

"Holy shit," Constance said. "You know who that is, right? You know who her father was?"

"Yeah, I know."

"Are we talking privately right now?"

"As far as I know."

"Just listen for a second. I don't know how much you know about Isaac Rojas, but I did a lot of research on him back when the zone first went rogue. Back when people inside could still contact us?"

"Right," Lennon said, glancing at Maisie and quickly away.

"That was a scary asshole, Lennon. He was about to go away for a double homicide when the virus hit. And he only got worse once the city was roped off and the jails emptied out. We think that we can attribute literally hundreds of murders to him. We had reports of him torturing people. He did whatever he could to seize control of the zone, and everyone knew that Dr. Lopez was just a friendly face to put on a dictatorship. I don't know a thing about his daughter, but you need to proceed with caution."

He swallowed, forcing himself not to look at Maisie again. It didn't seem fair to judge her by her father, but Constance did have a point. He barely knew Maisie. Or any of them.

"Got it. Will do. You're going to run with the video? Now?"

"Of course I'm going to run the video."

"Thank you, Constance. I appreciate it."

"You've talked to your father?"

"Let's just focus on the video for now, okay? I'll sit down with you as soon as I get out of quarantine on the other side."

He knew better than to give up any information about his father to a reporter without consulting the campaign first.

"All right." She sounded amused. *"I really hope this works out for you."*

"Me too."

"Bye, Lennon."

He couldn't help but notice that her *bye* sounded very final, like she thought it might be the last one.

He hung up the phone and passed it back to Hadley. "Okay. We're good. Should be on soon."

"In the meantime, we need to figure out how the hell we're going to get through Spencer territory," Maisie said. "I need a map, I guess?" She sighed. "But I'm not sure how helpful that will be. All our maps are years old. We don't even know which roads still exist. We always meet the shipment truck in the neutral zone at the border."

"Let me call one more person, and I can fix that problem," he said.

"How?"

"There's plenty of aerial footage of the zone. They haven't released images to the public in years, but some people who work for my dad have it. If we get them to send that to us, we can combine it with the old maps and figure out the best roads to take."

"That's . . . a really good idea," Maisie said.

"I'll try not to be insulted that you sound so surprised."

"Maps aren't going to tell you where the shipments are," Elise said. "Are you just going to go up there and drive around? The north is three times the size of the south, and you don't even have two days before this one needs to leave."

"We're just going to have to wing it," Maisie said. "North-gate is pretty small, and the shipment should still be there."

"Well . . ." Hadley winced. "I may actually be able to help with that."

They all looked at her.

"How?" Maisie asked.

"I've had contact with a Spencer."

MAISIE

MAISIE GAPED AT Hadley. "How? *Who?*"

"I don't know his name," Hadley said in a rush. "I'm sorry I didn't tell you, but Uncle Franco said that absolutely no one could know. No one besides the two of us."

"Explain," Maisie said.

"Okay." Hadley took a deep breath. "About a year ago—"

"A *year* ago?"

"Do you want me to explain or not?"

"Sorry."

"About a year ago, I got this message through the old radio. The one we used to be able to talk to Americans on? Anyway, it was this guy's voice, and he just said, 'Don't eat the queso.' And I was like, 'Excuse me, how dare you, I'll eat all the queso I want.' And he was like, 'Don't eat the queso on the shipment. Trust me.' And then he just kind of disappeared. So, I told Lopez about it, and we went down to check the queso in the next shipment. It was full of maggots."

"Gross," Elise said.

"All the jars had been opened. Someone had put the maggots in there. So, we just threw them all out, because hardly anyone buys that jarred queso anyway. I don't know why they keep sending it."

"It's really not very good," Elise said. "And now I'm never eating it again."

"Anyway, I tried to reach out to him, but he never responded. Then, one day, like a month later, he gives me another tip. And he's right again. So, eventually, I get him to actually talk to me and not just disappear like a big asshole. Turns out he's up in Spencer territory. Must be pretty well connected, because he knows a lot of stuff."

"But you don't know who he is?" Maisie asked.

"No. He never gave me a name. I just call him Queso. I don't even know which territory he's in, though I suspect it's Northgate. But I do have a way of contacting him. So, I could ask. I've asked about the shipment before, but that was weeks ago. He claimed it was coming, but maybe he knows something now."

"Seriously?" Maisie said. "And you didn't tell me about this?"

"I'm sorry! I was going to, but Uncle Franco told me not to tell anyone. And he used his serious voice. The one that meant some real bad shit was going to happen if I didn't listen."

Maisie made a face at Hadley, even though she kind of understood. She knew the voice that Lopez used when he meant business.

"I don't know," she said. "This Queso guy could be laying a trap."

"How could it be a trap?"

"I don't know! He lives in Spencer territory!"

"I really don't think that he passed along tips about queso to me on the off chance that a Lopez might one day sneak up north and he could use that to his advantage," Hadley said.

She sighed. "Fine. Feel him out, I guess. But don't pass along too much information if you're even a little bit unsure about him."

"Got it. I'll radio him now." Hadley bounced out of the room.

"Wait, can I listen?" Elise called after her.

"Yeah, but you can't say anything! It'll freak him out!"

Elise stood and followed Hadley out of the room, pulling her oxygen tank with her.

"I'll call about those maps," Lennon said, reaching for the phone again.

Maisie moved in front of it. "Wait."

He drew back, looking at her curiously.

"I need you to understand what it means, crossing into Spencer territory. I'm going to give you an opportunity to change your mind."

"I'm not going to change my mind."

"Just listen, okay?"

"Okay."

"First, you have to get across the border. That won't be a problem on our side—I'm sure the border patrol is still licking their wounds after we grabbed you—but I really don't know what to expect on the Spencer side. It looks barren out there, but we see drones sometimes. They monitor the area."

"Avoid drones, got it. What else?"

"It's thirty miles from the border to the northern gate. I think I can grab us a vehicle, but chances are we won't make it the whole way with it."

"Because of charging issues, or because it's too conspicuous?"

"The latter. I doubt we can just cruise down the road the whole way there. We're going to have to do a lot of walking, I think."

"Got it. Ready to walk. What else?"

"Well, just the fact that we are strictly prohibited from entering Spencer territory, and they will definitely try to kill us."

"People keep trying to kill or kidnap me everywhere I go lately, so that's not much of a change."

She rolled her eyes, but couldn't help the laugh that escaped her lips. "You're such a pain in the ass, you know that?"

"I've been told."

She held her hands up. "Okay. I just needed to be straight with you. The stories I've heard about Spencer territory are really fucking grim."

His smile faded. "Yeah. We heard them too, on the outside."

"And yet, here you are, being a pain in my ass about wanting to go up there."

"I have to try."

"Why?"

He cocked his head, his expression a little bewildered. "How would you feel, if you suddenly had to leave your home? Your friends? Your family? Everything you have?"

"Not great," she admitted.

"Yeah, not great. I at least have to try."

She pushed her hands through her hair with a sigh. "Okay. Call about those maps."

LENNON

LENNON CALLED HIS dad's campaign manager, who, after a brief freak-out, sent aerial maps within minutes. Maisie spread them out on the table, and then marked them up with some notes. Hadley returned from her call with the Spencer contact—*Queso,* a code name that Lennon found charming—and added some information.

Lennon peered at the maps and Maisie pointed. "We pieced everything together the best we could. There are still some spots where it's unclear if a road is being maintained. But we outlined some possible routes."

"And some helpful tips," Lennon added, pointing to the spot where Hadley had written, *You're probably screwed if you go here.*

Hadley shrugged innocently. "Just telling you what Queso said."

"These are the four Spencer territories," Maisie said, pointing. "They're ruled by four different Spencers. Used to just be one territory, but they can't get along for shit up there."

"Understatement," Hadley said with a short laugh.

"Just north of us is East Spencer and West Spencer," Maisie continued. "East is ruled by Nash Spencer, West is Arthur. West is weak and sparsely populated. East is . . . bad, by all accounts. We're going to try to stay west and avoid east altogether."

Lennon put a finger to the map. "That big highway that runs through West Spencer is still in use. We could take it nearly all the way to the next territory."

She nodded in a way that he suspected was just to humor him. "That next territory is the biggest one, known as Val's Territory. Valerie Spencer runs that one, with a gang known as the Vals. Mostly made up of women who fled East Spencer. Last we heard, Val and West have a tenuous alliance, and she helps protect them from East. It's notoriously difficult to cross through Val's Territory, but Queso says we can try here." She put her finger on the spot.

"He makes no promises," Hadley added.

Maisie pointed to the top of the map. "Northgate is the smallest territory, but arguably the most powerful. Ruled by Jonathan Spencer, who used to rule the whole north. The gate is at the northwest corner of the territory, so he controls everything that comes in and out. They've built the Spencer compound directly in front of the gate, which is really bad, but there are options for getting around it on foot."

Lennon had seen the Spencer compound on the aerial map—it was a large, walled compound that was most likely heavily patrolled and impossible to avoid if you wanted to get to the gate.

"Queso thinks he can help you get into Northgate," Hadley said. "But not to the gate. He is checking on the shipment location, though."

"And for the record, I'm still deeply suspicious of this cheese man," Maisie said.

Lennon studied her for a moment. "Are you sure we shouldn't bring a third person with us? Once we get the shipment, you have to be able to get it back. You'll be alone."

"I'd rather be alone," she said.

"I'd rather be alone," Hadley said, lowering her voice in a dramatic impression of Maisie. "Always alone."

"Shut up," Maisie said with a laugh, bumping her shoulder against Hadley's.

"He's right, though," Hadley said. "It would be better if you could take someone."

"Who? Elise isn't well enough to go; you can't leave the station for two days, especially in the middle of an emergency; and I can't think of a single other person who would volunteer to go into Spencer territory. Beto was my best shot, and he pretty much laughed at me."

"I guess that's true," Hadley said with a sigh. She grabbed a backpack from the table and pulled out a radio. "Stay in contact, okay? We don't know if your phone will work up there, so I'm sending you with this radio. This light right here? On top? It'll flash when I'm trying to get in contact with you. Make sure you check it occasionally."

"Got it." Maisie took the backpack and peered inside. She smiled. "Thanks for the snacks."

"You know I'm all about the snacks."

"Also, plenty of extra bullets," Elise said.

"And a second gun for Fancy-pants, if you trust him not to shoot you," Hadley said.

"Thanks," Lennon said dryly.

Hadley and Elise traded a glance, and he realized suddenly that they were worried. Scared for their friend.

"Listen, we were talking, and . . ." Hadley took a deep breath. "We wouldn't blame you. If you decided to just leave once you got up there."

Lennon looked between them in confusion. Why did they think Maisie could leave?

"I'm not leaving," Maisie said, clearly exasperated. She glanced at Lennon, and then quickly away. "Let's not—"

"No, seriously," Elise said. "They'll let you out. They've said so. Maybe it's time."

"Wait, who said so?" Lennon asked. "Why would they let you out?"

Maisie opened her mouth.

"She's immune," Hadley said, before Maisie could stop her.

"Dammit, Hadley," Maisie said with a sigh.

"Wait, what?" He looked at Maisie, baffled. "You're immune?"

"She's a special snowflake," Hadley said. "She's been immune for years. Hasn't caught the virus since she was a kid. That's why you have her antibodies."

His lips parted. "Are there others? Who are immune?"

"Nope, just her, as far as we know," Elise said. "They think it's a genetic thing. Her dad wasn't technically immune, but he barely got sick every time he got the virus."

"The CDC has been offering to let her come out for

years," Hadley said. "She'll have to go into quarantine for a few months, but if she's clear she can go out forever."

"Holy shit." Lennon put a hand on Maisie's arm. "They're right. You should leave with me."

"They didn't say I *should;* they said they wouldn't blame me." Maisie shook him off and crossed her arms over her chest. "But it's not happening."

"Why not?"

"What am I going to do on the outside? My home is here."

"If you really are immune, maybe they'll let you go back and forth. You could visit occ—"

He stopped as she shook her head. "They said no. In or out. No coming back once I'm gone." She put the backpack on the table. "I'm just going to go pee before we go." She turned and walked out of the room.

Lennon looked at Hadley and Elise. "How long has she been able to leave?"

Hadley scrunched up her face in thought. "Mm . . . I think it's been five years. She was thirteen, I think."

"Five *years*?"

"She's never even considered it," Elise said.

"She probably did consider it, at least for a minute," Hadley said. "I wouldn't blame her. But she'd also have to leave through the north, so it honestly wasn't even much of an option," Hadley said. "But now that she's going anyway . . ."

"She should go," Lennon said. "Don't you think?"

They both shrugged.

"If she wants," Hadley said. "I don't want her to, but I don't think it's fair to say that. She should make up her own mind."

"She could help, once she's out," Lennon said. "She'd be the face of the quarantine zone. She could advocate for your release. People would listen to her. She's spent eighteen years in here."

"Maybe," Hadley said. "But I doubt you can convince her of that."

"I . . . I think that I should try," he said slowly. "I know you guys will be sad if she leaves, but I think she could make a real difference if she left."

Hadley swallowed. "Like I said, it's up to her. Say what you want to her." Elise nodded.

Maisie walked back into the room, grabbing the backpack.

"I've got it," he said. She passed it to him, and he strapped it on.

"Well, I guess this is it, Fancy-pants," Hadley said. "Don't forget to tell people how cute I am."

He smiled. "I'll tell them you were very kind." He held his hand out, but she pulled him into a hug.

They hugged Maisie next, Hadley saying something in her ear that he couldn't hear.

She pulled away and turned to him. "Ready?"

"Ready."

MAISIE

MAISIE LED LENNON outside and onto the street. Hadley had given her the code for one of the cars in the Lopez garage, something that would *not* go over well with the family. She was taking an "ask for forgiveness later" approach to this whole thing.

The garage was about a mile away, and they walked in silence, Lennon occasionally stealing glances at her.

"Would you just say it?" she asked.

"What?"

"Whatever you've got going on in there. You keep looking at me."

"They told me that you've known you're immune for five years."

She sighed. "Of course they did."

"I can understand not going when you were thirteen, but have you ever reconsidered? Like after your dad died?"

"No."

"Why not?"

"My dad was my only blood relative in here, but he wasn't my only family."

"Do you have relatives on the outside? Do you know?"

"Yes. Both my mom's parents are still alive, and so are my dad's mom and his sister. I haven't heard that they've died, so I assume they're still out there in Texas somewhere."

"Have they ever let you talk to them?"

"No, but I didn't ask. I don't know them."

He was quiet for a moment. "Did Dr. Lopez have an opinion?"

"He said it was up to me. The medical team has taken enough samples to work with, even if I leave."

"But he didn't have an opinion about what would be best? Even when you were a kid?"

"Not that he shared."

"What about your dad?"

"My dad said that sometimes the devil you know is better than the one you don't. And the grass is always greener."

"Big fan of idioms, your dad?"

Her lips twitched. "Yes."

"And not in favor, it sounded like."

"He was not in favor of his only child leaving forever, no."

"Understandable," Lennon said quietly.

They turned a corner, and walked in silence for several minutes. They were in an area that was mostly businesses, near the lumberyard, and there weren't any other people on the street.

"Did you and your dad . . . get along?" Lennon finally asked.

She gave him a confused look. "You want to talk about my relationship with my father?"

"I've just . . . You know that we've heard of your father, right? Out there?"

"Ah," she said, understanding dawning on her. "Right. You want to know what the famous Isaac Rojas was like."

"I was just curious if he was different from the rumors."

She didn't need to ask what he'd heard. Her dad had already seen the inside of a prison cell—more than once—when the virus hit. And the Americans had a lot more access to information inside the Q back in the first few years. When they'd had internet inside, people had seen video of what was happening.

It made sense that her dad had argued so forcefully to control the news and internet inside. He'd done some pretty gruesome shit to get the Q under control.

Back when Lopez had first started supplying people with new organs, there were payment plans and deals. People who were in really bad shape could barter or beg their way into a new pair of lungs or a new kidney, with just the promise of repayment.

Trouble was, repayment rarely happened. Her dad had his hands full knocking skulls every day, and it never did any good. He couldn't keep up with the backlog.

So, he started repossessing the organs. He famously pulled a guy's lungs out in the middle of the square, in midday, surrounded by people—as a warning to others. He'd cut them out, wrapped them up, and shoved them into a bag.

When she was younger, she hadn't understood at first why he did that. They couldn't be reused. But later, she realized that he probably just liked the visual of sauntering off with a dead man's lungs swinging from his hand, blood twisting a path behind him.

Lopez had put a stop to all payment plans and deals after a few repossessions. He said he wasn't putting organs in people just to have them torn out by Isaac a few months later. It was a waste of resources.

It also wasn't great for morale. No one wanted to see their neighbors getting their chests ripped open in broad daylight. Made for a real bummer of a commute.

She also realized later that it was likely the plan all along to let her dad terrify people by repossessing a few organs so Lopez could swoop in and put a stop to it. They were good at always presenting Lopez as the good guy and her dad as the monster. But the truth was, everything that they did, they did together.

Maisie glanced at Lennon. "He's what you heard. But he was also a good dad."

He raised his eyebrows. "Yeah?"

"Yeah. My mom died when I was two—the virus—and he was actually pretty good at parenting by himself. Some of the other dads around here seemed to completely fall apart when their wives died, or they just had no interest in their kids. But Dad wasn't really like that."

"No?" He looked at her curiously.

"No. He took me nearly everywhere with him, when I was a kid. Even when he didn't have to. I used to sit on his lap during his poker games, even though all the other kids were in the next room. He seemed to actually like having me around."

"Wouldn't know what that's like," Lennon said, looking up at the sky.

"What?"

"Having a dad who likes having you around."

She hesitated, unsure what to say to that. Finally she swatted his shoulder lightly, with a smile. "Well, nothing like a little kidnapping to make your parents appreciate your presence, right?"

He laughed, his lips curving up into a bright, wide smile of his own. She hadn't seen him smile like that, and she realized suddenly that this must be his real smile. The one that wasn't tinged with terror or nerves.

"True," he said. "My parents and my sisters will never take me for granted again after this."

"You have sisters?"

"Yeah, two. Stella and Caroline."

"Are you close?"

"Not so much with Caroline, my older sister. She's always been the golden child, and since I was the screwup, there wasn't much common ground there. But Stella and I are pretty close. I'm three years older than her, which was just enough to fool her into thinking I was cool when we were younger."

"But not now?"

"No, now she's sixteen, so she's old enough to know better." He grinned at her.

She smiled, pointing to the garage ahead. "The car's there."

"Do you know how to drive?" he asked.

"Of course I know how to drive."

"Hey, I was just asking," he said. "Sometimes people in cities don't drive. A lot of New Yorkers don't."

"Dad taught me when I was twelve. I transported stuff for him back then; I had to learn."

She stopped in front of the garage and typed out the code on the pad. The gate creaked open.

Lennon hopped into the passenger's side of the small black car as she slid into the driver's seat. He put the backpack by his feet and grabbed the map from inside.

She drove out of the garage, rolling down the window to let some fresh air into the car. Lennon sat back as she pulled out onto the road, closing his eyes for a moment.

"Why do you look so relaxed?" she asked.

He smiled as he turned to her. "Would you prefer I look tense?"

"No. Yes. I don't know. It's just weird. Don't look relaxed around me."

"Don't look *relaxed* around you?"

"Yes! What happened to being scared of me? Go back to that."

He laughed, tilting his head back with the force of it. "I'm sorry. You're terrifying."

"Don't patronize me." She pressed her lips together, but a smile twitched at them anyway.

"Now *you* look relaxed."

"Shut up."

LENNON

LENNON STARED OUT at the rolling hills as Maisie drove. It was peaceful out here. They had to be close to where he'd landed, but he'd only noted how empty it was. The word hadn't been *peaceful.*

It seemed ridiculous now that he'd thought he could stay in one spot and not interact with anyone in the zone. What did he think they were going to do? Stand ten feet away while he shouted at them to send a helicopter to rescue him?

He glanced at Maisie. It was embarrassing that his fear had overwhelmed him and kept him from considering the upside of his predicament. He hadn't even seen that this could be an opportunity to actually see the area that had long fascinated him and talk to the people inside. He was mortified that he hadn't thought of them at all, except as a way to get a message to the US government.

A red sign along the highway caught his attention—NEUTRAL ZONE—NEXT TWO MILES.

"Have you ever been to the north?" he asked. "Like, as a kid? Before you guys split it up?"

"No, back then we weren't officially separated, but we'd still sort of carved out our spaces. Plus, the roads were a disaster. Totally clogged with cars that couldn't run without gasoline. We had to go everywhere on foot for a long time."

He nodded. "Makes sense."

She took in a breath, and he noticed that the knuckles of her right hand had gone white around the steering wheel.

They passed another sign—SPENCER TERRITORY—ONE MILE.

She hit the gas a little harder. Lennon held his breath as they crossed over.

SPENCER TERRITORY

He waited. They continued down the road.

He wasn't sure what he was expecting.

A checkpoint, maybe? Angry cannibals chasing them?

Maisie stared straight ahead.

A noise pierced the quiet suddenly, a high-pitched squeal. It was getting closer.

Something dropped onto the hood of the car. It was small, and metal, and the high-pitched noise was getting louder every second.

"Oh, shit." Maisie slammed on the brakes. "GET OUT OF THE CAR!"

He reached for the door handle, barely remembering to grab the backpack before he dove out onto the pavement.

The explosion knocked him off his feet. He hit the ground, curling into a ball to protect his head. The heat from the blast enveloped him as debris ricocheted off his back.

He peeked up. The top of the car was totally blown off, the inside on fire. Maisie darted around the hood and did a quick double-take as Lennon sprang to his feet, pulling on the backpack.

"Come on." She grabbed his hand, and then let it go as they began to run.

The squealing noise started again.

He looked up. Two metal drones flew overhead.

The bomb dropped at his feet.

He let out a yell, barely sidestepping it, and bolted forward.

The blast didn't knock him off his feet this time, but the sudden, sharp pain in his shoulder made him grimace.

Another bomb dropped on the road.

"That way!" Maisie pointed to the trees to their left. They were a good quarter mile away.

They veered off the road. The bomb exploded behind them.

He pushed his legs faster, but quickly pulled ahead of Maisie. Surprise colored her features as he slowed a little.

The drone dropped another bomb, and another. Heat licked at Lennon's heels as he ran, keeping pace with Maisie.

Finally, they were in the cover of trees. A bomb burst overhead, igniting one of them.

Maisie veered to the right, and they ran for several minutes, until they were deep into the trees and Lennon couldn't hear the squealing noises anymore.

He slowed to a stop as Maisie did. His heart was pumping too fast, and he braced his arms against his knees as he tried to catch his breath.

"Christ . . . you're fast," Maisie said, sucking in air.

His breathing started to even out, and he straightened. "I run a lot."

"Why?"

He laughed, his nerves beginning to subside. "Because I like it?" That was probably an understatement. Running was one of his favorite things. He loved how it felt impossible at first, and then it felt okay, and then it made his mind go blank. It was blissfully peaceful inside his brain, for several miles every day.

His shoulder burned suddenly, and he winced, twisting to try to see it. Something metal was poking out of his shoulder.

Maisie winced. "Ouch."

Now that he could see that he had a giant piece of metal sticking out of his shoulder, it really hurt. "What is that?"

"Looks like a piece of one of the bombs. Sit down. No, wait." She carefully lifted the straps of the backpack around the metal, pulling it off his back. She set it on the ground and unzipped it.

He sat with a wince.

"Really smart thinking, grabbing the backpack," she said as she dug through it.

"I try." He watched as she pulled out a small pouch. "Did Hadley pack a first aid kit?"

"She packed a lot more than a first aid kit." She held up a pouch that was labeled *For when you get shot.*

Lennon barked out a laugh.

Maisie held up another one: *For when you get stabbed.* "I'm gonna save that one for later. I think we just need some basic wound-closer for that." She grabbed the first aid kit and walked over to him, dropping to her knees.

A sharp stab of pain rippled across his shoulder, and he gasped. Maisie tossed aside the piece of metal.

"Jesus, you could have warned me."

"Did you think I was just going to leave that in there?"

"No, but—" He almost laughed. "Never mind."

"Take off your jacket and pull this arm out of your shirt, will ya?" She tapped his right arm.

He shrugged out of the jacket and gingerly pulled his arm out of the sleeve. He pushed it up closer to his neck, so she could see his shoulder.

Her fingers brushed against his back, soft and gentle, and he took in a sharp breath.

"Sorry," she said, her hand disappearing from his back. "Did that hurt?"

"Uh, no." It actually hurt *less* when she touched him like that. "How does it look?"

"It's not too bad. Just a little . . . gaping wound."

"Sure, doesn't sound too bad at all."

He tried to think of something else as she cleaned it. The burning intensified.

"You've done this a lot?" he guessed.

She laughed shortly. "Yeah. My dad had me patching him up pretty much as soon as I could hold a bandage. He was a practical guy. Didn't believe in coddling me."

"Was that . . . okay? Couldn't have been easy, patching up your bleeding father as a little kid."

"Eh, it was fine."

The way she said it was too casual, and he looked over his shoulder. Their eyes met, and her hand stilled on his back.

"Sounds tough," he said quietly.

One side of her mouth lifted, as if to acknowledge he was right. "I'm guessing your father didn't get into a lot of bloody fights? Or your mom?"

He laughed, turning back around. "No. I got into a fight in middle school once, and my parents made me go to the kid's house to apologize—*he* punched me first, by the way—and then write an essay about toxic masculinity."

"Wow," she said, her voice full of amusement.

"It was a pretty good essay for a twelve-year-old, if I do say so myself."

"Did it work? Did you get into more fights?"

"No, punching people was never my style. I preferred to piss off my parents in other ways."

"Like playing naked tennis?" she guessed.

"Like that," he said with a chuckle. "Though, in my defense, strip tennis was not my idea, and I didn't know there were cameras around. We were just being ridiculous." He glanced over his shoulder again, his lips curving up when he saw the smile on her face. Her fingers lightly grazed his shoulder in a way that felt intimate.

"Why'd you want to piss off your parents?" she asked.

"I don't know," he lied. "Didn't you enjoy pissing off your dad?"

"God, no."

"Right. Not really the kind of guy you want to piss off, I guess."

"He never would have laid a finger on me. I just . . . I guess I preferred to make him happy. Kind of desperate for his approval, actually." She muttered the last line, almost to herself.

"I don't think that approval was ever within my grasp," he said. "So I went the other way for a while. I did give it my best shot when I joined the campaign, though. Thought I could start over now that I'm older, impress him and everyone else. I'm not sure how well it worked." He'd probably been right when he was younger—his dad's approval felt like a lost cause, no matter what he did.

"Sure," she said quietly, and then stepped back. He immediately missed her touch. "You're good. Try not to swing that arm around too much for the next ten minutes or so, while that dries."

He carefully stuck his arm back into the sleeve and pulled his shirt down. "Got it. Thanks." He slipped his jacket back on.

"Anytime." She packed the first aid kit into the backpack and swung it on. She pointed straight in front of her. "We're going to have to keep going that way. The trees stay thick for long enough that we can lose the drones."

He pointed the other way, which he was pretty sure was west. "The main road was that way, right?"

"Yep." She turned in a circle. "I have a really bad feeling that we've already crossed over into East Spencer. Or we will, soon. And we can't risk going back west with those drones."

"So, the plan to *not* go to East Spencer and stay in a car for as long as possible didn't really work out so well."

"Not so much."

MAISIE

MAISIE GLANCED AT Lennon as they walked through the thick trees. He didn't appear to be bothered by the shoulder injury, though it must have hurt.

He'd handled the car getting blown up better than she expected. He was proving to be calm under pressure, which was not her initial impression of him. She was glad to be wrong.

"Listen," she started, and then cleared her throat. "Next time, you can pull ahead of me when we're running. It's fine. I'll catch up."

He gave her an utterly baffled look. "I'm not leaving you behind."

"You wouldn't be leaving me behind. I'd catch up. You're much faster than me."

"And what am I supposed to do if I get there first, and there's someone to fight off? Am I supposed to punch them in the face by myself? No, thank you. That's your job." He grinned.

She bit back a laugh. "Good point."

They walked in silence for several minutes. The sun was

starting to sink lower in the sky, casting an orange glow through the trees.

"What would my life be like, if I don't make it to the northern gate in time?" Lennon asked quietly.

She let out a short laugh. "Wow. Have you lost faith in me already?" She tried to sound flippant, but in reality, she was disappointed at the prospect of him not having faith in her. Since the moment they'd met, he'd looked at her like she was the scariest, coolest person he'd ever seen, and she didn't hate it. It was nice to have someone believe in her, for once.

"That's not what I was saying—"

"Just because the car exploded doesn't mean—"

"I was just curious—"

"Let's keep a positive attitude here. We came out with all of our limbs." She held up her injured hand. "So far, anyway. I break this hand again and I might have to get a new one."

He laughed. "I have no doubt that you could get us there in time, even if you only had one hand."

Heat crawled up her neck, and she quickly turned to hide her red cheeks. Maybe she should have told him how much she appreciated that, but she couldn't find the words suddenly. She couldn't find *any* words. He'd thrown her off balance, and he hadn't even seemed to notice.

"I just wondered," he considered. "Declan said to lock me up. What was he going to do with me later?"

She avoided looking at him as she tried to pull herself together. Having this many emotions over a kind joke felt deeply embarrassing. "Well, Beto told me to take you to Vacancies to get an apartment. Which I imagine is what Declan had in mind as well, eventually."

"They'd give me a place to live?"

"Yeah. Nothing nice. Probably a really small place, and you could work your way up. You'd be given a job, based on what was available and your skill level. You'd start earning credits and paying rent to the family like the rest of us."

"What would I happen if I didn't want the job that was assigned to me? Like, if I just didn't do it?"

"You'd be thrown out of the apartment and someone would come to kick your ass. You'd have a couple options at that point—you could go see if the Reapers would have you, and they'd provide a certain level of protection against us. Or you could try to join the border patrol, though they don't really like newcomers and you probably have a fifty-fifty chance that they decide to make you lunch instead of letting you join."

"Such appealing options," he said dryly.

"But then you'd probably die within a year anyway, because the virus starts shutting down organs in most people, and you need credits to get new ones. Plus, if you're not getting protection from the family, that also means you're not getting your regular screenings, so you won't even know when your organs are starting to go until it's too late. The Reapers have some medical skills, but nothing compared to ours."

"So, I should take whatever job they give me, is what you're saying."

"That is definitely what I'm saying."

"What would it be?"

"Garbage plant, probably, to start. Most people start there, or at least rotate in for a shift every once in a while."

He grimaced.

"After that, who knows? You can pick a trade, or train

under a professional. You might be useful in communications, since you seem into that. Hadley and Elise could probably put you somewhere."

"That doesn't sound too horrible," he said quietly.

"Why? Don't tell me you want to turn back now."

He shook his head. Quickly. "No. That's not what I was saying. I really was just curious."

"Thinking of the worst-case scenario?"

"No, no. The worst-case scenario is dying."

"Low bar."

"I think it could be helpful to tell people that, when I go back. A version of that," he said. "That you were all prepared to provide me with housing and a job. Just like that. I was dropped in here without warning and you were all just like, 'Sure, we can hook him up with a place to live, a job, and medical care.'"

"Yeah, make us sound all good and noble. Hopefully that will help with the not-getting-blown-up thing."

Maisie slowed as she peered ahead. The trees were thinning.

She did a quick survey of the sky. No drones in sight.

"Those were East Spencer drones, right?" Lennon asked.

"Yeah."

"So hopefully they didn't follow us west."

"Only one way to find out."

They walked out of the trees.

LENNON

GRASS STRETCHED BEYOND the trees. Lennon spotted an old road, overgrown and covered in weeds and grass. A deer trotted past several yards away.

Maisie's gaze was fixed behind him, and he turned to see a patch of buildings ahead. She knelt down, pulling a map from the bag.

She studied it, then pointed to the old road. "Let's follow that in. Looks like it will take us right along the outskirts of town. Hopefully we can duck in and grab a car." She folded the map back up.

He raised his eyebrows with a smile. "We're going to steal a car?"

"I'd really like to drive part of the way. It's going to be tough to get the shipment *and* get you to the gate in time if we have to walk nearly thirty miles."

"Good point."

"I don't know what their vehicle situation is like up here,

but they have something that transports the shipments from the gate to the neutral zone, so there's that at least," she said.

"Our satellites showed more vehicle movement on the roads up north than in the south. Significantly more."

"Huh. Interesting." She swung the backpack over her shoulder. "Should be easy, then." She sounded like she was trying to reassure herself as much as him.

They walked to the old road and started down it, darkness settling in as the sun finished setting.

Lennon's shoulder burned a bit, but he got the feeling that anxiety and nerves were keeping him from feeling the full brunt of the pain.

Plus, he was distracted by Maisie.

She'd often walk just a bit ahead of him, and the view was . . . well, he shouldn't have been looking at the view. He should have been keeping his eyes to himself.

But there wasn't much else to look at out here.

Not that it would have mattered. He would have enjoyed that view in the middle of a crowded street.

A light breeze was blowing an occasional whiff of Maisie's flowery shampoo his way whenever her ponytail flapped in the wind.

He needed to stop. He needed to focus.

He'd gotten so good at focusing over the last year. Tuning out distractions. His father's campaign manager had complimented him on how well he'd done since they'd hit the road. He'd even steered clear of starting a new relationship after his latest messy breakup, to avoid causing another scandal before the election.

Then he met Maisie, with her hair, and her cute little walk, and the way she'd looked at him when he'd made the joke about her punching people for him.

He was ignoring it. He was being good.

It didn't matter, anyway. She had shown no interest in him, beyond an appreciation for his running skills.

Well, she did seem to find him kind of funny.

But even if there was a spark, now was certainly not the time. They were in the middle of something. Something that might get them shot. Or blown up by drones.

The breeze blew over a whiff of her hair again. Dammit.

He just needed to think about something else. Like . . . his shoulder, which still hurt. Maisie fixing his shoulder. The way she was always so calm under pressure, and brave, and—

Dammit.

Maisie pointed ahead, to where the patch of lights was growing brighter and bigger. "Let's just go straight in, all right? Act like we belong."

"Always a solid plan." He looked down at his clothes. "Any idea if we'll fit in? You know anything about the fashion up here?"

"Should be similar. I've caught a glimpse of northerners when they drop the shipments in the neutral zone, and they weren't wearing anything too wild."

He tugged the mask out of the front of his shirt. "You think they do this? Sew masks into their shirts?"

"Probably. That started not long after quarantine was first declared, when it was just one big Q." She glanced at him. "Actually, put it on if you see a lot of people with theirs on. In

Lopez territory, we suggest people wear them during the more intense outbreaks."

"You don't really need one, do you?"

She shook her head. "I still wear it, though. Most people don't know the truth about me."

"Why not?"

"No need to be an asshole about it."

"Sure." He paused. "You know, just because they said you can't visit once doesn't mean that's the answer forever. We could try to convince them on the other—"

"Lennon, let it go."

"You won't even—"

"No. I don't want to live out there. They'd probably just lock me up and run tests forever anyway."

He frowned. "I don't think they'd do that. You could—"

"Lennon, seriously." Her tone turned sharp. "Drop it."

He couldn't even pretend to understand why she would want to stay here, but he smiled like he wasn't completely baffled by her life choices. Maybe he'd try again later, when they were closer. "Got it. Sorry."

The small town was clearly built post-quarantine. Lennon had compared an old map to the new, and he was pretty sure this area had been mostly suburban homes before the walls went up.

The homes were gone now, leaving fields of crops and a very odd town.

The structures were all very similar, built for function, not design. Row after row of matching square buildings along wide roads. They were all different businesses—a market, a hardware store, a clothing shop—but they were identical on the outside, save for the tiny signs in the large front windows advertising what was sold inside.

The streetlights were incredibly bright. Weirdly bright, in Lennon's opinion. Like they were trying to make sure no one could hide.

There were almost no cars on the road, and the sidewalks were nearly empty as well. The people he did see walked quickly, heads down. None wore masks, so he left his in his shirt.

"Yeah, this is not going to work," Maisie murmured. "It is way too quiet to grab a car here. If we can even find one. We're going to have to keep walking."

"Technically, we could walk the whole way," he said. "We could do thirty miles. We have over twenty-four hours still."

"We could, though I'd rather not. Especially if we're going to find someone to talk to about that shipment. Doesn't leave a lot of time." She looked at him meaningfully.

"Right. Good point." He smiled at her. "Plus, you know I'm very delicate. Who knows if I'd even make it? You'd probably have to carry me."

She pressed her lips together like she was trying not to laugh, and then lightly brushed her hand against his arm.

Dammit.

"Hey!" The voice came from behind them. They both froze.

Then slowly, they turned around.

Maisie put a hand on his arm again, though it wasn't light

and friendly this time. She wrapped her fingers around his jacket and held tightly, like she was trying to make sure they weren't separated.

The man who had called out to them was a few yards away. He wore a black uniform with a gun at his hip. Some kind of law enforcement, probably. He stalked to them, hand outstretched.

"Let me see your permit."

Lennon's gaze slid to Maisie, wondering if she knew what "permit" he was referring to. Her expression gave nothing away.

"We were just on our way home," she said smoothly.

"Permit," the man barked, opening and closing his fingers.

"Is that necessary? Look at us. We're harmless."

The officer's eyes flicked from Maisie to Lennon. Whatever he saw, he disapproved.

"Per-mit," he said, drawing the word out slowly. Rudely, in Lennon's opinion.

Maisie's hand slid down his arm, to his hand. She squeezed it.

"Oh my god, you're relentless with this permit thing," Maisie said, and then took off running, pulling Lennon with her.

MAISIE

"STOP!" THE PERMIT dude yelled from behind them.

Lennon had barely missed a beat when Maisie started running. Maybe it was the vise grip on his hand. She still had that vise grip.

"I said stop!" the guy yelled again, like they were actually going to listen. There was a hint of bewilderment in his words.

That seemed like a bad sign. He sounded like he was used to being obeyed, which meant that he was about to really lose it when they didn't.

"I need backup!" she heard him yell. "Immediately!"

"This way," she panted, pulling Lennon around a corner.

"Alert. Unauthorized visitors. Alert. Unauthorized visitors." The computer voice came from somewhere above them, and Maisie cast a baffled glance up at the sky. What the hell kind of neighborhood was this?

Headlights appeared at the end of the street. Four of them.

The two identical black cars took up the entire street as they barreled toward them.

"Oh, shit," Maisie said. Lennon dropped her hand and whirled around. He grabbed it again as soon as they sprinted back the way they came.

She ran as fast as she could, the sound of the cars' engines growing closer. She cast a glance over her shoulder to see them speeding toward them at an alarming pace.

They dove around the corner just in time, the cars whizzing past them. The permit man from before had a long black object in his hand. It was thin, like a baton, but with a green light glowing at the end. A Taser, maybe. He charged at them.

Lennon hissed in pain as the end of the Taser hit his arm with a bolt of electricity that Maisie could hear. The man grinned and took a step back, triumphant.

Then confusion crossed his face, like he'd expected that small hit to have a much bigger impact.

Maisie jumped forward and punched him in the face with her good hand. He stumbled, blood pouring from his nose.

The cars spun around to face them again, and Maisie grabbed Lennon's hand as they took off. She glanced at him, trying to judge if the hit to his arm was serious, but there wasn't a trace of pain on his face.

She heard the squeal of tires nearby. Another car coming their way.

A hand stuck out of the car heading straight toward them, and she jumped back, pulling Lennon with her. The hand aimed a gun at her.

She reached for the hand, yanking it so hard she heard a

pop. The man screamed, half his body hanging out of the car. He dropped the gun.

Lennon shot forward, grabbing the man by his arms. The car slowed. The man clawed at Lennon.

Maisie jumped forward, helping Lennon to drag him out of the car. He squirmed against them, knocking her on her butt.

She sprang to her feet. The man kicked her in the stomach, and she doubled over with a wheeze. He dove for the gun he'd dropped, but she was there first. She aimed it at his gut and pulled the trigger. He doubled over and hit the ground.

"Maisie, get in!"

She whirled around. Lennon was in the driver's seat of the car.

She raced to the passenger's side and jumped in. Lennon shifted the car into gear.

She twisted around to look at the cars behind them. "Are you okay driving this thing?"

"Yes."

They shot forward so quickly her head hit the back of the seat. She fastened her seat belt.

Lennon shifted again, pushing them even faster. They were racing down the road at an incredible speed. Maisie gripped the side of the door. She'd never been in a vehicle that moved this fast.

Lennon turned suddenly, practically taking the car onto two wheels.

"Jesus," she said, giving him a baffled look.

"You know how that news reporter said I was arrested four times?" He turned again.

Every muscle in her body was tensed. "Yeah?"

"Only one of those was for being naked."

"What were the other three?" She already had a guess.

A car appeared in front of them, and Lennon came to an abrupt stop that made her teeth rattle in her head. He shifted into reverse and hit the gas, grinning at her.

"Street racing."

LENNON

LENNON WEAVED THE car through the street in reverse, his heart pounding with excitement. He hadn't been behind the wheel of a car in months. The campaign had insisted that he be shuttled around everywhere by a driver. They said it was for his own safety, but Lennon knew it was because they didn't trust him.

They were probably right not to.

He hit the end of the street and turned the wheel hard. Maisie yelped as the car spun.

He put the car in drive and raced down the street. His arm burned from where the guy had Tased him, but he could barely feel it through the rush of adrenaline coursing through him.

Another identical black car turned onto the road in front of him, moving very slowly. He floored the gas pedal.

"Uh, Lennon?" Maisie sounded very alarmed.

He looked in the rearview mirror. A car was still following him.

He slowed just slightly as he took a sharp turn into an alley. He heard the crunch of metal as the car behind him slammed into the slow one.

Maisie let out a short laugh, twisting around in her seat to look. "Holy hell, man, that was amazing."

His lips twitched. It was nice, to impress her.

They flew down the alley and he took a turn north, onto a main road. He kept an eye on the rearview mirror, but no one was following them.

"Damn," Maisie said, leaning back in her seat with a sigh. "You do all the driving from now on."

"Agreed."

"How fast does this thing go?" She leaned over to see the speedometer.

"Seems to top out at about a hundred and twenty."

"What!"

"Why? How fast do you guys' cars go down south?"

"Fifty, maybe? And no one actually drives them that fast."

"Clearly different priorities up here."

"Clearly," she murmured. She reached down to dig through the backpack, then seemed to remember something, and straightened. "Are you okay? Did that Taser hurt you?"

He glanced down at his arm. "Not really. Stung a little."

"Huh."

"Maybe it was broken? He looked surprised it didn't affect me more."

"Maybe." She resumed digging in the backpack, pulling out the map. She opened it and studied it for a moment.

"Am I going the right way?"

"Yes. We're headed toward Val's Territory, though we still have a few more miles."

"How far can we drive until we need to go on foot?"

"I mean . . . we could go almost the whole way there, but . . ." She winced.

"What?"

"What do you think the odds are that they don't have GPS tracking on this thing?"

"Shit."

"Yeah."

"We probably shouldn't risk it, right?" He slowed.

"Let's . . ." She twisted around to look behind them. He glanced in the rearview mirror. Nothing but empty road. "Why don't you really step on it? Let's put a few miles between us and that city before we go on foot."

He smiled at her. "Sounds like a plan to me."

The car suddenly died five minutes later. The engine turned off, and it slowly rolled to a stop. It refused to start again when Lennon tried. Maisie grabbed the backpack and climbed out.

"They may have remote access to it," she said, glancing up at the sky. He followed her gaze, searching for drones. It was too dark to see anything.

"Or it could have just been out of power?" he said hopefully.

"Could have been." She pointed into the darkness. "Let's not stick too close to the road. If they were tracking it, we don't want to make it easy for them to find us."

They traipsed into the grass. The lights of another

neighborhood were visible up ahead. They also had an intense streetlight situation going on, from the looks of it.

"At least we covered a lot of ground." She bumped her shoulder against his with a smile. He bumped hers back.

Their eyes met briefly. He was doing a horrible job ignoring that little voice telling him to keep his distance.

And he was going to keep ignoring it, if she kept looking at him like that.

"I should probably check in with Hadley," she said. "Been a while." She pulled the backpack around to her front, grabbing the radio inside. She turned up the volume. "Hadley?"

"Oh my god! Finally! I've been pinging you for, like, twenty minutes. I was imagining the worst, FYI."

"Sorry. We were in a car chase."

"A car chase? What?!"

"Turns out Lennon's a very good driver."

"I know, I've been watching the news here."

"Seriously?"

"Yeah, Elise tried to stop me, but I know how to access it myself now, soooo . . ."

"Is something up?"

"Yeah. I have bad news."

Maisie sighed. "Tell me."

"Declan figured out that you took Lennon and went up north. And he did not love that, let me tell you."

"What did he do?"

"Well, first he yelled a lot, like a big baby."

Lennon almost laughed. He cleared his throat.

"Then some shit went down here, and now basically the Declan faction and Lopez faction are at war. But, like, a tense

*war. No-one-is-talking-to-each-other kind of war. And I can't
really tell who is on which side now. I think some people are siding
with Declan just to avoid getting killed."*

Maisie muttered something he couldn't understand.

*"And I think Declan knew that you wouldn't go up there just
to drop Lennon off, since you've been asking about that shipment.
So, he left. For the north, I mean. He's coming for you. And the
shipment. He took some guys with him and they have a stupid
plan to take on the Spencers."*

Lennon looked at Maisie worriedly, but she actually appeared amused.

"I wish him luck with that. We've encountered some serious shit here, and I don't know how he'd even find us."

*"Solid point, solid point. But Declan has also decided he wants
Lennon, by the way, since—oh! I forgot the most important part.
Lennon is there, right?"*

"Yeah, I'm here," he said.

"Dude, your dad won the election!"

Lennon stopped. He blinked.

He had somehow completely forgotten that the election
was *tonight.*

And his dad *won?*

"He . . . what?"

*"Yeah, he totally won. Hold on. Let me turn this up and you
can hear for yourself."*

It was quiet for a moment, and then he heard a familiar
male voice. A news anchor.

*"A historic night for the United States tonight, as Senator
Camden Pierce defeats President Howard, ending the over-twenty-
year reign of the Howard family. Senator Pierce looks to be winning*

by a landslide, and voters seemed to have turned against the presi-dent since news broke today that his campaign was responsible for dropping Lennon Pierce into the quarantine zone."

"Holy shit," Lennon breathed.

"So, congrats and all," Hadley said, the anchor's voice fad-ing. *"But now Declan's decided he'd like to keep the son of the next president."*

"And do what with him?" Maisie asked.

"I dunno. Smugly show him off once in a while? Threaten to murder him occasionally if they don't keep sending supplies?"

"That . . . doesn't sound great," Lennon said.

"They're not going to blow us up if the president's son is in here. Declan probably knows about that."

Lennon glanced swiftly at Maisie. Hadley might be right. He worried suddenly that she might also decide it was best to keep him here.

"Calm down," she said, rolling her eyes.

"What?"

"What?" Hadley echoed.

"I'm not going to make you stay here just because they might be less likely to blow us up," Maisie said.

His cheeks heated. "I, uh . . ."

"I said I'd take you to the northern gate, and I will."

He swallowed, embarrassed that she could read him so easily. He was usually really good at hiding his emotions and pretending everything was fine. It was unnerving, to have her so easily size him up.

"Anyway, mostly I think Declan's just pissed that Maisie didn't follow his orders," Hadley said. *"So, he's going up there to take charge or whatever."*

"Okay," Maisie said with a sigh. "Thanks, Hadley. We'll keep an eye out."

"Anytime. And answer your radio faster next time! I thought you were dead!"

Maisie's lips twitched. "I'll try."

She slipped the radio into the backpack, then smiled at Lennon. "Congratulations."

"Thanks," he said, still a bit shell-shocked.

"So, you're now . . . what do they call it? First son?"

"Yeah, uh, I guess so."

"First son and first person to leave the Q. You'll be famous." She tilted her head. "I guess you already are famous. More famous?"

His stomach lurched. *More* famous did not sound like a good time. He already hated the media attention, the way the tabloids twisted stories about him to sound as salacious as possible.

She was giving him a curious look, and he forced a smile.

"That's me. First and famous."

MAISIE

THE SECOND NEIGHBORHOOD they entered was similar to the first. It was mostly new structures, which fit with what Maisie knew about the north. The aerial maps showed that the north had destroyed a lot more of the pre-zone buildings than the south had. It seemed like a dumb use of resources to Maisie. She'd sat in meetings with her dad while the Lopezes discussed construction, and everyone had always been in favor of using existing structures wherever possible.

There were more people on the streets in this town, though. A lot of the shops were still open, and people walked casually down them, some of them swinging bags. That seemed like a good sign.

She felt a hand slip into hers—her good hand—and she jumped, almost pulling it away. Lennon tugged her a little closer, nodding at something ahead.

It was another man dressed in all black. They must have been some kind of police force for the area.

"Let's go this way," she said, ducking into an alleyway.

He glanced over his shoulder as they walked. The man continued down the street, swinging his Taser, and then disappeared from view.

She released his hand, encountering a tiny bit of resistance when she did, like he'd intended to keep it. His skin had been warm against hers, and she almost wished she'd waited to see if he'd pull away first.

She stuffed her good hand into her pocket, rolling her eyes at herself. Her last boyfriend was Declan, and clearly *that* had been the wrong choice. Now she was imagining holding hands with Fancy-pants from the other side of the wall. She was nothing if not consistent in her bad dating choices.

She looked over her shoulder again. The officer was at the end of the street, watching them.

"Shit," she murmured. Lennon followed her gaze. They both picked up the pace.

"Do we stand out somehow?" he asked. "Why do they keep finding us?"

They turned a corner, and she took a quick glance around. The clothes were varied, so that wasn't it.

Her gaze caught on something glinting in the bright streetlights. It was a large silver pendant on a chain around the neck of a woman rushing past. And on the guy next to her. And everywhere else Maisie looked.

"It's the necklace," she said. Maybe that was the "permit" the last cop had been talking about. Some kind of ID chip embedded in the piece of jewelry.

Lennon made an annoyed noise. "Crap, we should—"

"Stop!" a voice yelled from behind them.

"—run," Lennon finished.

She took off, Lennon beside her. They needed a car. Or, at the very least, they needed to lose this officer.

They turned another corner.

She cursed.

There was nothing but open space in front of them. A park, with a dirt walking path, and a few small trees. They needed a crowded street. To get lost in a rush of people.

Maisie pulled her gun out of her waistband. She didn't want to use it—the sound would only attract attention—but she didn't have a choice.

She dared a glance over her shoulder. The officer pumped his arms, feet flying over the pavement, his brow lowered in fury. He was gaining on them.

He stopped. He lifted his arm, pointing his Taser at her. His lip curled.

She stopped, and aimed her gun.

She wasn't fast enough.

The shock rocketed through Maisie's body like a bolt of lightning. She gasped, and swayed.

The world went black.

LENNON

LENNON DOVE FORWARD to catch Maisie. She landed heavily in his arms, and he grunted as he struggled to keep his balance.

The officer aimed his Taser at Lennon. He winced, bracing for impact.

The jolt hit him. He jerked as the current of electricity passed through him. It was uncomfortable, but it subsided quickly.

The officer frowned, and slowly lowered his Taser. He stared at Lennon.

He reached for the other gun in his pocket.

Shit. That was a real gun, with real bullets.

Lennon dropped Maisie as gently and quickly as he could. He grabbed her gun from the ground. The safety was already off.

He winced and aimed low, for the legs. The first bullet ricocheted off the ground. The officer took quick steps forward, aiming his gun at Lennon's head. He was approaching fast. Too fast.

Lennon fired again. And again. The officer yelled and hit the ground only a few feet from him, clutching his leg. His gun skittered across the pavement.

Lennon grabbed it, and then used his own gun to whack the officer across the head. He collapsed with a grunt.

"Sorry!" Lennon yelled, reaching down to scoop up Maisie. He shoved both guns in his waistband, barely remembering to put the safety on before he did. Maisie would never let him live it down if he shot himself.

He caught a glimpse of something shiny around the officer's neck, and he knelt down, pulling it over the man's head. He put it around his own neck. There was a chance that they could use it to track him, but it was a risk he was going to have to take. Clearly, he couldn't move through the city without one.

He took off as fast as he could with Maisie in his arms, glancing at the officer behind him. Still motionless. He went back the way they'd come, away from the park with all its dangerous open spaces.

"Maisie," he said breathlessly. Her eyes popped open.

He turned a corner and skidded to a stop. "Oh, thank god. Can you wal—"

Her body convulsed, her mouth opening in a silent scream. She went limp again.

"That's a no." He held her tighter and ran, ducking in between buildings until he found a tall patch of bushes on a quiet street. It wouldn't hide them for long, but he just needed a minute to figure out what to do.

He gently lowered her to the ground and pulled off the backpack. He fished out the radio and pressed the *talk* button.

"Hadley." He waited. Nothing. "Hadley. It's an emergency."

"I'm here." Hadley's breathless voice came through too loud, and he quickly turned the volume down and glanced around. They were still alone.

"Maisie's hurt," he said.

"What? Hurt how?"

"I don't know. The cops here have some kind of Taser. They hit us with it. I'm fine, but Maisie is unconscious."

"Unconscious?" Hadley screeched.

"And she was convulsing. I don't—" He cut himself off and took a deep breath. "I need to know what those Tasers are and what it did to her. Can your contact tell us where to go? Is there a hospital or something? Can I even take her there? They keep asking for our permits and I—" He stopped abruptly again and took in a breath. Calm. He couldn't afford to panic.

"Hold on, I'm trying to contact him now. Are you in East Spencer?"

"Yes."

"That's not great, but we're going to have to work with it. Give me a minute, okay?"

"Sure."

The line went silent, and he looked down at Maisie. She convulsed, and moaned. He put a hand on her arm. She immediately shook it off.

"Okay." Hadley's voice came through the radio a few minutes later. *"It's not the best news, but, um . . ."*

His heart seized in his chest. He barely knew Hadley, but he could hear the fear in her voice.

"*Those Tasers are some real dickhead technology that sends a tiny device into your body to attack artificial matter.*"

"Artificial—"

"*Like, most of her organs.*"

"Oh." That was bad.

Don't panic.

"*And it sends out electric currents that—never mind, never mind. Queso gave me an address. It's not a hospital, but they can help. If you get her there quick, they might be able to . . . they might be able to do something. But it works fast. Really fast.*"

He swallowed. "I'll go as fast as I can."

"*Okay. You have your map? Queso walked me through how you can get there.*"

Lennon ran as fast as he could with Maisie in his arms, following the route Hadley laid out for them. The location wasn't far, but he had to stop twice and prop Maisie up until a cop passed by, angling her toward him so they couldn't see she was missing a necklace. One of them gave Lennon a knowing smile after his gaze skipped from the necklace to Maisie slumped against him, and he'd had to resist the urge to smash his gun against this guy's head too.

The address was in a residential neighborhood, blessedly free of cops. The homes were all identical little brown boxes, and he was sweating and panting as he ran up the driveway of the last one on the street.

The door opened before he could knock. Lennon took a small step back, holding tighter to Maisie.

The woman in front of him was tall, nearly as tall as him, and probably twenty years older. She peered at him over her glasses.

"The kidnapped one," she said.

"That's me. She needs—"

"I know, I know," she said, cutting him off. "Come in."

He stepped inside the house. It was tiny, and so full of books that it was like they'd taken on a life of their own. Books in every corner, on every surface, stacked so high they blocked out most of the light from the street.

"I took this necklace from a cop," he said in a rush. "It doesn't have a tracker, does it?"

"You mean from one of the patrols?" She glanced back at him with an impressed look. "No, it doesn't have a tracker."

She led him through the living room, and he held Maisie closer, carefully weaving around the towers of books.

They went down a narrow staircase and into a basement. Medical equipment had been set up in the corner of the room—some machines Lennon couldn't place—and a tray full of instruments. Two large cabinets were against the wall, shelves labeled with various supplies. There were three cots against the wall, all empty.

"Put her there," the woman said, pointing to the cot closest to the equipment.

Lennon gently lowered her onto it.

"What's her name?"

"Maisie—" He cut himself off before he said her last name. He had no idea how much this woman knew, and maybe it was best if they didn't hear the name *Rojas*. "And I'm Lennon."

"You can just call me Doc."

"Sure." He watched as she grabbed a long white wand that resembled an ultrasound probe. She slowly scanned it over Maisie's body and eyed the screen next to her, where Lennon could see the faint outline of a skeleton.

"That's weird," she murmured.

"What?"

"I don't see it."

"Should you?"

She nodded, pushing her glasses up her nose. "The device splits once it's inside a body. There should be at least three. . . ." She peered at him. "Do you know where it hit her?"

"It was on her left side. Probably her arm or her side?"

Doc moved the wand up to her left arm. She continued scanning down it. "There's one." She grabbed for a metal contraption on the table. It was short and round, like a soda can, but had four scary sharp pieces sticking out the top.

"What is that?" Lennon asked.

She pointed to the sharp pieces. "These will go into her skin. It sends out a signal that brings the pieces of the device close so that I can easily extract them."

Maisie stirred, her eyes popping open. She took in a sharp breath, her gaze darting around the room.

"Where—"

"Hold her down; this is going to hurt," Doc interrupted.

Maisie started to sit up, and Lennon hesitated. Doc pushed her back down.

"Either hold her down *now* or this thing will start destroying her lungs."

Lennon jumped forward, using both hands to press Maisie's shoulders into the table. She grabbed both his arms. The look on her face suggested he was about to get punched.

Doc ripped Maisie's left hand away from him and Maisie yelped in protest. She tried to push him away.

"What are—"

"Just trust me for a minute, okay?" Lennon said, his words coming out in a rush as he held tighter to her. "Remember how when we met you kept saying you were trying to help me and I didn't believe you? Don't be a dumbass like me."

He hadn't actually expected that to work, but she stilled. Her fingers dug into his arm, her eyes wide as she stared at him.

Doc jabbed the device into her arm. Blood seeped out around it as the sharp pieces burrowed into her skin. Maisie gasped, her body jerking.

"Dammit, didn't get it." Doc threw him a furious look. "Hold her tighter. I'll knock her out in a second, but I have to get this one first."

He leaned his body into hers, pressing his hands firmly to her shoulders. She screamed, burying her head in his chest.

"I'm sorry," he whispered into her hair.

"Almost . . ." Doc jammed the device into Maisie's arm. She shook against him. "Got it!"

Maisie slumped against the table, her eyes half closed.

Doc blew out a breath. "Okay. Two more."

Lennon woke with a start.

"Sorry," a voice behind him said.

He blinked, rubbing the back of his neck. He'd fallen asleep in the chair beside Maisie's cot. He couldn't have been out long, but he was sore.

He glanced back at Doc, who had spoken, and then at Maisie. She was still on the table, unconscious. Her chest rose and fell peacefully. Doc had knocked her out after the first extraction, and she hadn't woken up yet.

"I was trying to be quiet," Doc said. She grabbed the bloody instruments from the table and put them in her bucket. "She should be up soon. She'll be groggy, but should be good to go within an hour of waking."

He glanced down at Maisie's watch. Nearly seven a.m. Twenty-four hours to make it to the gate. And find the shipment.

He took a breath and tried not to think too hard about it.

"I saw you on the news," Doc said.

He stood, walking to her. "You guys have American news in the north?"

"Not officially, but a lot of us watch it anyway. More than the south, I think?" She looked at him for confirmation.

"I don't really know, I was barely there," he said, even though he thought she was right. He didn't want to spill information about the south if he wasn't supposed to. If there was one thing he'd learned being a politician's kid, it was to always say as little as possible, as nicely as possible.

"There's a truck headed up to Northgate, going through the compound to the gate. The driver will let you on it if you leave . . ." She looked at her watch. "Within the next half hour."

His heart leapt into his throat. "Really?"

"Goes straight there. You'll be there by eight a.m."

Eight a.m. Nearly twenty-four hours early. Less exposure to the virus inside the Q. He could be back inside a comfortable quarantine room at the CDC by this afternoon.

But. He glanced back at Maisie.

He'd promised to help her find the shipment.

Of course, he'd be gone before she woke up and realized what he'd done.

His stomach twisted guiltily. He couldn't do that to her. He'd promised. And he wouldn't just abandon her—unconscious—in hostile territory.

"No," he said. "Thank you, but I have to help her with something first." He gestured to Maisie.

"You sure?" Doc paused at the bottom of the stairs, lifting a skeptical eyebrow.

"Are you sure?" He could see his mom in front of him. And Caroline. They both had this skeptical way of looking at him whenever he did something that wasn't totally selfish. Like they thought there must have been a catch or that he'd change his mind.

He tried not to be too insulted about it—for years, he'd been the black sheep of the family, the one rolling his eyes when his dad started lecturing about acts of service. (His dad was insufferable at times, but he also practiced what he preached. It was both annoying and a point of pride for Lennon.)

But he couldn't help but think that his family had never expected quite enough of him. Maybe they should have had a little more faith.

"Yeah," he said to Doc. "I'm sure."

MAISIE

MAISIE'S EYELIDS WERE glued together. She tried opening them and failed.

She tried again. Light crept in. Pain shot through her left arm. She moaned.

"Hey," a male voice said. "Don't try to sit up. You're probably groggy from the sedative."

Lennon. She squinted, blinking again until he came into focus. He was sitting in a chair. The room slowly took shape behind him. Some kind of makeshift medical station.

The Taser. The pain. Lennon pushing her into the table and looking down at her with those intense green eyes. It all came rushing back, and she ignored his advice and tried to sit up.

The world spun violently, and she collapsed back onto the soft surface. She groaned.

"Doc said you'll only be groggy for about an hour," he said.

"Doc?"

"Hadley made a call to her friend, and he directed us here,"

Lennon explained. "Those Tasers shoot devices that destroy your artificial organs."

"What? That's sadistic."

"I know. But honestly you got really lucky, because two of them got stuck on the metal plate in your hand. And Doc got the other one out before it got past your arm. She thinks it was stuck for a while too, but managed to get free."

"Why were they so painful?"

"It's a feature, apparently. It's supposed to be that only the cops can remove them, so people have to immediately turn themselves in or die, but a few people are able to remove them now." He made a face. "Gotta tell you, not feeling great about the north so far."

She rubbed her hand across her eyes. "Same."

Something occurred to her suddenly, and she quickly checked her watch. Nine a.m. "Shit. We lost so many hours. I'm sorry."

"It's not your fault." He sat back in his chair, his expression unreadable. "We still have nearly twenty-four hours."

"That should be plenty of time," she said with confidence that she didn't actually feel.

"Do you want some water?" He reached for the table behind him and handed her a glass.

She took it, barely lifting her head to take a few small sips. "Thank you."

"There's some food when you're ready for it, too."

She felt slightly nauseous, so she just nodded, her brain racing through everything she could remember from the last few hours.

There wasn't much. A vague memory of being with him on the street. A gunshot. She did a quick scan of his body for injuries. He noticed her gaze and looked down at himself curiously.

"Did you shoot someone?" she asked.

"Oh. Yeah. The cop who shot you with the Taser. In the leg, though."

Damn. She hadn't thought he had it in him to even grab a gun in time, much less aim and hit a target who was also shooting at him.

"And then I hit him over the head," he said. "With the gun. Which is probably ridiculous, but, you know. Never killed anyone before. I'm not super-eager to start."

She just nodded. She didn't want to look too startled. She didn't want him to think she was surprised that he'd managed to get them away from the cop.

Because it wasn't that, exactly. The image of Lennon running away from their car had been on a constant loop in her head. He was so fast. It was . . . well, it wasn't entirely horrible, watching him run.

But he could have just bolted. He could have left her on the ground and taken off. He had the maps.

It seemed rude to let him know that she was surprised he hadn't abandoned her.

"Thank you," she said softly.

"For what? Catching you when you fainted? No problem." His voice was full of humor.

She tried for annoyed when she turned to him, but a smile spread across her face. "I did not faint."

"Yes, you did. You're very delicate."

She laughed despite her best effort not to. "Shut up."

He laughed too, leaning closer to the cot. His ridiculous hair was in his eyes, and she almost reached up to touch it before he shook it back into place.

"For getting me here," she said.

His gaze was a little soft, in a way that she didn't hate. "Sure," he said quietly. "Anytime. And by that I mean, please never do that again because I will probably die next time."

Maisie forced herself to eat some food, and managed to get upright about half an hour later. Doc peered at her disapprovingly as they headed up the basement stairs.

"You know you're running around with a broken hand?" she asked.

"The stabbing pain makes it hard to ignore," Maisie responded.

"It hurts?" Lennon asked. "Did Hadley pack any pain meds?"

"Yeah, there's some numbing cream. I'll put some on in a minute." She smiled at Doc. "Thank you."

"No problem. I knew your father."

Maisie's smile faltered, because it was hard to know if people meant that in a good or bad way. She nodded.

"We were friends, pre-zone," she said. "He helped me a few times. Figure we're even now."

Maisie thanked her again and followed Lennon out the door. She pulled the numbing cream from the backpack and spread some on her hand. Pain meds would be better, and she had some, but she couldn't afford to be foggy right now. She still felt a little off balance from the sedative.

"Doc thinks we'll have an easier time now that curfew has passed," Lennon said. "We probably shouldn't have tried to move at night at all. Patrol is really heavy then, apparently."

Her gaze caught on a flashing light coming from the radio in the backpack. She pulled it out. "Hey, Hadley."

"Hey! You're awake!"

"Yeah, I'm up. We're just leaving Doc's."

"Oh good, I was—wait, 'we'? Why is Lennon still with you?"

Maisie looked at Lennon in confusion. "Why wouldn't he be with me?"

"Queso told me that Doc was offering you a spot on a truck to the gate! They didn't tell you, Lennon?"

Lennon ran a hand through his hair. "No, they did. I didn't go."

Maisie gaped at him. "Why not?"

"Because I promised to help you get the shipment first."

His eyes met hers, and her stomach flip-flopped.

"That's nice, but very dumb, Lennon," Hadley said.

"Very dumb," Maisie echoed softly.

"I was supposed to just leave you unconscious in some strange woman's house in the worst territory in the north?" One side of his mouth lifted.

She was blushing. Shit. She wanted to touch his stupid hair again.

"I was actually about to figure out just how deeply Maisie was screwed now that she was alone," Hadley said. *"So, I'm glad you're not, hon."*

"Me too," Maisie said faintly. She tore her gaze away from

Lennon's because that half-smile was really distracting. "Uh, we're fine. We should have an easier time now that it's daylight, and we're not far from Val's Territory. I'll call you when we get there, okay?"

"Okay."

LENNON

LIKE DOC HAD said, the walk was much easier in the daylight. They stuck to the edge of town, and were able to veer off into an old, unused back road as they got closer to the edge of East Spencer territory. The narrow two-lane road wasn't fit for cars anymore—there were huge holes and debris in the road—but it was beautiful. The trees on either side were huge, providing shade as the sun rose higher in the sky.

Lennon glanced at Maisie. She'd been quieter than usual the last couple hours.

"You feel okay?" he asked.

She started at the sound of his voice, almost like she'd forgotten he was there.

He, on the other hand, was intensely aware of her presence, and every time her hand accidentally brushed against his. He was intentionally staying on her right side, because he couldn't brush up against her injured left hand.

"Yeah, fine." She smiled sheepishly. "Better than you, probably. I actually got to sleep."

"I slept for an hour or so, I think." He didn't feel tired.

"I would have understood, you know."

"What?"

"If you'd gone. If you'd taken that truck to Northgate. I wouldn't have been mad."

He laughed. "Come on, you would have been a little mad."

She considered for a minute. "Okay, I would have been *a little* annoyed. At first. But then I would have realized that I'd been unconscious for hours, and you did what you had to do."

He watched as she pushed a strand of pink hair behind her shoulder. "I know."

She frowned. "You know?"

"Yeah. You're obviously a very logical person. I know we just met, but I already got that about you. I didn't think you'd be mad. Still doesn't mean it was the right thing to do."

She stared at him for so long that he had to look away before his face betrayed his emotions. The way she kept watching him with a new kind of intensity was making it hard to concentrate on anything else. He hadn't known he wanted someone to look at him that way—like she was both surprised and deeply intrigued by him—but now he never wanted her to stop.

"You're not," she finally said. "A logical person."

He laughed. "Not really, no. I mean, sometimes. But I'm more of a 'go with my gut' person."

She nodded. "I like that about you."

He couldn't hide his surprise. He wasn't exactly surprised that she liked that about him, but that she would say it so openly.

She stopped suddenly, putting her arm out to stop him, too.

Ahead, two cops were in an off-roading vehicle, blundering through the grass.

Maisie grabbed his hand and pulled him off the pavement and behind a tree. She crouched down, and he followed suit.

They waited until the cops lumbered over the road and onto the grass on the other side. Maisie stood as they disappeared in the distance.

"Honestly, of all the stupid things to carry over from the US," Lennon grumbled as they stepped back onto the road.

"What?"

"Cops. Why you would create your own society and then decide, 'Hey, how about we give a bunch of power-hungry assholes the power to kill you?' is completely beyond me."

She let out a laugh, eyebrows raised. "Are they like that on the other side of the wall too?"

"Not exactly, but definitely similar."

"It sounds terrible over there."

"Does it?"

"Well, yeah. Apparently, you have some of those"—she waved her hand in the general direction of the disappearing cops—"and you've had the same family in charge for years, even though you're supposed to be a democracy, and apparently you get kidnapped if you go to a place called Georgia."

"That last one is just me. Georgians would want me to clarify that it's actually a very nice state where people usually don't get kidnapped."

"It doesn't sound great. Though . . ." She trailed off, her gaze distant.

"What?"

"Dad used to talk about the ocean. He had family in south Texas—what's that area called? Rio something?"

"The Rio Grande Valley?"

"That's the one. He'd go down there and see them and they'd go to the beach. I've always wanted to see the beach."

"It's nice," he said softly. "Maybe you will, one day."

She shrugged. "Maybe."

He took a moment to gather his thoughts before speaking, trying not to sound rude. "Does it feel small in here? Do you feel trapped?"

"No. Not usually. Sometimes, if I think about it. . . ." She glanced at him. "My mom, she was British."

"Yeah?"

"Yeah. She was in Austin visiting friends when it all went down."

"Christ, that sucks."

"Yeah. And I can't really, like . . . conceive of that distance. Between the US and the UK. Or even imagine what a whole other country would look like. My dad's parents were from Mexico, and he only went there a couple times, but I can't really understand that, either. Even though there was no ocean involved with them, I can't imagine traveling that distance. This"—she gestured around them—"felt nearly insurmount-able." She shook her head. "That probably didn't make sense. I think I mean that I don't really feel trapped unless I think about it too hard. It must have been much harder for my parents. And everyone else who remembers life before the wall."

He nodded.

"I do actually understand why you're so desperate to get

out of here," she said. "I know that it must feel much smaller for you than it does for me."

"It's not that," he said. She shot him a look. "I mean, yes, it does feel small, but it's more about my life outside the walls. My family and my friends. I was going to go back to school next year." As he said it, he realized that he wasn't going back to the same life he'd left. His dad had won the election. He was going back to a new world of secret service protection and politics and he was actually going to get to, like, hang out in the White House. It was both exciting and terrifying.

"What's this expression?" she asked with a laugh. "You look freaked out suddenly."

"I was just realizing how different things will be when I get back. We're going to be moving to the White House. Stella must be losing it."

"Your sister?"

"Yeah. She's super into history and old buildings. Getting to live in the White House is her dream come true."

"But it's not yours?"

"It's cool, I guess, but I think that both Stella and Caroline are better suited for that life. Caroline will probably be thrilled to help Mom with all the holiday decorating and picking china or whatever. I'll just . . ."

She looked at him expectantly.

"Maybe it's best I'll be back in school next year," he said. With secret service trailing him everywhere he went. With the entire world watching him, deciding if he was living up to his father. It was hard enough being compared to his dad *before* he was president, when he was just the senator who'd grown up poor, worked his way through college, and earned the reputation as the nicest guy in Congress within a few weeks of first being elected to the House of Representatives.

Lennon hoped everyone got used to disappointment.

"I'm sure you'll find your place," she said.

He shot her a grateful look. "I know you're probably not going to come with me when we get to the gate, but just know that if you ever change your mind, I'll help you. You wouldn't have to navigate the world out there by yourself."

"You're right that I won't come." She smiled at him. "But thank you."

MAISIE

THE BORDER BETWEEN East Spencer and Val's Territory was a makeshift fence. Some places were an actual chain-link fence, and other spots were open but patrolled by cops.

Maisie and Lennon walked about half a mile to the spot where Hadley's friend had suggested they cross over. It wasn't the best spot. That spot was miles away, on the route they could have taken if their car hadn't immediately gotten blown up upon crossing into Spencer territory.

This spot was the only option they had, at the moment.

It was beneath a crumbling overpass that someone had only recently dug through to make accessible. According to their friend, the cops in East Spencer hadn't found the hole yet, so it wasn't monitored on their side.

The other side, though? That was a mystery.

"I think I see the spot." Lennon pointed. "There are the black rocks Hadley was talking about."

She followed his finger to where a pile of black rocks sat on the front of the rubble. That was the spot.

She glanced over her shoulder, checking for cops. All clear.

Lennon hopped up the rubble, reaching for the black rocks. "What do you think our chances of getting crushed to death in here are?"

She surveyed the crumbling overpass, which was bound to cave in one day. "I'd say fifteen percent."

He stopped for a moment, flashing her a smile that made her heart leap. "I was going to say twenty. I like that optimism."

She returned the smile, and his eyes lingered on hers for a moment past normal before turning back to the rocks.

God, she was an idiot. And so was he. They were a couple of idiots maybe about to be crushed to death.

She considered, for a moment, leaning into the stupidity. It was a cool, clear day, and they could go sit in the grass and take a break instead of possibly getting crushed to death. She would like that—to just take a few moments with him. His shoulders had tensed up when they talked about his family, and they'd never gone quite back to normal. Maybe they would, if she ran her fingers across them.

But she was being ridiculous. They'd already lost hours because of her. He needed to get to the gate in time, and she wouldn't be the reason he didn't make it.

Especially not because she was dreaming about running her hands across his shoulders.

Lennon climbed up the rubble to the top, just beneath the bridge. He grunted as he pushed aside a big rock, and then braced his hands against his knees as he peered inside. "Yeah, this is the path."

Maisie used her good hand to hoist herself up the rubble.

Lennon extended a hand down when she got close, helping her the rest of the way.

"You go first," he said.

She nodded, ducked, and stepped into the tunnel. It was cold and dark, and she had to crouch down. Lennon stepped in behind her, then shuffled around to put the rocks back into place to hide the entrance.

"You don't have to wait for me," he said.

"If one of us is getting crushed to death, both of us are getting crushed to death."

He let out a sound between a laugh and a grunt as he pulled the final rock into place. It was dark, light barely filtering in from both sides of the tunnel.

"Stop it, you're making me blush."

She blushed too, and was suddenly very glad for the darkness.

His hand was warm on her back suddenly, and she shuffled forward, toward the light.

She squinted in the sun as she stuck her head out of the hole.

She was met with a gun in her face.

LENNON

LENNON HEARD MAISIE'S tiny intake of breath before he saw the gun.

And then, when Maisie climbed out of the hole, the girl behind the gun.

And then, all the other women with her, also holding guns. Lennon counted seven of them—most of them young, and all of them armed to the teeth. He saw guns strapped to hips and legs, sheathed knives, canisters on belts that looked terrifyingly like some kind of explosive.

This must be the Vals.

Lennon climbed out of the hole and down the rubble. He put his hands up. Maisie did not.

The girl in front—a tall brunette about Lennon's age—jerked her gun at the hole. "Go back." She had a very cute splash of freckles across her nose, which he decided to focus on instead of the weapon in his face.

"Just give me thirty seconds," Maisie said calmly.

The girl cocked her gun. "I could give you thirty minutes,

but there's nothing a couple of assholes from East Spencer can say that's going to change my mind."

"We're not from East Spencer," Maisie said. "I'm from the south."

The girl waited, expression curious.

"My name is Maisie Rojas."

"Oh, shit," one of the women said.

Maisie tilted her head toward Lennon. "And he's from the other side of the wall."

The girl lowered her gun, a baffled expression on her face. "He's from where now?"

"It's true," he said, putting his arms down.

The women all stared at them.

"We just need to pass through to get to Northgate," Maisie said. "We—"

The girl barked out a laugh. "You're not passing through shit. Ladies, put them in the truck."

Lennon was handcuffed again.

This time, it was old-fashioned metal handcuffs instead of zip ties. He liked them better. More comfortable. The chain between the two cuffs let him move a little more freely than a zip tie.

He laughed. Maisie, also handcuffed and sitting beside him in the back of an ancient pickup truck, looked at him like he'd grown a second head.

"It's my fourth time being kidnapped just in the last week," he said over the wind blowing around them. They were lumbering down a dirt road, four women sitting across from them in the back of the pickup. They all appeared interested in him suddenly.

He'd been trying not to think about where they were taking him. If they were going to separate him from Maisie. If they had weapons like East Spencer. The weapons they had just strapped to their bodies seemed bad enough. He didn't want any more deadly Tasers as well.

He needed to distract himself, and he needed to endear himself to these women so they didn't kill him or Maisie.

"Fourth?" Maisie repeated in disbelief.

"The guys in Georgia, and then the cannibals, and then you—"

"I did not kidnap you!"

"I wasn't exactly willing, so I'm counting it."

"I helped you—"

"Still counts!"

Across from him, one of the women pressed her lips together like she was trying not to laugh.

He was good at this. He'd always been good at this.

"And now this time," he continued. "So, four just this week. Five total."

"Five *total*?" Maisie repeated.

"A woman grabbed me at a fair when I was four. She didn't make it very far, though."

"Jesus Christ, man, maybe you should reconsider your life choices," the woman across from him said.

Maisie threw her head back with a laugh.

"Coming from my fifth kidnappers, I feel like I should really take that into consideration."

The woman snorted.

He felt Maisie's arm brush against his, sending a jolt of warmth through him. He didn't move, hoping she wouldn't, either.

She didn't. In fact, she leaned into him, her cheek pressing against his shoulder. He suddenly hated these stupid handcuffs. He wanted to wrap an arm around her waist and pull her against him.

"I saved you from getting kidnapped by Declan, so I think that should cancel mine out," she murmured.

He chuckled, turning so he could rest his chin on her head. "Deal."

The truck stopped outside a large building a few minutes later. The exterior was like one of those huge department stores that barely existed anymore. The sign had long been taken down, and the windows at the front were covered in colorful artwork, obscuring what was inside.

Lennon jumped out of the truck after Maisie, his heart thumping as the women marched them inside. If Maisie was nervous, she didn't look it. He found that oddly comforting.

It occurred to him suddenly that if he died in here, he'd likely made things worse for the people inside the walls with that video. He'd been so focused on crafting a narrative for people to follow that he hadn't considered that. Death hadn't seemed like a real threat at the time. Even when Maisie had warned him about the north, it hadn't quite sunk in.

Try thinking about someone besides yourself every once in a while, Lennon, Caroline had said to him a few weeks ago, with an eye-roll. *Just to mix things up.*

The building was surprisingly empty on the inside, with some chairs and a table in one corner, and boxes stacked in another. The floors were bare concrete, and their footsteps echoed in the emptiness as they walked to a room at the back of the building.

The door was open, and an older woman, probably in her fifties, sat at the desk. Her brown-gray hair was pulled back in a ponytail, and she was writing on a tablet with a stylus. Her intense concentration made Lennon a little nervous.

The girl who had greeted them with a gun stepped forward. She stood a little straighter when she talked to the woman.

"Why are you bringing me people from East Spencer, Anna?" the woman asked. She kept writing.

"Because they're not from East Spencer. That one"—she pointed at Maisie—"claims to be Maisie Rojas, and the dude says he's from the other side of the wall."

The woman's head snapped up. She looked from Maisie to Lennon.

"We thought you'd want to decide on these two for yourself, Val," Anna said.

Beside him, Maisie took in a quick breath at the name *Val*. The woman who ran the whole territory.

"Maisie Rojas," she repeated. Lennon almost laughed. He'd thought that the shocked look on her face was because of him.

Maisie took a small step forward. "I'm sorry to just barge in. I would have contacted you first, but I didn't know how."

"Dr. Lopez knows how." Val stood, and Lennon noted the weapons strapped to her body. A huge knife in a leather holster at her hip. A gun in a shoulder holster. Another knife strapped to her leg, which he only caught a brief glimpse of before she stood. The people in this territory were prepared for the worst. He didn't love it.

"Lopez doesn't know I'm here," Maisie said.

Val eyed her suspiciously. Lennon wondered how long it would take for news of Lopez's death to spread to the north. Maybe it already had, and Val was about to catch Maisie in a lie.

"No, I can't imagine that he'd approve this," Val finally said. She jerked her head at Anna. "Take their handcuffs off, will ya, Anna? And then give us a moment?"

Anna hurried forward, unlocking Lennon's first, and then Maisie's. He noticed her wince as Anna pulled hers off. Val seemed to have noticed it too. Anna walked out of the room, leaving the door open behind her.

Val plopped back down in her chair, swinging her feet up onto the desk. "Go ahead, tell me the story. This oughtta be good."

MAISIE

VAL WAS QUIET after Maisie finished the story. She looked between Maisie and Lennon, and seemed deep in thought for several moments.

"How many shipments?" she asked finally.

"Just the one truck," Maisie said. "But it was a big one, and we need it. People are going to start dying. We can do without the food, but we have to have the medical supplies."

"And, what? You're just going to go up to Northgate and take it?"

"Take it and avoid a bloody war, is what I'm hoping. I assume you'd like to avoid that as well?"

Val snorted. "*I* would like to avoid a bloody war, yes. My brothers might welcome it. In fact, I'm fairly certain that Jonathan has been holding up the shipments in Northgate with the intention of forcing conflict."

"He's going to get it. And the south will have to go straight through your territory to do it."

Val dropped her feet from the desk. "Last I heard, Maisie

Rojas was a loyal soldier to Dr. Lopez. How did you get here without him knowing?"

She hesitated. Her first instinct was always to protect the family, to not give out information until it had been approved.

But the family was fractured, and it was only a matter of days until everyone found out anyway.

"Lopez is dead," she said.

Val's eyebrows shot up to her hairline. "How?"

"Declan killed him. He's making a play for the south, and then the north, too."

"Jesus." She ran a hand over her mouth. "That's bad."

"Declan is going to need support from a lot of people in the south to launch a full-scale assault, and he might get it if I don't bring back the shipment. I have a—"

A yell from outside made her stop.

Val jumped to her feet and bolted out of the room. Maisie followed.

The front doors banged open.

She saw Declan first. He was so easy to recognize, with that annoying swagger and his mouth open to start yelling.

He had a gun. The men around him had guns. There were about ten of them. She immediately recognized a few members of the Lopez family, all armed. Her eyes widened as she spotted Beto, rifle pointed at them.

She, on the other hand, didn't have a gun. Her backpack was still in Anna's hands.

Around her, the Vals leapt into action. Maisie grabbed Lennon's arm, pulling him closer to her. The clicking noise of the safety being removed from a gun sounded all around her.

"I just want my people!" Declan yelled. "I don't want to hurt any of you."

Val glanced back at Maisie and Lennon before strolling over to Declan. "That's a rude way to introduce yourself."

Maisie could see the moment Declan spotted her. He had this way of looking at her, like he was both interested and disappointed.

He lowered his gun, returning his attention to Val. "Declan Myers. I've come for those two." He pointed to her and Lennon.

"So you said. What do you want with them?"

"They're my people. Doesn't matter what I want with them."

"They're *your* people?"

"Yes, they're my people," Declan said impatiently.

"Are you the new leader of the south?"

Declan hesitated, his eyes on Maisie again. He was clearly trying to work out what she had told them. "Yes."

"Self-appointed, I take it."

"I've been second-in-command to Lopez for years. I'm just trying to keep things together in his . . . absence."

"Mm, sure, very big of you. But, you know, it's weird—last I heard, the daughter of Isaac Rojas was being groomed to be the next leader of the south. Which is"—Val pointed over her shoulder without turning around—"that young woman right there."

Lennon looked down at Maisie, but she avoided his gaze.

"First I've heard of it," Declan said.

The lying bastard. Everyone knew she was expected to take over for her father. Declan had just decided to ignore that the past few years and hope it went away. If he acted like the heir, he'd magically become it.

It had worked, Maisie realized with a start. She'd even sort of believed it.

She caught Anna's eye, gesturing to the backpack at her feet.

Please, she mouthed.

Anna kicked the backpack over to her.

"Well. I guess that conversation I had with Dr. Lopez last week was . . . wrong?" Val shrugged. Declan's face turned red. "Anyway, you're in my territory now, so it doesn't really matter."

Declan stared at her. His gun twitched up, just a tiny bit.

Maisie grabbed the guns from the backpack, as discreetly as she could. She slipped one into Lennon's hand.

"Safety is on," she whispered. He nodded.

"Don't test me," Declan said, his voice low.

A chill ran up Maisie's spine. She knew that tone. Declan had never used it with her, but she'd heard it directed at other people.

Usually just before he killed them.

Val put a hand behind her back and pointed one finger straight up.

Pop-pop-pop.

Smoke suddenly filled the room, choking her and stinging her eyes. Maisie lowered her gun and stumbled back. Everyone started yelling at once.

Someone crashed into her left arm and she let out a yelp as pain shot through her hand. She squinted at the woman as she rushed past, wearing goggles.

An arm circled her waist. Lennon. She reached into her shirt, pulling out her mask and tying it around her nose and mouth. It wouldn't do much, but it was better than nothing.

She reached into Lennon's shirt and pulled his out as well.

"Oh, right." He coughed, dropping his arm from her waist as he put the mask on.

She turned, squinting in the thinning white smoke. No one was firing—too risky when they couldn't see—but she heard grunts.

A hand grabbed hers. The bad hand, and she let out a loud curse. They held tighter.

"What the fuck are you doing, Maisie?" Declan growled.

She yanked her hand free, resisting the urge to scream in pain. The smoke had thinned enough for her to see his furious face. His mouth was twisted in disgust.

"What you wouldn't."

"I gave you an order—"

"I don't take orders from dumbasses."

His nostrils flared.

From behind her, she heard Lennon yell.

She whirled around.

He was gone.

LENNON

SOMEONE GRABBED LENNON roughly from behind. Maisie disappeared in the smoke. He yelled in protest, and was rewarded with a punch straight to the face.

The world spun and darkened at the edges. His knees went weak.

Oh god, he was going to faint again.

He was getting *kidnapped again.*

The world came back into sharp focus. He tasted blood. A man had him in a choke hold.

Lennon dug his heels in, twisting against the solid arm. It disappeared.

He stumbled back, gasping for air. He ran a hand under his nose and saw blood on his fingers.

The man who'd had him in a choke hold lunged and took him by the collar. Another grabbed his hands, holding them behind his back. Around him, chaos.

"Get him on the bus *now*," a familiar voice said. "Just go.

Don't wait for us. Get him south as fast as you can. Got it, Bruce?"

The man released his hands and Lennon looked over his shoulder to see Declan darting away.

The other man—Bruce, presumably—tightened his grip on his collar, and Lennon snapped his attention back to him. He made a fist, reeling back.

Lennon spun out of his grasp just in time to miss the punch.

Another pair of hands grabbed him. Then, the now-familiar feeling of a plastic zip tie against his skin.

No. He was not getting kidnapped again. He drew the fucking line at five kidnappings.

He tried to yank his arms apart, but it was too late. His wrists were bound together.

The man spun him around.

Lennon lifted his knee and drove it into the man's groin.

The man yelled and doubled over. Lennon darted to the side, narrowly avoiding another pair of hands. A girl whizzed by him, nearly knocking him down.

Gunfire sounded nearby, and he instinctively ducked. Bruce's face appeared in front of him, and Lennon quickly turned, ducking and weaving in between the women around him.

Bruce yanked on his shirt collar again and Lennon hit the ground, rolling away from him. Someone stomped on his leg. He scrambled to his feet.

"Get them!" a woman yelled.

A hand grabbed the front of his shirt. Lennon looked up. Declan. He pointed his gun at Lennon's face.

"If you—"

Lennon drew his head back and slammed it straight into Declan's.

Stars danced in his vision. Christ, that hurt. Of all the stupid ideas.

He heard several loud curses, and then more gunfire. His hands were free suddenly. Declan was on the ground. Lennon whirled around, ready to run, but he smashed directly into another body.

It was Anna, knife still in hand. Maisie darted over to them, grabbing his arm.

Blood was trickling down his lips again. He reached up to wipe it away.

Anna took a step back, looking at Maisie in amusement as she pointed her knife at Lennon. "Dude, your friend is crazy."

Tick-tick-tick.

The noise drifted over the yelling.

The amusement faded from Anna's face. "Oh my god."

Tickticktick. It was getting faster.

"Run!" Anna yelled. "Everybody run!"

Lennon took off, holding tight to Maisie's hand.

The world exploded around him.

MAISIE

EVERYONE WAS YELLING.

Maisie loosened her grip on Lennon's shirt and slowly pulled away from him. They'd been crouched down together behind an overturned table. She'd managed to pull him behind it just in time.

"Stop him!" She heard Val's voice, harsh and furious, and she turned to see Beto darting around rubble, making a beeline for the exit. Two women tackled him.

She surveyed the rest of the area. There were several dead bodies, and most of them were Vals. A few women raced around, tending to the injured.

Maisie looked over at Lennon. Blood trickled from his nose, but he was in shockingly good shape, considering he'd just headbutted Declan.

"They're gone, Val!"

Maisie turned to see Anna striding across the room.

"They took all of them," Anna continued. "And they're gone."

Val cursed.

"Took what?" Maisie asked.

"Explosives," Anna said. "Those things that they threw, with the warning ticks? Those are ours."

"It must have been what he was after the whole time," Val said. "He charged in here pretending to want you two and . . ." She trailed off, shaking her head.

"And his men took what they really wanted," Maisie finished.

"Word has gotten out," Anna said, with a hint of pride.

"Word has gotten out?" Maisie repeated.

"About Val's weapons. The smoke bombs, the ten-second-warning bombs that they took—Val developed them herself. And those aren't even the best ones."

Maisie kind of wanted to know about the best ones.

Val stormed past them, glancing over her shoulder. "Anna, with me. You two, stay here."

Maisie nodded, watching as Val and Anna joined a few other women at the back of the building.

Lennon was wiping the blood under his nose with the back of his hand, and she pulled off her backpack and dug inside. She produced a tissue and handed it to him. "Sit down."

He did as ordered, plopping down on the ground and pressing the tissue to his nose. She knelt down across from him.

"I can't believe you headbutted him." She pushed his hair back to examine his forehead. No bruise yet.

"It seemed like the best option at the time." He pulled the tissue away from his nose. It had stopped bleeding.

She let go of his hair and sat back on her heels. "You can actually really hurt yourself doing that. You're lucky you hit him in the nose. I hope you broke it."

A smile tugged at his lips. "Me too."

"But seriously, cool it with the headbutting from here on out."

"I didn't want to be kidnapped again."

"I mean, that's fair." She couldn't stop the smile that spread across her face.

His eyes lingered on hers, making her stomach flip-flop in a pleasant way. She moved a little closer to him, until her knees touched his.

"Your nose isn't broken, is it?" she asked quietly.

He shook his head. "I don't think so."

"Good. It's a nice nose."

He smiled again. "Thank you." His fingers brushed the hand she had on her knee, and she didn't move away.

"I guess you've ruined your streak, huh?" she said. "Of not fighting since middle school? Your parents would make you write another essay if they were here."

"I would title it 'Why Declan Deserved It.' Alternate title, 'I Hurt Myself as Much as I Hurt Him, So Please Give Me a Break.'"

She laughed. "I'd read either of those." She moved her fingers, letting them barely intertwine with his. It was getting harder not to touch him. "I've actually been wondering what you plan on telling your parents. About everything that's happened to you here."

"Are there things you don't want me to say?"

"No." She winced. "Well, I wouldn't mind you leaving out the border patrol."

"Don't worry, already planned on that."

"Thank you. But I actually meant more about you

specifically. Like, do you want to tell them about headbutting Declan? About shooting that patrol guy? About throwing a Molotov cocktail? Are they going to judge you for that?"

He looked down at their joined fingers and was quiet for a moment. "Maybe? I think they might tell me that they understand that I did what I had to do. But . . ."

She moved her thumb across his hand. "But?"

"But I actually think it'll be used against me, in a way." He winced. "I don't mean that to sound as bad as it does. I just mean that my parents were always telling us that we didn't get to do things in private, the way other kids did. People were always watching, and everything that I did reflected back on my dad. It's sort of why I was such a pain in the ass when I was younger, because I was so annoyed by that. I didn't choose to be the son of a wildly famous congressman. *He* chose that for me.

"So even though they'll be understanding, there's also a part of them that's going to be disappointed. If I tell them the truth, their faces will fall, like they always do. They won't get the story they want, which would be something about me making friends in here and rising above the violence or whatever fantasy they have out there about how they'd act if the situation were reversed. And then we'll have to come up with some media narrative that's a shiny, highly edited version of the truth. Might as well just skip the truth altogether and give them what they want."

He met her gaze, laughing self-consciously. "Sorry. That was way more than you wanted to know, right?"

"No," she said softly. She moved a little closer to him. "I absolutely wanted to know all that."

He smiled, covering their intertwined fingers with his other hand. "Thanks, Maisie."

She wanted to know more, actually. Part of her wanted to say, *No, keep going. Tell me everything about you because I think you're the most interesting person I've ever met.* She wasn't sure when she'd become so deeply curious about him, but she was suddenly dying to know it all.

"Hey!" It was Beto's voice, from across the room. *"Maisie!"*

She tensed. She wasn't sure she wanted to know why Beto was here. With Declan.

"You're being summoned," Lennon said. She saw him take a quick glance at her lips, like he was thinking about kissing her, and she didn't want to move.

"Yeah, but it'll piss him off if I just ignore him for a while, and I can't let that opportunity pass me by."

He laughed, squeezing her hand.

"Maisie!"

"You want to come with me?" she asked.

"Yeah, okay."

She was slow to get up, waiting until the last minute to drop his hand. She glanced at her watch as she stood. Eighteen hours to go.

"Mais—"

"Yeah, I'm coming, shut up!" she yelled, cutting him off. She strode across the room, Lennon falling into step beside her.

Beto sat on the floor, handcuffed, five Vals surrounding him. His eyes were still red from the smoke, and blood dripped from a cut on his eyebrow.

"What the hell are you doing here, Beto?" she asked. "With *Declan*? The man just killed your father."

"He doesn't know I know that," he muttered to the floor. "And it was all I could think to do. If I just sat back and let him come up here and take those shipments, the Lopez family is done. We'll lose control of the south. The Reapers were already starting to make moves before I left."

"The Lopez family is going to be done anyway, because you're all going to be dead after you start a war with the north. What's he doing with those explosives?"

He looked up at her. "I swear I didn't know that he was after those. He said that we had to grab you before you did something stupid and—"

"Before *I* did something stupid?" She laughed. "I'm pretty sure that y'all have the market cornered on stupid."

"He knows about Pierce winning the election and he said that we needed to keep him here. And he's right, honestly. With the son of the president in here, they're going to make damn sure that nothing happens to the Q."

She had no response to that, because he was right. Lennon had promised to advocate for them on the outside, but it was certainly true that there were benefits to keeping him in.

"Keeping him here against his will is going to cause a whole host of other problems," she said, avoiding Lennon's gaze.

"I guess."

"You mean, 'Yes, Maisie, what an excellent point.'"

He rolled his eyes. "Declan saw that stupid video you made. You left that part out when you told me you were coming up here."

"What do you care?"

"I care because you told the Americans that you're going to deliver their golden boy back to them, and when you fail it's going to be a huge disaster and they're going to hate us even more."

"They were assuming the worst about me in here," Lennon said. "At least now they know I was safe and someone was trying to help."

"It doesn't matter, because we're going to make it to the gate," Maisie said. "We still have time, and we already crossed through the two biggest territories."

"One, you're not out of Val's Territory yet. And two, Northgate makes East Spencer look like a damn party."

She just shrugged, unwilling to tell him that she had a man on the inside in Northgate.

"Can we . . ." Beto regarded the women surrounding him. "Can we talk privately for a minute?"

"Yeah." She grabbed his arm, hauling him to his feet.

"Excuse me, what are you doing?" one of the Vals—an older woman with a serious face—demanded.

"Just let me talk to him for a minute, okay? We'll be right over there." She pointed to a corner. The Val frowned, but didn't move to stop them.

Maisie turned to face Beto once they were out of earshot.

"Listen," he said quietly. "I didn't get the whole plan because Declan didn't trust me—"

"Smart," she interjected.

"—but he's definitely going up to Northgate to do what he did in the south. He wants to take out as many members of the Spencer family as he can. Jonathan Spencer, especially. He wants control of the gate, and I don't think he's wrong."

"That'll start a war. You'll get everyone killed."

"Are you totally sure that *you're* not going to start a war, traipsing over to the gate and stealing the shipment?"

She blew out a breath. "Maybe."

"You mean, 'Yes, Beto, what an excellent point.'"

She resisted the urge to punch him. "I'm going for covert here. My plan was to grab the shipment, get Lennon out, and hightail it back south. I'm not trying to take over the entire territory, and I'm certainly not killing any Spencers in the process."

"Declan doesn't think you can do it."

"One, fuck Declan, and two, how exactly do you plan to take control back from him after this? If, by some miracle, he succeeds, what were you going to do?"

"I was going to . . . murder him?" He scrunched up his face.

"Jesus Christ, Beto, are you asking my permission?"

"No, I just . . ."

"I don't think you should murder someone if you have to phrase it like a question. I think you need conviction in this particular situation."

"Shit, Maisie, I don't know. I'm sorry if I didn't have every-thing perfectly figured out after my father was suddenly killed by his lieutenant."

She softened, just a little. She'd known Beto her whole life. She'd grown distant from him—and a lot of the Lopezes—since her dad died, but they'd been close once. Beto was three years older, and he often got stuck with the job of babysitting her. She'd spent one terrifying night locked in a closet with him while their dads fought off Reapers. At the time, she'd felt safe with him, but he'd only been nine or ten years old. He must have been scared shitless.

"I'm sorry," she said quietly.

His eyebrows drew together, like this sentiment confused him.

"About your dad. And I think I punched you earlier. So, I'm sorry about that, too."

"You did." He paused. "I'm sorry I held a gun on you a few days ago."

"It's fine." She glanced over at the Vals, and at Lennon, who was making conversation with a few of them. Maisie was momentarily distracted—and impressed—by how Lennon could so easily adapt to any situation. From headbutting to chatting with the women who'd kidnapped him in a snap.

She returned her attention to Beto. "What do you say we try to do this without getting everyone killed?"

LENNON

MAISIE HAD BEEN talking to Beto for a long time. Lennon kept glancing over at them, expecting they'd be done, but they were still talking quietly, heads bent together.

"Wait, so they just dropped you out of the plane?" Jessa, a younger Black teenager with long dreadlocks, was staring at him with a dumbfounded expression. She and Anna had apparently been elected as the Vals tasked with keeping an eye on him.

He nodded, returning his attention to them. "Yeah. Strapped a parachute on me and pushed me out."

"Damn," Anna said.

"But what if you'd panicked and didn't open the parachute?" Jessa said. "Or if you'd, you know . . . done it wrong? Isn't it hard to land?"

"I would have died, I guess. And yeah, it is hard to land. But I did all right." He considered for a moment. "And by that I mean, I didn't break anything. It wasn't exactly graceful."

Jessa laughed. "I would have liked to see that."

"I've been wondering," he said. "Why is this called 'Val's Territory'? When everything else is just east and west and north?"

"Because it used to just be those three," Anna said. "When Val split off, she took the territory south of Northgate, but north of East and West Spencer. What was she going to call it? Mid-Spencer?"

"Doesn't have a nice ring to it," Jessa said.

Anna nodded. "Plus, I think that she just liked naming it after herself. Going against her brothers was a big deal. They were all about 'traditional family values' or whatever, which they took to mean that the men were in charge of everything."

"That's why she split off and made her own territory?" he asked.

"Yeah. I mean, family values are nice and all, but things started getting really grim for women, especially in the east. They were talking about only letting girls take cooking and homemaking classes at school. They didn't let women have any positions of power, anywhere. They were using the virus and the Q as an excuse to take women back to the nineteenth century."

"Gross," Lennon said.

"So Val was like, 'Fuck you, have fun by yourselves, boys,' and took off with, like, three-fourths of the women in East Spencer." Anna laughed. "I bet they regret their choices now. There are, like, five men to every woman in the east."

"Men started defecting up here because of it," Jessa said. "We don't take them anymore, but back in the early days, we let some in. That's how Val got so powerful. She didn't even have to convince people to come to her territory after a while. They were begging to get in."

His mom was going to love that when he told her. She often joked about forming a girl gang like the ones she'd read about in books when she was a teen. She'd probably secretly be jealous.

Anna glanced at something behind him, and he turned to see Maisie approaching. Beto had gone back to the Vals who were guarding him.

"Making friends, I see," she said with a smile.

"They were explaining why East Spencer is terrible," he said.

"And Lennon was telling us about getting dropped in the Q," Jessa said.

He'd actually told the story twice since Maisie went to talk to Beto. The first time to Val, who had listened quietly and then disappeared.

Maisie's hand rested lightly on the back of his head, in his hair, and he took in a sharp, quick breath. Her fingers brushed the nape of his neck and then landed on his shoulder.

He really wished they were alone. He might have turned around and kissed her right then.

"How's your head?" she asked.

"Better. They gave me a painkiller," he said, gesturing to Anna. "I think it's starting to kick in."

"You took pills from your kidnappers?" she asked, amused.

"I took one first," Anna said, before he could. "And the Vals have never poisoned anyone, thank you very much." She looked at Jessa. "Have we?"

"I don't think so. Not Val's style."

Val emerged from the back of the building, beckoning at them. "Maisie, Lennon, I need a minute."

He stood and fell into step beside Maisie. "What was that about, with Beto?" he asked quietly.

"Just making a deal," she said.

He tried to ignore the twinge of jealousy in his chest. The two clearly had history, and the way they'd looked at each other was sort of . . . well, they were fond of each other. Lennon wondered just how much.

It wasn't like it mattered, though. He was still on track to be out of here in less than eighteen hours. It would be years before he saw Maisie again, if ever. He wasn't sure he'd even be able to communicate with her at all once he got back.

What a depressing thought. He kept his gaze on his feet as he walked.

Val was back at her desk, waiting for them.

"I'm sorry about him," Maisie said. "Declan. I had no idea what he was planning, but I know you lost some people."

"We did. It's safe to say that Declan Myers is on my forever shit list." She ran a hand down her face. "We need to figure out what to do with you two."

"I have a proposition," Maisie said.

"Does it have anything to do with that long conversation you were having with one of the men who killed my girls?" Val asked.

"He swears he didn't know about Declan getting those explosives. He thought they were just here for me and Lennon."

Val looked skeptical.

"He's Beto Lopez, Dr. Lopez's son."

Val lifted her eyebrows but said nothing.

"I have a contact in Northgate who's going to help us get to those shipments," Maisie said. "If you let us go, and let us cross your northern border, we can get it and I'll drop Lennon at the exit gate. Then we'll go back and never bother you again."

Val squinted at her. "There are so many holes in that plan that I don't know where to start."

"I know it's not perfect, but we're running out of time and—"

"It's certainly not perfect," Val said with a snort. She pointed at Lennon. "And you're only running out of time because of this guy. You're really that committed to getting him out of here?"

"I promised," Maisie said softly.

The words made Lennon's chest squeeze. He brushed his hand against hers.

"And what's it going to look like, if we keep him here against his will?" Maisie continued. "If we can't transport him thirty miles in three days? Three days! The people on the other side of the wall are already talking about killing us all. If he doesn't show up when the CDC gave us a way to get him out, we're never going to recover. We might all be dead."

Val sighed heavily. "You're not wrong about that. I keep up with the news out there best I can, but it's scary as hell at times. Sometimes I wish I didn't know what they were saying. Seems easier not to know."

"It was definitely easier," Maisie said, a bit wearily. Lennon felt a stab of guilt. He could have just not told her.

"But it's better to know," she continued. "We can't make things better if we don't know."

Val considered this for a moment. "And how does Beto factor into this?"

"He agreed that if I can get the shipment, he'll help me get it back south, and he thinks he can convince most of the family members who were backing Declan to abandon him. He doesn't even have enough people for a full-scale assault now; he can't afford to lose more."

"You need more than that," Val said. "You need reassurances that this won't keep happening. You need a plan for the future."

Maisie threw her hands up. "I wish I had one, but what I have right now are people who desperately need the medical supplies in that shipment. And a guy on a deadline." She gestured in Lennon's direction.

Guilt crawled up his spine. He hadn't really considered the mountain of problems that he was leaving for Maisie. Was she even going to be able to get back to the south? And even if she did make it back, she was returning to a south in turmoil. Dr. Lopez was dead and everyone was making a play for his spot.

Val leaned back, gesturing at the girl in the doorway. "Go get Beto Lopez for me, will ya? Bring him here."

The girl nodded and disappeared.

Val scratched her cheek. "He should be here if you two are making big plans together."

The girl returned a moment later with Beto. She unlocked his handcuffs before walking back to the doorway. He shook out his hands.

"Beto, Maisie has been telling me about your agreement,"

Val said. "And I was just about to tell her how friendly Dr. Lopez and I were."

Beto nodded. "I know."

Maisie looked at him quickly. "What?"

"We worked together," Val said. "Made life easier for each other."

"You did?" Maisie asked.

"I helped ensure those shipments made it down south. I negotiated with Jonathan in Northgate. Part of the reason that the shipments aren't making it anymore is because they've started playing hardball. They're . . . well, I don't know what's going on up there, but it's something. They may also be dealing with some mutiny." She tapped her fingers on her desk. "Tell you what. I'll make you a deal."

Maisie perked up. "I'm listening."

"First off, I will have one condition if I'm going to help you." Val pointed at Maisie. "I want her in charge of the south."

MAISIE

MAISIE BLINKED. "YOU want *me* in charge of the south?"

"Not immediately, but yes. Soon. It's what your father and Dr. Lopez had planned." Val walked around to the front of her desk and leaned against it. "A Lopez would take over as head of the family, and Maisie would run the day-to-day, like her father did. That was always the plan, according to what Franco told me."

Maisie looked over at Beto. "Did he tell you this?"

"No." Beto frowned.

"You told your father you didn't want the responsibility of running the south," Val said.

"Yeah, but that was before . . ." He trailed off, swallowing.

"Before you realized Declan was going to take it from you? This was never going to be an easy transition, son. Maisie's a good choice. It won't ruffle feathers."

"It won't?" She was increasingly baffled.

"Well, you'll never please everyone. But according to Dr. Lopez, you have strong relationships in the community."

"You just want her because you think you can control her," Beto said. "You make a deal and basically run the south. Sounds like you've already taken West Spencer."

"I haven't taken anything, son. And I'm not taking the south. I'm helping the south. The men of the Lopez family could stand to learn the difference."

Beto sighed, and then looked at Maisie. "Dad did tell me once that he was having you out collecting for the past few years because he wanted you to build strong relationships with people. Everyone knows that he was grooming you for something."

"For something when I was older, maybe," she protested. "Everyone said I was too young last year, when Dad died."

"Maisie, let me give you a tip," Val said. "You will never be old enough for them. You will always be too young, or too inexperienced, or too much of a woman. You can either let them keep pushing you aside, or you can take this opportunity and tell them all to deal with it."

She took in a slow breath. Declan had taken it, back when her father died. He'd swooped in and grabbed his spot before the body was cold. He'd acted like he deserved it, and maybe part of her had agreed.

He wasn't even that much older than her. And now that she thought about it, she'd been old enough to be his girlfriend, but not old enough for his job? Why hadn't that seemed like a load of crap at the time?

Maybe because she'd heard her father's voice in the back of her head, telling her that no one would respect her if she didn't toughen up. Declan was so much like her father—willing to kill and destroy people to get things done. It had seemed like the only way to be a leader, at the time.

"And I'm not saying that you take your father's place immediately," Val continued. "But I want Declan gone, and for you to start working with the Lopezes to take that spot. Perhaps they can partner you with someone? I'll expect an update, if you agree, and assurances that you aren't being pushed out."

"Beto has a point," she said, meeting Val's gaze. "If you think that putting me in charge means you run the south, you're wrong. Just so you know that."

A smile twitched at her lips. "Understood."

"What do you want in return?" Maisie asked.

"I want to continue to work with the south, just like I did with Dr. Lopez. I'll expect assistance when we really need it, and you can count on the same from me. Also, Dr. Lopez was very generous in sharing his research and techniques to help us save lives up here, and I want that to continue. We're not heavy on medical personnel in this territory."

She nodded. "That sounds fair. I—I can try. To be the one to lead the south."

"I'll need more than *try.*"

"I'll do it." She tried to sound confident. She didn't even think this was something she could promise. There was no guarantee that the family would accept her, even if it had been Dr. Lopez's plan.

"All right." Val laced her fingers together. "Tell me, who is this source you have?"

"We don't know his name. But he's been feeding some information to one of my friends. He gave me some tips on making it into your territory and into Northgate. And he's meeting us once we get there."

Her eyebrows shot up. "Really."

"Yeah."

"Could be a trap."

"Could be, though I don't know for what purpose. We only asked about the shipment, so he may not even know about Lennon. If he does want Lennon . . ." She winced.

"I'm notoriously easy to kidnap," he said.

Val gave him an amused look. "If the source has been feeding you information for a long time, then I'm cautiously optimistic. Like I said, a lot of mutiny. I'd definitely like to know who has gone as far as reaching out to the south, though. That's some high-level betrayal right there."

She paused, considering for a moment. "Here's my offer. I'll send two of my girls with you. They'll help you procure the shipment. They get to meet the source."

"I'll need to have my friend run that by him first."

Val waved her hand. "Fine. Once you're back here with the shipment, I can get you safely back south."

"Seriously?" Maisie said.

"Yes. I control one of the roads in West Spencer. The west is weak; they need my protection. They'll look the other way."

"That would be amazing."

"And I want you to keep your word about calling off this nonsense," she said to Beto. "I don't care how you get Declan under control; just do it."

He nodded.

"If this falls apart, and Declan takes over the south, trust me when I say you will all regret it. I don't want to partner with

Arthur and the east to get the south under control, but I will do it if I have to. And you won't like it."

Maisie and Beto exchanged a nervous glance.

"We won't let that happen," she said.

"Good." Val clapped her hands together. "Let's do this, then."

LENNON

LENNON STOOD OUTSIDE the building with Maisie as they waited for the Vals to send out the two girls accompanying them. She'd been quiet since their conversation with Val, occasionally pulling on her hair and making faces like she was deep in thought.

"So," he said.

She looked up at him.

"Is there, like, a title to go along with this position? Do I call you *consigliere* now?"

Her brow furrowed. "I have no idea what that means."

"It's Italian. From *The Godfather*?"

"Oh right, that old movie about the mafia. My dad loved that movie."

Lennon held back a laugh. Of course her dad loved that movie.

"No title, then," he said.

"No. I . . ." She shook her head. "It's not real anyway. I'm going to get back and Declan's going to do something or the Lopezes are going to revolt and it's all going to fall apart."

He turned, leaning his shoulder against the building. "Then you won't let it fall apart."

She lifted a skeptical eyebrow.

"You heard Val in there. You're going to take it. And honestly, I've only known Declan for, like, a day, but he kind of seems like the worst. You're definitely going to do better than that guy."

She smiled, turning to face him. They were close now, close enough that he could have leaned forward a few inches to kiss her.

He considered it for a moment.

"I think it'll look good out there too," he said.

"Out there?"

"In the US. When I get back. They've all already seen you. When I say, hey, that girl—the one who worked so hard to get me out—she's going to be leading the south. I think they'll like that."

"Yeah, I'm sure that having a teenager in charge will really instill a lot of confidence."

He leaned a little closer, which was dangerous, but he couldn't help it. "Don't do that."

"What?"

"Don't be self-deprecating. My dad always says to act like you know what you're doing, all the time. People will eventually believe it."

She rolled her eyes. "I'm sorry, but that is the most white-dude advice I have ever heard."

"I'll give you that." He laughed. "Sometimes it results in

guys like Declan shoving themselves into places they don't belong. But sometimes it means people like you actually getting a shot and not letting dudes like Declan steamroll over you."

She twisted a lock of hair in her fingers. "My dad always told me I wasn't tough enough. Scary enough. He ruled through . . ."

"Fear, I know. We heard on the outside."

"I was never good at that."

"You don't need to be good at that. You didn't get here by being a scary asshole, did you?"

"I got here because you kept hounding me to bring you here." Her lips curved up.

"You struck a pretty good deal, from what I remember. Not to toot my own horn, but I've been very helpful making it this far."

"That was one hundred percent tooting your own horn."

He laughed, reaching out and gently poking her arm. "Well, it's true."

"It is, actually. You're very . . . adaptable."

He cocked his head. He wasn't sure what word he'd been expecting after *very*, but that wasn't it.

"Adaptable," he repeated.

"Yeah. I don't think most people would have adjusted to all this the way you have." She paused, her gaze steady on his. "I think you're pretty okay up close too, you know."

"What?" He was distracted by the freckle near her mouth.

"You said that you're great from a distance. I think you're great close up, too."

The door to the building opened before he could respond, and Anna stepped out, a girl trailing behind her.

"We ready?" she asked.

No. He wasn't ready for anything. Maisie had turned away, but he was still rooted in place, trying to remember when he'd said that he was great from a distance.

Right. When they were watching the news. He'd said it off-hand and then regretted it, because it was too honest. He'd been too honest nearly every moment since he'd arrived in the Q, and he wasn't entirely sure why.

No, he knew why. Because there weren't any cameras or people staring at him. No one on the street recognized him. No one was analyzing his every word and reporting back to his dad's campaign staff.

And so, he'd said *I'm great from a distance* to Maisie because, one, it was true, and two, he didn't think it mattered. Even then, when he was still convincing her to take him to the exit, he was certain he was getting out. It didn't matter what he said or did in here.

But it mattered to Maisie, apparently. She'd heard it and remembered it and now she thought he was great close up, too.

He wondered if she'd still think that in a week, or a month, or a year. Probably not.

My god, you looked like so much more fun in the tabloids, an exasperated girlfriend had said to him once, voicing the exact thing that he'd felt from several girls before her.

Of course, no one here had access to those tabloids. And there was a little nagging voice in the back of his head, saying that all those ex-girlfriends would probably really like this more honest version of him.

"Lennon." Maisie's voice pulled him out of his own head.

He straightened. "Sorry."

Anna pointed to the pale, freckled redhead to her left. "This is Ivy. We're going to make sure you don't die."

"Great," he said. He didn't know whether to be impressed by or terrified of the number of weapons both Anna and Ivy had on their bodies. Guns, knives, smoke bombs, real bombs— they looked like they were going to war.

Beto walked out of the building, casting a nervous glance over his shoulder.

"Did Val threaten to kill you in a really gruesome way if you betray us?" Ivy asked cheerfully.

He swallowed. "Yes."

Anna smiled. "Perfect. Then we're ready to go."

MAISIE

ANNA LED THEM to a truck and climbed into the cab with Ivy and Beto. Maisie jumped into the truck bed with Lennon, and she glanced over at him as they started to move.

He'd had a distant look in his eyes since their conversation earlier, and she wasn't sure what it was about. So much of him was still a mystery. She'd thought she had him pegged right away—rich, spoiled kid from the other side of the wall, terrified and disgusted by all of them—but she had to admit that her assumptions about him were probably wrong. She had no idea what was going on inside that head.

She inched closer to him. Her shoulder brushed his, and he looked over with a small smile.

God, that smile. She watched the way his lips curved up with more than a little interest.

"You okay?" she asked.

He nodded. Her hair blew across her face, and he reached over, his fingers brushing her skin as he tucked it behind her ear. He lingered for a moment longer than necessary, making her heart skip a beat.

"Nervous?" She couldn't help prying.

He shook his head, and then laughed as he seemed to reconsider. "Well, yes. I think I've been nervous nearly every moment since getting dropped in here."

"Sure."

He drew his knees up, slinging an arm across them. "It was really nice, what you said. About me being okay close up, too."

Her cheeks warmed. She almost hadn't said it. But his words had popped into her head, and she couldn't let him think that about himself. Especially when it wasn't even close to true.

"'Great,'" she corrected. "I said you were great up close."

He turned, his eyes burning into hers.

"Did someone say you were better from a distance?" she asked.

He leaned back, turning his gaze to the empty field on the other side of the truck. "A girlfriend mentioned something about that once. But I already knew it, even before she said it. I could tell by the way people interacted with me, how they had all these preconceived notions about me from reading articles about my family or from the tabloids. They'd already created a version of me in their heads, and it didn't match the reality."

"Who do they think you are?"

"Fun. Everyone thinks I'm a nonstop party. And I'm sure they thought I was a spoiled rich kid, which was true. That was fair. But I started noticing that people didn't want to be around me for the harder stuff. They didn't know what to do if I was sad or angry or just having a bad day. I was Good Times Lennon. They didn't want to hang out with the guy the day after the party, who just got dumped by his girlfriend." He glanced at Maisie, an embarrassed expression crossing his face. "I'm sorry. I sound like such a whiner. Forget I said any of that."

"No." She put a hand on his arm. "You don't sound like a whiner. That actually sounds kind of terrible, to have everyone think they know everything about you from a few pictures and articles."

His eyebrows drew together. "Isn't it sort of the same for you, though?"

"How so?"

"People must make assumptions about you because of your father. I did, a little." His expression was apologetic. "And you said it yourself. Your dad didn't think you were tough enough. There was automatically an assumption that you were supposed to be like him."

"Oh." She'd never thought of it like that. "I guess so."

"And . . . forgive me if I'm overstepping here." He hesitated, but she squeezed his arm, letting him know it was okay to overstep. It didn't feel like there was anything he could say right now that wasn't okay. "People must have wondered— *I* wondered—what it was like to grow up with a father who was so notoriously brutal. What kind of person that made you."

"Yeah," she said softly, considering that for a moment. "Declan used to tell me all the time that I needed to be more of a 'badass bitch.' He'd always say, 'I thought you were your father's daughter. I thought you were more than this.'"

"Every time I learn something new about his guy I hate him more," Lennon said.

"Yeah," she said dryly.

The truck came to a stop, and she twisted around to see that they were in an empty parking lot in front of a church.

She started to drop her hand from Lennon's arm, but he grabbed it, lacing their fingers together.

"I think you're pretty great close up too," he said softly. "You don't need to be more of anything."

His thumb brushed across her hand, and she felt it through her entire body. She tried to smile, but it was hard when she felt like she was about to melt into a puddle in the back of this truck.

She'd been wrong when she'd chalked her attraction to him up to another bad dating decision. He didn't belong in the same category as Declan. It seemed absurd to compare them now.

In fact, she thought that Lennon could have ended up being the best choice she ever made, if she'd actually had a chance to make it. But he was leaving, and she was staying, so she would never know.

A door slammed as Beto, Anna, and Ivy piled out of the cab, and he slowly dropped her hand. She climbed out, head down to hide the conflicting emotions probably splashed across her face.

Anna pointed west. "We're about half a mile from where your friend said to cross. We walk from here."

Maisie nodded, swinging the backpack over her shoulder, but Lennon reached for it.

"I've got it," he said, smiling at her as he put it on his back.

"Thanks." She could only hold his gaze for a moment. It

felt like something had shifted between them, and she didn't know where to look.

Beto looked from Maisie to Lennon and back again, and then rolled his eyes at her. She punched him in the arm.

"Hey, so your dad is really going to be the president out there?" Ivy asked Lennon. Luckily, he seemed to have missed that exchange between her and Beto.

Maisie fell into step beside Anna, and Beto walked on her other side. "Can I ask you the obvious question here?"

Anna peered at her curiously. "Sure."

"Where are all the men?"

"Oh." Anna laughed. "I don't even notice anymore. They're around. We were telling Lennon earlier about how some defected here after Val established her territory. But we're still heavier on women. And Val doesn't usually let men work for her. There are a few, but we're mostly women and nonbinary folks." She glanced at Beto. "Isn't the Lopez family heavier on men?" He nodded.

"I mean, there are maybe thirty percent women, so there are some," Maisie said.

"I do not envy you that situation."

"What situation?"

"Taking over as a woman. That's going to be a rough transition, yeah?"

Maisie swallowed. "Yeah. Probably." She looked at Beto again.

"Maybe not," he said quietly, and then shrugged. "No one has united around me or the other Lopezes, which means their other option is Declan. So you have that going for you, at least."

"Ah, yes. The old, 'At least I'm better than that guy' argument."

"You used to date that guy." Beto's lips twitched.

"Ew, really?" Anna said.

"One mistake!" Maisie said, exasperated. "One stupid mistake and no one will let me forget it."

"In your defense, he is *really* cute," Beto said.

"Thank you, Beto, I appreciate that." She bumped her shoulder against his.

They walked for a few more minutes, until Anna signaled for them to stop. They were in an open area, mostly just grass and a few trees around them.

"It's there," she said, pointing to a totally empty field. In the distance, she could see the outline of a few buildings, but they were too far away to be used for surveillance.

Maisie checked left and right. "It's not guarded at all."

"Well, it doesn't need to be. It's chock-full of land mines."

A head popped up in the distance, over the weeds. Anna, Beto, and Ivy drew their weapons at the same time. Maisie moved a little closer to Lennon, but left her gun in her holster.

The person stood and slowly, cautiously made their way to them. A man, probably. He wore a black face mask that covered everything from the nose down. His blond hair was being ruffled by the breeze.

He stopped. "Maisie?"

She let out a breath. "Yeah," she called. "Hadley's source? Queso?"

He nodded. The others lowered their weapons.

He drew closer, and when Maisie could see his feet, she

realized he was keeping them in a straight line, stepping extremely carefully.

He stopped not far from them. He was very tall, probably close to six foot five, and on the lanky side. Most of his face was covered, but he seemed young. Bright blue eyes stared out over the mask.

"Are you sick?" Anna asked.

"No," he said.

"You don't want us to see your face, then?" Ivy asked.

"Not really."

"What about a name?" Maisie asked.

"I don't really want you to have that, either."

Anna sighed. "Listen, Val is trusting you, so—"

"Later," he said. "Okay? Let's get out of this field and I'll . . . I'll think about it."

"Yeah, okay," Maisie said. Anna frowned but didn't argue.

"What do we call you, then?" Ivy asked.

"Hadley calls me Queso."

"Queso?" Ivy repeated.

"It's a whole . . ." He shook his head. "Never mind. Can we talk after? Standing in the middle of land mines makes me nervous."

"Reasonable," Beto said.

"Okay, listen, this is really important," Queso said. "There's a clear path through the land mines, but you need to stay exactly on it. One foot in front of the other. It's carved out in the dirt, and it can be a little hard to see, but it's there. We're going to go in a straight line. Follow the person in front of you exactly, okay? One wrong step and you're going to blow us all up."

"No pressure," Lennon muttered.

Queso carefully turned around, so he was facing the way he'd come. Anna and Ivy fell into line behind him, Beto behind them, and Maisie gestured for Lennon to go in front of her. She took a spot at the end.

Queso took a step forward. Lennon looked over his shoulder at Maisie.

"We're going to be fine," she said.

"Or we're going to die," he said.

She let out a short, startled laugh. "You've been here too long. You're getting dark."

"I'll take that as a compliment." He returned his attention forward as Anna took a step. He followed her, and Maisie followed him, staying exactly on the path.

They went that way for several minutes, no sounds around them but the buzzing of crickets. It might have been peaceful, if not for the fear of getting blown up.

"Oh no," Queso said suddenly.

Everyone stopped.

"What do you mean, *oh no?*" Beto called.

"Duck!" he yelled.

Maisie lifted her chin to see a bird heading straight for them. A shiny, silver bird.

"Don't move your feet!" Queso yelled.

The bird was soaring straight toward Maisie's face with alarming speed.

She bent her knees, careful to keep her feet planted. She covered her head with her hands.

Cold, hard claws landed on her hands. She yelped, trying to shake them off. She felt a scratch, and then a flap of wings.

"What are those things?" Ivy yelled.

She felt metal again on her hands. A beak pricked her left hand, and she yelped, swinging her arms out.

Her feet moved, just a little. She froze.

Ahead of her, Lennon looked over his shoulder. He started to turn.

"No, no, don't—"

The bird dive-bombed her face again. She put her hands up, desperately trying to keep her feet in place. She grabbed a wing.

It was metal. Not an animal at all, but human-made, shaped like a bird.

The bird flapped its other wing, squirming in her grasp. She threw it.

It sailed through the air. One wing sagged uselessly. She'd broken it.

The bird dropped. A bomb shook the ground.

In front of her, Lennon lost his footing and swayed dangerously.

She leapt forward, grabbing him around the waist. They both tilted to the right, but she wrapped her arms tightly around him, holding him steady. They stilled.

She felt him let out a breath. His hands covered hers. "Thank you."

"Sure."

In front of them, Ivy, Anna, and Queso were all watching over their shoulders. Maisie carefully stepped back, keeping her feet in line on the dirt path.

"What the hell was that?" she asked.

"Watcher birds," Queso said. "They're fucking with all the

Spencers right now. And this is a Spencer field, so they must have assumed."

"Watcher birds?" Maisie repeated. "Who controls them?"

"If the Spencers had figured that out, they'd be dead," Queso said.

"Are you part of the Spencer family?" Maisie asked.

Queso turned around. "Let's go. We're almost there."

LENNON

FOR THE RECORD, Lennon thought land mines were stupid. Whoever invented them was stupid, and whoever put them in that Spencer field was stupid.

Or just evil.

He was still having a hard time breathing, ten minutes after clearing the field. He might never breathe right again, actually. His nerves were shot for life.

Queso had put the five of them in the back of a van and then left them for unknown reasons, and Lennon leaned his arm against Maisie's. There. That was almost better.

She smiled at him, and he pointed to her left hand, which was now swollen, bruised, and covered in tiny, angry fake-bird bite marks. "That looks worse."

"It really does."

"Does it hurt?"

"Some."

Some probably meant *a lot.*

She pressed her cheek to his shoulder. He loved how she kept doing that.

He slipped an arm around her. Beto and Ivy leaned forward, talking to Anna in the front passenger's seat, and it almost felt like they had a bit of privacy in the very back.

He turned, his lips barely brushing against her forehead as he spoke quietly. "You want me to grab some alcohol and numbing cream? We have more."

She reached her good hand up to lace her fingers through his, shaking her head. "Can we just take a minute?"

"Yeah," he said softly, holding her a little tighter. He could feel her relax against him, her body going loose and soft. He liked that she felt comfortable letting her guard down with him. He suspected it wasn't something she did with everyone.

They sat in silence for several moments, until Queso opened the front door of the van and climbed into the driver's seat. He started the engine. "Everything looks clear. The shipment is still on the truck, and it's just down the road."

"Seriously?" Maisie said. She straightened, and Lennon reluctantly slipped his arm from her shoulders. Their eyes met briefly, and she gave him a soft smile.

"Yeah. Or it was, when I checked last night." He looked Anna up and down. "I'd heard Vals were always armed to the teeth, but damn."

"Thank you," she said.

"What is that?" He pointed to something on Anna that Lennon couldn't see.

"Smoke bombs."

"Really? How do they—" He cut himself off with a shake

of his head. "Anyway. We should be able to get to the shipment pretty easily, and then I can tell you the best road back to Val's. Might not be totally smooth sailing, but there's a chance they might not stop a Spencer truck." He pulled out onto the road.

Anna lightly punched his shoulder. "I like you."

Lennon opened the backpack. "We should let Hadley know we made it." He grabbed the radio to see that the light was blinking.

"Hey, Hadley."

"Are you there? Did he meet you?"

"Yeah, we're in the car with him right now. We just managed to not get blown up."

"Oh, in the land-mine field? That place sounds stressful. Hi, Queso!"

Lennon glanced up at Queso, but his eyes were on the road, and he didn't reply. He wondered how much he and Hadley told each other.

Maisie leaned forward. "Is there any chance of negotiating with Jonathan Spencer?"

Both Ivy and Beto turned around to look at her like she'd lost her mind.

"What?" Maisie said. "It worked with Val."

"No," Queso said. "Jonathan is not Val. He hates Val, actually. If you manage to get the truck, you need to get it out of here before they notice it's missing."

"The thing is, I need to get Lennon to the gate," Maisie said.

"I saw that you made some pretty big promises," he said, glancing at them in the rearview mirror.

"You have access to American news here?" Lennon asked.

"I have access to a lot of things."

"*Ooh, fancy,*" Hadley said.

"I can . . . I might be able to help with that," Queso said with a sigh.

"Why?" Maisie asked.

"Why what?"

"Why are you able to help with that? What do you want in return?"

"Well, I'd like you not to attack the north, for one. But I do actually sympathize, believe it or not. I know it's tough not getting the shipments. People will die."

Lennon could hear his dad's voice in his head suddenly. *"People want to do the right thing; you just have to let them."* He'd be incredibly smug when Lennon told him about this. Even Caroline would find it touching, and she loved pretending that she didn't have emotions.

"And if the Americans are going to let Lennon out, I really don't care if he wants to go," Queso continued.

"Seriously? You're doing this out of the goodness of your heart?" Anna asked skeptically.

Queso took a turn. He abruptly stopped the van.

"Oof," Ivy said, bracing her arm against the front seat.

"It's gone," he said softly.

Lennon leaned forward. They were approaching a ware-house. And a totally empty parking lot.

"What?" Beto said.

"The truck. The shipment." Queso sat back with a sigh. "It's gone."

MAISIE

MAISIE SAT ON the floor of the van, her legs hanging out the open door, and watched as Queso paced back and forth with his phone pressed to his ear. They'd parked in front of the warehouse while he tried to track down the shipment. Beto, Ivy, and Anna stood a few yards away, talking.

"Give me your hand."

She looked down to see Lennon kneeling in front of her, the backpack open beside him. He pulled out an alcohol wipe. She stretched her sad, mangled hand out as ordered.

"After this heals, maybe you should invest in some brass knuckles or something," he said, running the wipe over her cuts.

She laughed and then winced as the alcohol stung her skin. "You have *definitely* been here too long."

He glanced up, his expression a bit wistful. "It feels like I've barely scratched the surface of what I could see here."

He tucked the wipe into the empty wrapper and tossed it

back in the bag. She wasn't sure what this expression on his face was. Pensive, maybe. Or sad, even.

"You'll miss us a little when you go, won't you?" she said, a hint of amusement in her voice.

He smiled at her. "Maybe. A little. Not your border patrol, though."

She laughed. "That's fair."

He sat down on the edge of the van with her. "Do you want me to tell people that you could leave, if you wanted?"

She stretched her legs out, considering. "I don't know. Do what you think is best."

He raised an eyebrow. "Seriously?"

"Yeah. Why?"

"I don't think you should put that much faith in me."

She let out a startled laugh. "Why not?"

"I can't make that decision! No one in their right mind would trust me with that big of a decision. People on my dad's campaign used to pick out my clothes every day."

She made a face. She got the impression that his life on the other side of the wall wasn't exactly happy. He kept casually mentioning how people didn't like him, or didn't trust him. While she didn't exactly believe that, there was clearly someone out there making him feel that way.

"Maybe they should have focused more on not letting you get kidnapped and less on your clothes," she said.

He laughed. "I'm going to mention that to them, actually. I'm going to get some really great mileage from that guilt." He leaned back on his hands. "I'm not going to tell anyone. About you."

"No?"

"No. It'll become a huge story, and I'll have to explain your reasoning over and over and . . ." He shook his head. "I shouldn't speak for you. You can tell people one day, if you want."

She bumped her shoulder against his. "See? I should definitely put my faith in you."

"What?"

"That sounds like a pretty great decision to me."

He looked down, like he was embarrassed, and then back up at her. They held each other's gazes for several seconds past normal, and heat began to crawl up her neck. She could still feel the warmth of his body against hers, when he'd put an arm around her in the van. The way she'd been able to feel his heartbeat. The moment had ended far too quickly.

She wished they had another day. More than a day. She wanted more time with him to ask about his family and his life and whether it was painful to play tennis naked.

"I appreciate that," he said softly. "The faith."

"Well, it's only right for me to return the favor. You've put a lot of faith in me."

His eyebrows drew together, like he was confused. "Why wouldn't I?"

She barked out a laugh to hide how absolutely delighted she was by that question. "Because you've only known me for a couple days?"

"That is *more* than enough time to realize how amazing you are."

Her cheeks warmed, but she didn't try to hide the blush this time. Maybe she wanted him to know the effect he had on her.

She felt his hand lightly on her back, and then he slipped his arm around her waist, drawing her closer. The way he tucked her into his side felt so easy, so natural, and yet it made a thrill of excitement race up her spine.

"I've got a lead."

Queso's voice broke the spell, and they both turned to him.

"I think they moved it to the service center, where we fix the trucks."

"Is it close?" she asked.

"Yeah." He walked to the driver's side.

Lennon hopped up, offering her his hand. She took it, and then held it for longer than necessary. A soft smile spread across his face, and he squeezed her fingers.

Queso drove them about ten minutes, to an area that looked more like a junkyard than an auto shop to Maisie.

"Wait here," he said, pushing the door shut and walking toward the small building at the front of the mess.

He returned a minute later. He pulled open the van door, holding up a hand when Ivy, Beto, and Anna started to climb out.

"Just one of you," he said. "Preferably someone who knows how to drive a big truck, because I don't."

Lennon unbuckled his seat belt. "I can drive anything." He hopped out.

"Why just one?" Maisie asked, with more than a little suspicion.

"Someone needs to stay here and watch the van. You don't just leave your shit parked wherever here. And I need you guys to leave in about ten minutes, okay? If something goes wrong, we'll walk to the end of the road and meet you there."

"And all four of us need to stay to do that?" Maisie asked.

"I can't go over there with a whole crew; it'll look suspicious," Queso said impatiently. "Do you want the shipment or not?"

"It's fine," Lennon said, his eyes on Maisie. "I can take care of myself. Occasionally."

Beto snorted.

It wasn't that she didn't trust that Lennon could take care of himself. It was just that she was suddenly feeling a little panicky at the thought of something happening to him. She wanted him here, with her, where she could slip her hand into his.

"I won't let anything happen to him," Queso said. "You can trust me."

"I literally *just* said I can take care of myself," Lennon said.

Queso gave Lennon a skeptical look, and threw the door shut.

Maisie watched them go, an uncomfortable feeling in her stomach.

"Well," Beto said. "Let's hope Hadley's right about this guy."

LENNON

LENNON GLANCED BACK at the van as he walked toward the junkyard with Queso.

"She definitely doesn't trust you," Lennon said. "Maisie."

"No reason she should."

"What are we doing, by the way?"

"Maybe *you* should learn to be less trusting. You probably should have asked that first thing," Queso said.

"I'll keep that in mind next time."

Queso pointed ahead, to an area where a few men were gathered, drinking something.

"Your name is John," he said. "One of the Cartwright brothers, if they ask."

"Okay . . . ?"

"They're going to call me Bobby, but that's not my name."

"Starting to think you don't have a name, to be honest."

They stopped as they approached the men, Queso pulling himself up to his full height. It was an impressive height.

Lennon was six foot two, and Queso had a couple of inches on him.

"Hey," he said, and Lennon could have sworn he made his voice a little deeper. "Tim said I should see you about the meds."

The men were all older than them—probably closer to thirty than twenty.

"You got the money?" one of them asked.

Queso handed it over. Lennon tried to hide his surprise. He hadn't realized that the north was still using paper money. Or that Queso was willing to fork it over for them.

"Why don't you go grab those girls you left in the van and hang out for a while?" another guy asked. He nudged his friend and they both laughed.

"Trust me, you don't want anything to do with those girls," Queso said with a forced laugh.

"I want something to do with all girls," the guy said, and then stuck his tongue out in a way that made Lennon wish he didn't have eyeballs.

"You've got three of them in there," the guy said. "Don't be greedy."

"We can't stick around," Queso said. "If I don't get this stuff back to my boss, he's gonna be pissed. And the girls are, uh, for him."

"Your boss sounds fucking greedy," the guy muttered. "Whatever. Third row, in the middle." He tossed him a set of keys. "Put the crates back like you found them."

"Got it."

Queso turned, and Lennon fell into step beside him as they walked away.

"They think you're just grabbing something from the truck?" he asked under his breath.

"Yes."

"What?"

"Cold meds."

"And how are they going to react when we drive that whole truck out of here?"

"Not well, I imagine." He looked at Lennon. "You're sure you can handle a truck?"

"Oh yeah."

Queso appeared skeptical.

"I totally can. Trust me."

"Absolutely not. But I will let you drive because I'm honestly really nervous that I'm going to kill someone if I do it."

"I wouldn't be super upset about it if it was one of those guys, though."

Queso snorted.

They weaved around broken-down cars to the back of the lot, where three eighteen-wheelers were parked. Two were ancient and dirty, but one was in excellent condition. Queso walked to that one and hopped up to the driver's side. He stuck the key in the lock, and pulled the door open.

"Did you have to pay a lot for those cold meds?" Lennon asked.

"Yes." He climbed over the driver's seat and disappeared to the back of the truck.

"That was nice of you."

"Not really!" he called. "This is it. I see the stuff."

"Not really?" Lennon repeated. He climbed up into the driver's seat.

Queso appeared from the back of the truck. "Money isn't an issue."

"Oh. That's nice." He wondered what Queso did up here that money wasn't an issue.

Queso slid into the front seat beside him, glancing at him as he buckled his seat belt. "Wait to start the engine until you see the van leave."

Lennon nodded, finding the van in the distance, still parked.

"Those guys don't know you?" Lennon asked. "It's a small territory."

"I'm wearing a mask."

"Still. I can recognize people with a mask on."

"I don't get out much."

"Why not?"

"I was sick a lot, as a kid. Now . . ." He shrugged.

"Now?"

"I don't know. It's just easier to be by myself." He slouched down in his seat, stretching his absurdly long legs out as far as they could go. Lennon imagined that his legs didn't fit most places.

"I bet you could ask Maisie to go back south with her," Lennon said. "If you don't like it here, I mean. I bet she would be okay with it, after everything you've done."

Queso leaned his head back against the seat and was quiet for a moment. "She probably would. But I can't."

"Why are you helping them? Do you hate the Spencers? You're not one of those drone people, are you? With the birds?"

"God, no." He rubbed a hand across his jaw. "I don't hate

the Spencers. Not all of them, anyway. I'm just trying to do the right thing for once."

"I hear that," Lennon said quietly.

In the distance, the van's lights turned on. Lennon straightened. It began moving slowly down the road.

"Here we go," he said. He stuck the key in the ignition. The engine roared to life.

Lennon put the truck in reverse. "I probably should have asked this before, but you don't care if I run over anything, do you?"

"No."

"Good, because I'm definitely about to destroy some shit."

He hit the gas, and the truck lumbered backward. He scraped against the back of the truck next to it as he pulled out. He pressed the gas again.

"You do know that a truck this big will tip over if you take corners too quickly?" Queso sat up straight and white-knuckled the armrest.

"Yeah, yeah," Lennon muttered, but he did ease up on the gas as he approached the edge of the yard. He turned the huge wheel.

He saw the men as soon as he rounded the corner. They were running. One had his hands in the air, waving frantically for him to stop.

The truck fishtailed as Lennon straightened it. The waving man scrambled out of the way.

Bullets pinged the back of the truck. Beside him, Queso pulled out his gun. He looked over his shoulder, a pained expression on his face.

"Don't. I've got this," Lennon said. Queso cast a relieved glance at him, but he poised his finger over the button to roll down the window, like he wasn't sure he believed that Lennon really had it.

The sound of gunfire disappeared as the truck barreled out of the junkyard. Lennon swerved onto the road, straightened, and then hit the gas harder. Queso returned his gun to its holster and smiled at him. "Well, you did it. Ready to go home?"

Lennon turned a corner. His stomach fell to his feet.

The van was in the middle of the road, riddled with bullets. A black SUV sped away from it.

Lennon accelerated, then slammed on the brakes when they were close. He jumped out of the truck and raced to the van.

The tires were all still intact, but there were bullet holes in all the windows. The front windshield had been hit and had a spiderweb of cracks running across it.

Ivy was sprawled out on the ground, blood seeping onto the road. Anna was on her knees next to her.

"Oh god," he heard Queso say from behind him. Anna sat back, wiping her arm across her wet cheeks.

Lennon's eyes flew to Beto, who had a bloody hand pressed to his side.

He didn't see Maisie.

"Where is she?" he gasped.

Beto winced. "He took her. Declan took her."

MAISIE

MAISIE STRUGGLED AGAINST the arm gripping her waist. She bit the hand over her mouth.

"Ow! Dammit, Maisie!" Declan yelled.

She bucked against him, but he held firm. They were on the floor of the SUV, just in front of the door.

They started to pick up speed. He released her and moved to sit in one of the seats.

She dove for the door. It was locked from the inside.

She took in a slow breath before turning around. The inside of the SUV was dark, and he reached up and flipped the overhead light on. She wished he'd kept it off, so she didn't have to see his smug face.

At least he looked terrible. That made her feel a little better. His nose was swollen, and a black eye was forming from Lennon's headbutt.

"What the hell are you doing?" She tried to keep her voice steady and didn't move from the floor. Sitting next to him felt like admitting defeat.

"I'm taking you back south. Or, Vic is." Declan pointed to the driver. "I've got business to finish up here."

She frowned at him. "Beto told us all about your plan to kill Jonathan Spencer."

Declan sighed, leaning against the side of the van. "I knew I shouldn't have brought that asshole. He was so insistent, promising that he'd convince all the Lopezes to unite behind me. Told me I was the best man for the job."

She rolled her eyes. Declan would believe anything if you stroked his ego enough.

"But, yeah, I guess it's not a secret now. I'm going to kill him and his guys, take the shipment, and head back south."

She opened her mouth. Shut it. Clearly Declan hadn't known why they were on that road. Lennon and Queso should have been almost to them with the truck, but she hadn't seen them as Declan shoved her in the SUV. Clearly, he hadn't either, and had no idea that they'd already taken the shipment back.

"You'll start a war," she said slowly.

"Obviously."

"Only an idiot starts a war on purpose."

"I think pretty much every war in the history of mankind has been started on purpose."

"Exactly my point."

He laughed, leaning his head back. "I swear to god, Maisie, it's so hard to stay mad at you."

"I don't share that feeling."

A smile slid across his face that made her want to punch him.

"Just let me out, Declan." She was starting to get nervous.

They were getting so far from Lennon and Beto and the Vals.

"No."

"I promised Lennon I'd get him to the gate! And if I think I can get the shipment without killing anyone I should—"

"Again, no," he said, with more than a little condescension. "I don't know how you're planning to get the shipment without killing people, but it won't work."

"How do you know my plan won't work if you haven't even heard it?"

"Because it can't be done."

"Sure, since you haven't thought of it, that must mean it can't be done."

He sighed. "I don't want *one* shipment. I want to control all of them. So, frankly, I don't care if you can get one stupid shipment without killing people."

"That is not—"

"Maisie. I know what I'm talking about, okay? And you should be thanking me for—"

"*Thanking* you?"

"Yes, thanking me! I just saved your life by kidnapping you. That little shithead can get himself to the gate if he wants out that badly, I don't care anymore." He snorted. "I wish him luck with that."

"You were trying to grab him a few hours ago."

"I was trying to grab both of you. I decided I didn't need him. I'm not sure how helpful the son of the president will be in here, anyway."

"I still think we should have kept him to help convince the

Americans not to blow us up," Vic called from the front seat. "The president won't order a hit if his own son is in here."

"Yeah, well, the brat has proved difficult to kidnap," Declan muttered.

Maisie almost laughed. Lennon would be so thrilled to hear that he was difficult to kidnap.

"And I can't waste my time on him," Declan continued. "You and Jonathan Spencer are my priority. Now you're safe, so we're on track."

"You have a weird definition of *safe*."

"How are you not safe right now?"

"You just grabbed me against my will!"

"For your own good!"

"Declan." Maisie tried to make her voice gentle. He wouldn't listen if she got mad. He was smart enough not to accuse her of being "hysterical," but he usually stopped listening to her if she got even a little bit upset and would just start kissing her instead.

He looked up at her. His expression was guarded, and she was reminded of the night they first got together. He'd been leaning against the wall of the shop, trying to hide the fact that he'd just been checking her out. She'd thought his expression was sort of endearing.

There was nothing endearing about it anymore.

"What if . . ." She took a breath, choosing her words carefully. "What if we get the shipment, and I agree not to fight you on leading the south? I won't tell anyone what you were going to do up here. I'll give you credit for getting the shipment."

"I don't need you to give me credit." Declan shifted,

adjusting his gun. "And I told you, I don't want one shipment. I want to control them all so this doesn't keep happening."

"We can negotiate—"

"Would you give it a rest? It won't work. Stop being naive."

She could tell he saw the irritation flicker across her face.

"It's true, Maisie. I know that you think you can do everything by charming people, but the world doesn't work like that."

"It's gotten me this far. And neither of us has any idea how the world works."

He frowned. "What?"

"All we know is what's inside these walls. We're part of a much bigger world that we knew nothing about."

"I'm fine with that."

"Are you?"

"Yes. That world out there . . . that world belonged to our parents, not us. We'll never get out of here. Nothing on the other side of the wall matters."

"Of course it does. What we do matters. How we handle this shipment—this conflict—matters out there. And not just because Lennon can tell them. They know what we do in here. Not only through surveillance. The Spencers communicate with them."

"I look forward to putting a stop to that when I take over Spencer territory."

"The solution to our problems is more communication, not less, Declan. As much as I respected Lopez, he was wrong to isolate us like this."

"That's one of the few things I agreed with Lopez about, actually."

Her father had agreed as well. In fact, he may have been the one to push hard to cut off the Q from the rest of the world. *We take care of our own, Maisie.* He'd always say that, pretending that whatever he wanted was for the best for everyone. There was no negotiation, no changing his mind.

Declan was watching her, clearly waiting for her to keep arguing, but she just leaned back with a sigh. Like her father, there was no use arguing with him.

Maybe she'd liked that about Declan at first, that he reminded her of the father she'd just lost. It was easier to just try to be what they wanted, instead of carving out her own path.

Lennon had been right, when he said that she had gotten here by doing her own thing. By going against Declan, and the path her father would have wanted. She already had the shipment that Declan claimed she couldn't get. She had the help of Val, and of Queso. Those were two more allies than Declan had ever made.

"Hey, Declan?" Vic said, looking over his shoulder.

"What?"

"We have a tail."

LENNON

"OH MY GOD, WHY DID I LET YOU DRIVE?"

Queso gripped the armrest like his life depended on it. Lennon had jumped in the van to try to catch the SUV, and Queso had protested, seeing how it was his van and all.

But Lennon refused to let his slow ass drive. Queso had settled for jumping in the passenger's seat.

He pressed the pedal to the floor. The van roared forward, even riddled with bullet holes. Apparently, they hadn't hit anything important. "Jesus, this thing goes fast."

"I hate you," Queso said.

Just ahead, the taillights of the SUV came into view through the cracked windshield. They were also flying down the road at incredible speed, but he was easily gaining on them.

Lennon let up on the gas just a little as they drew closer. He wasn't sure what to do next. Keep following them? Try to run them off the road? That option seemed too likely to possibly hurt Maisie.

Out of the corner of his eye, he saw headlights coming toward them from the left.

"Oh, shit," Queso said.

It was another SUV, barreling through the grass as it headed for them. Queso pulled his gun out.

The SUV wasn't slowing as it got closer. Lennon let up off the gas, just a little more.

A man hung out the passenger's-side window with a gun.

"Duck!" Lennon yelled, reaching over and pushing Queso's head closer to the dash. He turned the wheel, hard, to the right.

Bullets sprayed across the van, and he tensed, bracing to be hit, but they stopped as soon as they started. Queso looked up. His mask had slipped down to his chin, revealing his face. He yanked it off.

Lennon straightened, squinting to see through the cracks in the windshield. The two SUVs turned a corner and disappeared into the dark.

Lennon drove the van back to where they'd left the truck. Their headlights caught Beto and Anna standing on the side of the road, and he pulled the van to a stop next to them.

They did a double-take when they saw Queso without his mask. Lennon glanced over at him as he climbed out, his face illuminated by the lights from the van.

He was as young as he'd seemed, maybe the same age as Lennon. He had the sort of face that his mom jokingly called a "favor face." The guy you send to ask for a favor, because everyone likes his face.

Beto's shirt had a large, dark spot on it at his waist, and blood was drying on his hands.

"Are you okay?" Lennon asked.

"Yeah, just a scratch," Beto said.

"Ivy?" he asked, even though he already knew.

Anna shook her head, her eyes red. "She's gone. We put her in the truck."

"I'm sorry," he said quietly.

"Yeah, well, no time to sit around crying about it," Anna said, clearly trying to sound tough, and failing a bit when her voice shook. She was holding Ivy's shoulder holsters in her hands, and she passed the one with smoke bombs to Queso. "Here. You can have it."

He took it slowly. "I can?"

"You only have one gun. It makes me nervous. Plus, I noticed you keep staring at those."

"Thank you." He took one off the holster and turned it around in his hand. "I've been curious how they work."

"Just don't press that button unless you want a mess," Anna said, and then returned her attention to Lennon. "I see you didn't track down Maisie."

"No, it was . . . it was a dumb plan. They fired on us, and I had to let them go. We both almost died."

"Well, *you* almost died," Queso said. "When people are firing on you in a car, you should turn so that you're farther away from them, not closer. Remember that next time."

"But then *you* would have been closer to them," Lennon said.

Queso squinted at him like he was trying to process that.

"That looked like a West Spencer vehicle, didn't it?" Anna asked. "The SUV?"

"Yeah, it is," Beto said. "Declan negotiated one."

"Oh, Val is going to be *pissed*," Anna said. She pulled out her phone and jerked her head at Beto. "Come on, I need to call her to tell her the plan has gone to shit, and you need to tell her everything you know about Declan talking to the west."

"Wait, we need to find Maisie," Lennon protested.

"Not until I check in with Val!" she called over her shoulder as she walked. Beto trailed behind her.

Lennon swallowed, trying to keep his nerves in check. What if he didn't find her before the deadline? Was he really going to leave without seeing her again?

Was he even going to be able to make it to the gate without her?

"Why is Declan Myers here?" Queso asked. "The second-in-command of the south, right? That's who they're talking about?"

Lennon hesitated, unsure how much he was supposed to tell Queso.

"He's looking for the shipment too, I think," he said, and then quickly changed the subject. "Are you going to tell us your name now?"

"I'm still thinking about it."

"Is it bad?"

"What?" Queso gave him a confused look.

"Your name? Is it bad? Embarrassing, I mean?"

He rolled his eyes. "Coming from a guy named *Lennon*."

"What's wrong with Lennon?"

"It's weird, and I think it's a girl's name."

"Names can be any gender."

Queso's lip twitched like he was trying not to smile. "Fair point." He checked his phone again, the expression fading back to worry.

"Something wrong?" Lennon asked.

"No, I'm just . . ." He slipped his phone back into his pocket with a shake of his head. "It's nothing."

Anna walked back to them a few moments later. "All right. Val left it up to me whether to stay and keep helping or go back now."

Lennon winced, waiting.

"We're going to stay. We—" She threw up her hands. "Why do both of you look so shocked? Thanks for the faith, dudes."

"Sorry!" Lennon said. "I just . . . you know. Ivy died. You almost died. I wouldn't have blamed you."

"Whatever, I almost die all the time." She cleared her throat, blinking quickly like she was trying not to cry. "Since we know it's a West Spencer SUV, Val's sending a drone to track it down. She'll send us the location."

Lennon let out a breath, relieved. "Seriously?"

"Yeah, it shouldn't be a problem. But you, my friend, are going to the gate. Val's orders."

"No," Lennon said. All three heads swiveled to him.

"No?" Anna repeated.

"No. I still have a few hours. I'm going to get Maisie and help her secure the shipment, like I promised."

"We have the shipment."

"*We* have the shipment. Maisie doesn't. I need to make sure it gets back to her so she can get it south."

"Thanks for the trust," Beto said dryly.

"Why would I trust you?"

Queso nodded. "*That* is the right attitude."

"Hey!" Beto said, clearly insulted.

"Beto and I will help her with the shipment after you're gone. Trust me, she'll understand," Anna said.

"She absolutely will understand. Answer is still no."

"Val's orders are to—"

"No disrespect to Val, but I don't follow her orders. I'm helping Maisie. End of story."

Anna put her hands on her hips. "Has anyone ever told you you're a pain in the ass?"

"Just a few dozen times."

MAISIE

"BOSS, THERE'S A problem."

Maisie perked up, leaning forward to look at Vic, still driving the SUV.

Declan held up a finger, stopping him. "Not in front of her."

The SUV came to a sudden stop, and she grunted as she fell against the front seat. Declan hopped out of the van and then reached back in and grabbed her by the ankle.

"Get off," she said, kicking her foot and hitting him in the arm.

"Damn, Maisie," he said, rubbing it.

She scooted out of the van, surveying the area. It was too dark to see much. The headlights of the SUV were pointed at a small wooden building with boarded-up windows. A faded sign said Bar. She spotted another van on the other side of the building.

Declan and Vic spoke in hushed tones a few feet from her, and she turned in a circle, considering if she should run. From what she could see in the moonlight, the area looked pretty flat. If she took off, Declan could watch her run for quite a while before lazily climbing into his truck to follow.

"All right, do you trust me?"

Maisie turned around to find Declan's attention on her. She gave him a baffled look. "Are you talking to me? Of course I don't trust you."

"Maisie, come on, I've known you your whole—" He took a deep breath, shaking his head. "Never mind. Doesn't matter. Just know that I'm coming back for you, okay?"

"Coming back for me?"

"We've had a situation with one of the other vehicles, and I can't spare anyone to take you back right now. And I'm sure as hell not taking you with me."

He took a step forward, grabbing her arms. She immediately squirmed in his grasp, and then stopped.

Wait. It sounded like he was going to leave her alone. He had to be, if he was saying he'd come back for her. She'd be much better off if he was gone, even if he was going to tie her up. She had a knife in her boot that he likely wouldn't think to take from her. She might be able to get it and free herself from whatever restraints he was planning on using.

He gripped her tighter and she let her shoulders slump like she was defeated. He marched her into the old bar, which had obviously been abandoned for years. The lights were on, so the electricity clearly still worked, but no tables or chairs remained, just the long bar on the far wall. There were clean square spots on the floor that dust had settled around, like something large had just been moved.

He pushed her shoulders into a beam, and she almost laughed. That was just great. She wished Lennon were here so he could see how the tables had turned.

He pulled out a zip tie and secured her wrists together behind the beam. He patted her pockets, but they were empty since he'd taken the gun.

Just like she'd hoped, he did not check her boot for the knife.

"No one comes out here," he said. "If you need to pee . . ." He turned in a circle. "Shit. I don't see any buckets. Whatever, I guess you couldn't have used it anyway with your hands tied. I'll just grab you some new pants for when I come back."

"Thanks," she said dryly. "I'll just wait here in my own piss, then."

"Happens to the best of us," he said, clapping her on the shoulder.

She didn't try to hide her incredulous expression. "Declan, what—and I mean this with all of my heart—the fuck?"

He laughed, looking at her with genuine affection. It was maddening how completely he didn't see her as a threat.

And maybe he was right. She'd posed a problem for him, very briefly, and he'd quickly scooped her up and dealt with it. She was a temporary annoyance, at best.

She slid to the floor, careful to keep her arms away from the beam so she didn't get splinters. She sat down and leaned against it.

"I'll be back . . . before dawn, probably? Maybe a little later." He headed to the door, pausing to look over his shoulder at her. "I really will be back for you."

"I know." It wasn't even a lie. She was sure he would be.

She just hoped that she'd be gone by the time it happened.

He smiled like she'd said something kind. She resisted the urge to roll her eyes.

He turned and walked out, leaving her tied to the beam, alone.

She waited ten minutes after the sounds of the van faded to reach for the knife. The only way to get to it was to take the boot off and hope it fell out close enough to her.

She carefully toed off her right boot. The knife clattered to the floor. She used the heel of her foot to slide it closer to the beam, giving it a tiny kick as she aimed it at her hands.

It slid past them.

She cursed, looking over her shoulder to see how far it had gone.

She heard the sound of a car coming to a stop outside. Then, doors slamming. Yelling.

She turned back toward the door, and froze.

"They were here!" an unfamiliar voice yelled. *"A bunch of southerners!"*

The beam dug into her back as she reached desperately for the knife. Her fingers closed around it. She angled it so the blade was against the zip tie and began sawing.

"Check inside," another voice said. *"Send a bird down the road to look for cars."*

She sawed as fast as she could, taking in a slow breath. Panic would not help right now. If she dropped the knife, she was done.

Outside, footsteps drew closer.

Pain slashed across her palm as the blade cut her, and she winced. She angled it back toward the restraints.

The zip tie snapped off her wrists. She leapt to her feet.

The door banged open.

LENNON

"IT'S STILL MOVING back toward the center of Northgate," Anna said, leaning forward to talk to Lennon in the driver's seat. "The SUV."

"How far are we from where they were?"

"Only a couple minutes."

"Okay. We'll see where they went, look for any sign of Maisie, and then double back to them if we don't see her."

"You are literally going as fast as this van will go," Queso said. He had one hand on the dashboard like he was bracing for impact and hoping for a broken arm. "We can't double back."

"It's an expression." Lennon pressed his foot harder on the gas. "And *now* we're going as fast as this van will go."

"I deeply regret letting you drive again."

Lennon let up on the accelerator a little as they approached a curve in the road. It was dawn, the first hints of light making it easier to see and reminding him that he was very quickly running out of time.

Something smashed into the windshield.

Everyone in the van screamed, and Lennon slowed, swerving as they rounded the curve. The van bounced as they rolled into the grass, and he swerved again, getting back on the road.

A piece of a metal bird was lodged in the windshield. He could barely see through it now with all the cracks.

Out of the corner of his eye, he saw something move, and he quickly turned to see a small figure running toward the road. Maisie.

Two men were chasing her.

He slammed on the brakes.

"Oof," Anna said as he felt her hit his seat.

Maisie swerved, running in the opposite direction from the van.

"No—hey!" He flung open the door and cupped his hands around his mouth. "Maisie!"

She looked over her shoulder without stopping. Their eyes met for a brief moment, and he felt it deep down in his chest when her expression changed from fear to relief.

He shot back into his seat, hitting the gas. She couldn't change course again—the guys were gaining on her—so he was going to have to go to her.

He raced forward, getting so close to the guys that he heard one thump against the side of the van. The other yelled, swerving to avoid them. He came to a stop, and Anna slid the van door open. Maisie leapt inside. Lennon took off again.

"Oh god," she said, breathing heavily.

"Who was that? Are you okay?" Anna asked.

Lennon glanced back to see Maisie sitting up, pushing her hair out of her face. She shot him a weak smile.

"I'm fine. Some guys looking for us. They were talking about catching the southerners. Declan left me tied up there."

"He what?" Lennon tightened his hands on the steering wheel.

"It's fine, because he said he'd come back for me." Her voice dripped with sarcasm. "I managed to get free right before those guys got me."

"That's a relief," Anna said.

Maisie leaned forward between Lennon and Queso, doing a double-take when she saw the latter. "Hey! It's your face."

"A very nice face," Anna whispered.

Lennon tried to pretend he didn't feel a twinge of jealousy when Maisie looked back at Anna, the two of them sharing an expression he couldn't see.

"Did we get a name, too?" she asked.

"No," Queso said.

"I mean, if my nickname was cheese, I'd probably be fine with keeping it too," Anna said.

"Wait, where is Beto?" Maisie said, a hint of panic in her voice. "He didn't . . . ?"

"No," Anna said quickly. "He's fine. He's with the shipment. Ivy didn't . . . Ivy didn't make it, though."

"Oh. I'm so sorry."

Anna cleared her throat. "Yeah, thanks."

Lennon glanced in his rearview mirror, but he didn't see anyone following. No more birds, as far as he could tell.

"They were looking for us?" he asked Maisie.

"That's what they said."

"They would have seen us crossing that field," Queso said. "The birds have cameras." He sighed. "I picked that field instead of the road because it *doesn't* have cameras. So much for that plan."

"You really have no idea who they are?" Maisie asked. "You said the birds are messing with the Spencers, but does that mean they're organized? Val said there was some mutiny here."

"I don't know how organized they are, but those damn birds keep popping up everywhere. And they definitely don't like the Spencers, whoever they are."

Anna kicked the back of Lennon's seat. "Let's get this idiot to the gate, and then we can all go home."

Lennon tightened his fingers around the steering wheel. The clock on the dash said 6:45. A little over an hour to make it to the gate. He didn't know if this feeling in the pit of his stomach was because he was nervous he wouldn't make it, or because he was dreading what waited for him on the other side.

He wanted to see his family again. He really did. He wanted to have ice cream with Stella, and watch Caroline try not to look impressed when he told her about his solo skydiving landing. She didn't approve of things that were "dangerous for no reason," but she'd confessed once that she secretly dreamed about skydiving.

And he wanted to congratulate his dad, and tell his mom about the Vals and reassure her that no, he was not deeply traumatized. (She would not believe him. There was more therapy in his future.)

But the uneasy feeling in the pit of his stomach remained.

"Yeah," he said quietly.

MAISIE

LENNON DROVE THEM back to where Beto was waiting with the shipment, squinting in the early-morning light.

She hopped out of the van behind Queso, who caught the keys Lennon tossed him.

"My new life goal is to never get into a vehicle that you are driving, ever again," he said.

"I actually take it as a compliment that you hate my driving so much."

"You really shouldn't," Queso said. But he cast an amused look over his shoulder, and Maisie was struck by how Lennon so effortlessly put people at ease. Everyone he'd met—minus Declan—seemed instantly endeared to him.

Queso and Anna walked ahead, but Lennon stopped, turning to face her. He scooped her into a giant hug, her feet practically coming off the ground. She circled her arms around his neck and held him tightly, her body relaxing against his.

"I'm the only one here who is supposed to get kidnapped," he said, the words muffled against her hair.

"Sorry," she said with a laugh.

He held her for several more seconds, and she let her good hand linger on his neck as they pulled away. She might have kissed him, if they were alone. And the way he was staring down at her with those intense green eyes suggested he felt the same.

She dropped her hand, forcing her gaze away from Lennon's. Beto smiled as she headed over to him.

"You actually look relieved to see me," she said.

"I am." He shrugged. "Declan would never hurt you, though, so I wasn't really worried about that. He'd happily murder the rest of us, but not you."

"Your ex sounds great," Anna said with fake cheerfulness.

"Please don't call him that," Maisie said with a moan. "But speaking of murder, we need to . . ." She trailed off, glancing at Queso. He had no idea what Declan was up to. She'd wondered if it was safe to tell him, but he kept proving himself.

Lennon walked over to her, lightly touching her left arm.

"Seriously?" he said incredulously. "Did you injure that hand *again*?"

"Oh." She laughed, holding up her left hand. There was a new shallow gash across her palm, up to her wrist. "I used the knife in my boot to cut my zip ties. I had to do it in a hurry, so I wasn't exactly careful."

"At this point you might just want to get a new hand."

"Tempting." She smiled at him. "Thanks for coming to get me." She looked past him at Queso and Anna. "All of you."

"Anytime," Anna said. "Now, can you finish that sentence that started with 'Speaking of murder'? Because I'm getting kind of nervous."

"Right. Sorry. So." She turned her attention to Queso.

"Declan stole a bunch of explosives from the Vals. And he's making a play for Northgate. That's why he's here. But he's focused on Jonathan Spencer and his men, specifically. Killing them."

Queso went very still.

"So?" Beto said. "Let him."

"If he kills Jonathan, he's going to start a war," Maisie said. "I came up here to get the shipment so I could stop that from happening. Now Declan is saying that he doesn't care about the shipment. He wants to control the gate. And he's going to do that by taking out—"

She stopped abruptly when she saw the look on Queso's face. He'd gone so white he was practically see-through. His gaze caught hers. She could actually see the panic unfolding on his face.

"I . . ." He took a step back, taking in a huge breath.

"What?" Anna asked.

"I need to . . ." He couldn't seem to finish a thought.

"You know some Spencers you don't want to see get hurt?" Maisie guessed.

He hesitated, then nodded.

"Maybe you know a lot of Spencers?" she guessed. The expression on his face. The way he had access to high-level information.

Queso didn't respond.

"What's your name?" she asked.

He let out a sigh of defeat. "Ethan. Ethan Spencer."

"What!" Anna yelled.

Lennon cast a confused look at Maisie.

"Jonathan Spencer's only son," she said.

"Yeah," Ethan confirmed.

LENNON

"THE JONATHAN SPENCER who Declan wants to kill?" Lennon asked. "The one who runs this whole territory? That's your dad?"

"Yes," Queso—Ethan—said quietly.

Anna and Beto both pulled their guns out, but left them at their sides. Maisie held up a hand.

"What was the plan?" she asked Ethan. "Are you screwing us, or your family?"

"I—I don't want to screw anyone. I wanted to help you because it's not right that the people in the south should die for some stupid turf war."

"Oh, he's noble," Beto said with an eye-roll.

"And you were willing to betray your family for that? For a bunch of people you've never met?" Maisie asked. "Why reach out to Hadley in the first place?"

"Because I always listened to her program and when I found out that the shipments were being tampered with, she was the one I thought of. I don't know, I guess I felt like I knew her."

It's just easier to be by myself. Ethan's earlier words replayed in Lennon's head.

And *I'm just trying to do the right thing for once.*

"The Spencers are notoriously brutal on traitors," Maisie said. "Why risk it?"

"Because whatever they do to me isn't going to be much worse than my life now," Ethan snapped.

Maisie's expression softened.

"I wanted to mess with them a little," Ethan continued. "Make my dad's life as miserable as mine. And, yes, he's the fucking worst, but I don't want him to get blown up. With my mom and my cousins and—" He cut himself off and took a breath. "I'm just going to take the van and go, okay? I swear I didn't do this to screw you—I don't even know how that would work; I just *helped* you—but I won't say anything about the shipment or where you are or about Lennon going to the gate; you can just go and—"

"Ethan," Maisie cut in gently. The way she said his name made Lennon's chest squeeze in a pleasant way. He already knew what she was going to say, and he adored her for it. "I was going to say that we should try to stop Declan from killing Jonathan."

He blinked. "Oh."

"I'm not on board with that," Beto said. "It's Jonathan Spencer! He's a murderer and psychopath, by all accounts."

"He's not a psychopath," Ethan grumbled.

"You really want to start comparing fathers here, Beto?" Maisie asked. "Neither of us has much room to judge."

Beto glared at her. "I'm still not helping."

"I was going to suggest that you and Anna stay with the

shipment anyway. We can't just leave it. Lennon will go with me." She glanced at him. "I'd ask if you were cool with it, but I can already tell you are, from that look on your face."

"You know my looks so well," he said affectionately. She smiled at him.

"I can stay with the shipment, but I do not need you running around trying to save Spencers when the smart thing to do is to just get out of here as fast as we can," Beto said. "You've just told a Spencer; he can go warn them. You've done enough."

"I could, but . . ." Ethan put both hands in his hair and released a giant breath.

"Then you'll have to tell them how you know," Maisie finished.

"Make something up," Lennon said. "Tell them you heard us talking or something."

"It would take work even getting any of them to listen to me long enough to explain it," Ethan said. "I could warn my dad, I guess. He might murder me after, but . . ."

Lennon wondered if Ethan meant "murder" literally. He was worried that he did.

"Do you want me to punch you? Make it look like you had to get away from us?" Beto asked.

Ethan took a step back. "No. Thank you. Just . . . give me a minute to think."

"We don't really have a minute," Maisie said. "Lennon needs to get to the gate in . . ." She looked at her watch. "Like ninety minutes. Which means we are cutting it incredibly close."

"He's the one who insisted on saving you before going to the gate," Anna grumbled.

Maisie met his eyes, her lips twitching up. "Thanks for that."

"Anytime."

"But seriously, we don't have time to go around anymore. We have to go through the Spencer compound to the gate if we're going to make it before the deadline. And it sounds like you have access to it?" she asked Ethan.

"Yeah," he said hesitantly.

"We can get to the gate from there, right?"

"Yeah. There's a main road that runs through it for trucks. Once you exit the other side, you won't have any trouble at the gate. We have a strict no-violence policy in that area, because it's monitored by the US government."

"Trust me when I say that the US government is monitoring a lot more than you think in here," Lennon said.

"That's . . . horrifying," Ethan said. "But if anyone found out that I let a Lopez family member onto the compound, they'd literally kill me with their bare hands."

"Declan's got to be going there," Maisie said. "He may already be there, for all we know. So, there are going to be a lot of Lopez family members on the compound. And if it helps, I know a lot of people who would be horrified to hear that I followed the son of Jonathan Spencer around Northgate."

"It helps a little," Ethan muttered.

"After I drop Lennon at the gate I'll come back and help you," she continued. "Try to smooth things over. Assuming Declan and your dad haven't killed each other."

"That's quite an assumption," Ethan said.

Lennon felt a stab of guilt as he thought about Maisie turning around and going back inside Northgate after he went through the gate. He'd return to his normal life, but she was left with this mess.

"I'm just saying, we can help each other out," Maisie said. "You let us onto the compound, and I will do my very best to stop Declan from killing your family."

Ethan hesitated for a moment. "Okay. But we have to go to my hub first. Just for a few minutes. It's right next to the compound."

"What is your *hub*?" Maisie asked.

"It's where I talk to Hadley. I have a whole setup. I've hacked into the cameras across our territory, so I can see everywhere. I even set up a few of my own that my dad doesn't know about."

"That's both creepy and impressive," Lennon said.

"I may be able to find Declan and his guys. See if they've chosen a spot to launch an attack. If I can access the cameras, I can see and warn my dad about it. He won't even suspect I was helping you if I just report what I saw on a camera."

"Sounds like a plan," Maisie said, heading for the van. Lennon followed. "Stay with the truck, okay?" she called over her shoulder to Beto and Anna. "If you run into any big problems, just go. I'll find my own way back south."

"I think this is dumb, for the record!" Beto called.

"Noted!" Maisie replied.

Lennon climbed into the back of the van, and Maisie slid into the passenger's seat, next to Ethan.

She twisted around to look at Lennon. "Hand me the radio, will ya? I need to update Hadley on everything."

He handed it to her, and she paused, her finger poised over the button. She glanced at Ethan.

"One thing, though," Maisie said. "On a scale of one to ten, how mad will you be if I punch your dad? Not saying I'm planning on it, it's just . . . if the opportunity presents itself."

Ethan started the van. "Zero."

"Perfect."

MAISIE

ETHAN DROVE THEM across Northgate. The front windshield was so damaged that they had to smash it a few more times and remove it completely. Lennon had claimed he could see well enough through it to drive, but Ethan had been firmly opposed to that idea.

Cool morning wind blew through the empty spot where the windshield had been. Ethan took them down a back road that was only dotted with a few homes, and it was quiet and almost peaceful.

Maisie glanced back at Lennon, but he was staring out the window. They had a little over an hour to get him out. He must have been nervous.

She, on the other hand, was trying desperately to ignore the sad, sinking feeling growing in her chest as they got closer to the compound.

"What are those?" Lennon asked.

Maisie turned to see what he meant. About twenty cars, all different vibrant colors, were lined up on the side of the road.

They were all small, with seats for only two people, and looked more like rockets than cars. The front ends were sleek and pointed, with tail fins extending from the end. She couldn't imagine them being very useful for anything.

"They're for racing," Ethan said.

"I need one," Lennon said.

Ethan snorted. "My dad would be so thrilled by that reaction." He glanced at her, seeming to consider his words for several moments before speaking. "I appreciate you standing up for me, by the way. With Beto. About my dad."

"No problem. It's true, that neither of us has room to judge."

"Isaac Rojas . . . My dad told me once that he was scared of him. And my dad isn't scared of anyone."

She laughed. "I wish he was still around so he could hear that. He would have been smug for *days.*"

Ethan gave her a confused look. "Was he not scary, then?"

"Oh no, he definitely was."

From the back seat, she heard Lennon laugh softly.

"But, not to me," she continued. "The way he treated other people was . . . well, not great. But I knew a different version of him."

"I don't know how to deal with it sometimes," Ethan said quietly, his eyes on the road in front of him. "Everything my dad's done."

"*This* seems to be your way of dealing with it," she said, gesturing to herself, and then Lennon. "Helping us."

"Yeah. I guess so."

She hesitated, looking down at her bruised hand for a few moments. "I kind of compartmentalized it all for a long time.

Just tried not to think about everything my dad had done, or made excuses about how he didn't have a choice. But now, especially with everything's that happened recently . . ." She trailed off, turning to look out the window. "It's harder to justify lately. Now that I'm faced with similar choices."

She felt a hand on her arm, and she turned to see Lennon leaning forward, a soft expression on his face. He squeezed her arm. "You can love someone who did bad things. He was still your dad. And a pretty good one, from what you've told me."

She smiled at him, but it was tinged with sadness.

Damn, she was really going to miss him.

"Same goes for you," Lennon said, clapping Ethan on the shoulder before sitting back.

Ethan frowned. "Why are you so nice all the time? It creeps me out."

"Dude, you have so many issues," Lennon said with a laugh. "I'm honestly kind of sad that we don't have time to unpack that."

Ethan frowned harder.

Maisie pointed straight ahead. "Is that the compound?"

"Yeah."

It was surrounded by a massive stone wall, like they'd watched those old zombie movies and were preparing for the worst. She could see a few taller buildings inside, but for the most part, whatever was on the other side of the wall was a mystery.

Straight ahead of them, at the end of the road, was the entrance. Ethan took a turn and rolled past it, to a small rundown building about a quarter mile down the street. He parked the van in back, behind a dumpster.

"I'm going to need a minute to figure out how to explain"—
Ethan gestured to all the bullet holes as he climbed out of the
van—"all of this. Hopefully no one will notice it over here.
Or maybe I can just play dumb. I don't think anyone knows I
took it."

"Is there a reason your hub is outside the compound?"
Maisie asked as they walked toward the building. "Don't you
live inside?"

"Yeah, that's exactly why. Everyone is breathing down my
neck in there. Mom used this building for storage, but she said
I could have it if I cleaned it out myself."

He led them to the door, where he typed a code on the
panel. The door unlocked.

They walked through a dark, empty front entryway and
down a hallway to the room on the left. He flipped on the
lights as they stepped inside.

"Uh, wow," Lennon said.

One side of the space was completely covered in computer
equipment. There were four different monitors, three laptops
that Maisie could see, and stacks of hard drives and other
equipment. Four huge screens were mounted across the wall
above it all.

There were stacks of old technology all around the room—
she could see two ancient CD players, mountains of old
phones, tablets galore, and even some things she didn't recognize.

Lennon approached a tower of matching plastic cases.
"Are these CDs? Are you opening a museum?"

"I saved some stuff from old libraries and bookstores," he

said. Maisie noted that there were no actual books in the room. Maybe he put those somewhere else.

"Why?" Lennon asked.

"I like knowing how stuff works. And how stuff *used* to work." He plopped down at his desk chair and his screen sprang to life.

Maisie edged closer to the end of his desk, where an old radio sat. It was scuffed up and the blue back panel didn't match the rest, which was black. "This is how you talk to Hadley?"

He glanced at it. "Yeah."

"Did you build this yourself?"

"Yeah. I mean, most of it. I put it together from a few parts."

"You built the computers, too, huh?" Lennon asked. He was examining a laptop at the other end of the desk.

"Yes."

Ethan pressed a few keys on a keyboard, and all the screens in the room flickered to life, showing an image of his main screen. "Cameras two and seven," he said. The images changed to show exterior views of the compound. "Cameras five, three, and one."

Maisie leaned closer. "Where do you think Declan would come in?"

"Hard to say. Not the back; it's too hard to get there. Probably the north or south sides." He pointed to the two cameras. "But, seriously, anyone's guess. Keep your eyes open."

"Do you have an alarm system?" Lennon asked.

"Not exactly, but there is someone monitoring these

cameras all the time. They should see as soon as we do. In theory. Most people aren't stupid enough to try, so I don't know how well they're being monitored right now."

"Declan does enjoy being stupid," she said. "Do you have more cameras on the inside? It's entirely possible they're already in there."

Ethan cast a worried look in her direction. "You think so?"

"I don't know, just to be safe. They were headed somewhere right after abandoning me. It could have been to the compound."

He nodded, typing again. The screens split into four different images as he added more cameras.

"Are you armed?" Maisie asked him. "We may be in an intense situation soon if Declan is already here."

"Of course I'm armed." Ethan moved his jacket aside to show the gun in his waistband and Ivy's smoke bombs in the shoulder holster. "I may be the worst Spencer, but I'm still a Spencer."

She almost laughed. "Good."

"I don't see anything yet, though," Ethan murmured, scanning the camera feeds. He glanced over at Lennon, and then hit another button. American news appeared on one screen. "You can see how things are going out there, if you want. I haven't checked it in at least a day."

"You have American news here?" Lennon asked.

"Yeah, I hacked my dad's network."

There was a clock at the bottom of the screen, showing just under fifty minutes left, with the words *Lennon Pierce Deadline*. A news anchor was talking about the new president-elect, and a screen to the left side of his head showed the front of the gate on the other side of the wall. Cameras and lights had been set up, and there was a huge crowd of reporters and spectators behind the fence. Even more than last time he'd seen the news. He spotted a sign that read WELCOME HOME, LENNON.

"Wow," Maisie said.

"I hope you make it," Ethan murmured. "Otherwise, they're going to be real disappointed out there. It's all they've been talking about on your news channels." He pressed a button and the news disappeared. "Sorry, we can't watch for too long. Someone might notice. My dad's tech team isn't the best, but they're not totally incompetent."

"*Ethan? Who are you talking to?*" The woman's voice was distant, on the other side of the door, and they all froze.

"Closet!" Ethan whispered, pointing frantically to a door across the room.

Maisie dove around the piles of electronics and jumped into the closet with Lennon. Boxes were piled high here too, and they had to squeeze together next to them.

Lennon pulled the door shut. She held her breath.

"Ethan." The woman's voice was much closer now, and full of disappointment. She was in the room.

"Hi, Mom. What are you doing up? It's the middle of the night."

"It's almost eight."

"Oh. Really? Wow. I guess that's why it's light outside, huh?" He laughed nervously.

Lennon shifted, and Maisie felt his hand on her arm, near her elbow. They were so close she could feel the heat of him.

"Who were you talking to?" Ethan's mom asked.

"Myself," Ethan said. "And the computer."

"Did you stay in here all night again? I've told you that I don't want you outside the compound all night."

"I, uh—I lost track of time."

"Maybe you should do something besides stare at that screen all damn day and night." She sighed. "At least come make yourself useful."

"What?"

"I've got to run to the market before they open, but the truck won't start again. Come help me get it going."

"The market? That's a great idea!" he said, too enthusiastically. He was clearly thrilled that his mom would be safely away from the compound.

There was a short pause. "Do you want to come?"

"No! No. Thank you. I just, you know . . . we need food?"

"Ethan, just come help me. And seriously, hon, you should leave this room occasionally. You're getting weird."

"Right. Sorry."

Maisie listened as footsteps shuffled out of the room and faded away.

"So do we stay in this closet or . . ." Lennon whispered.

"Let's just wait another couple seconds to make sure she doesn't come back right away."

His hand was still on her arm, and she barely had to reach out to touch his chest.

"Maisie," he said quietly.

"Yeah?" She could barely see the outline of him from the light filtering in around the sides of the door.

"I didn't consider how bad it would be if I didn't make it to the gate."

"Are you losing faith? I know we're cutting it close, but it's just on the other side of the compound. It should only take a few minutes to get there once we're inside."

"No, I'm not, it's just . . ." He pushed open the closet door a crack and looked around. "I think we're in the clear."

She dropped her hand from his chest and stepped out. She walked over to the computer, but the screens were blank now. Ethan must have hidden the images when his mom walked in.

"It's just, when I insisted that we make that video, I wasn't thinking about you guys in here," Lennon said.

"I'm aware, Lennon."

His face fell. "You are?"

She gestured at the computers. "It seemed voice-activated, right? Hopefully it's not programmed only for Ethan's voice." She leaned a little closer. "Cameras two and seven." They appeared onscreen. She called up the rest of them, and then glanced at Lennon. "You were sort of thinking of us. It's true that they needed reassurance out there that you were okay."

"Yeah, but I could have just said I was fine. I should have said I'd be fine no matter what. I shouldn't have promised I'd make it there in time."

She paused, checking the cameras. "No, probably not."

"I'm sorry."

She reached for his hand, giving it a squeeze. "It's okay, Lennon. I admire your sense of self-preservation, honestly. You're damn good at getting what you want."

"Thank you?"

"It was meant to be a compliment."

He leaned one shoulder against the wall, watching the screen with cameras three and four. "Do you think we could find a way to communicate, once I'm out there?"

"I hope so." She edged closer to him. "I'll try, okay? I don't know what things are going to be like in the south after all this, but since Lopez is gone . . ." A lump formed in her throat. She hadn't fully processed that. She couldn't picture the south without Lopez.

"I just don't want today to be the last time I talk to you," Lennon said quietly.

She smiled. "Hopefully it won't be. But I can't make any promises."

"I know." He looked from the screen to her, and their eyes met. There was an intensity to his gaze that made her stomach flip. She wanted to tell him that she was more upset than she was letting on about the (strong) possibility that she'd never see him again once he disappeared through that gate. She wanted to tell him that she'd been working out reasons he should stay, and just didn't have the courage to say them.

His hand brushed against hers, and she caught it and laced their fingers together. He took a step closer to her.

She should have been watching the cameras. Or listening for footsteps. Instead, all she could focus on was the little lift on either side of his lips.

It was too hard to resist touching him. She let go of his hand and brushed her fingers across his jaw, lightly tracing the hint of stubble there. He took in a sharp breath, like he didn't mind.

She felt his hand on her waist. Her eyes went back to his lips. She couldn't help it.

His palms pressed to her back, warm and strong, as he pulled her closer to him. He leaned toward her, until their foreheads were almost touching.

"I can make a promise," he said softly.

"What's that?"

"I promise that I'm going to think about you every day after I get out of here."

She still had her fingers on his jaw, and he caught her hand in his, tucking it into his chest. It took a moment for her to speak, and when she did, the words shook, just slightly. "I'll think about you every day too."

His forehead brushed against hers as he held her a little tighter. "What do you do on dates here? What would we have done, if I'd had the chance to ask you out?"

She laughed softly. "I don't think I've ever been out on an official date. We all already know each other here, so we just . . . hang out."

"That's boring. I would take you on a real date."

"What do you usually do on a real date?"

He considered for a moment. "Back home, I'd probably find something interesting for us to do, like go to a local festival or show or something. Because I'd want to impress you."

"I'm already impressed," she said quietly.

He smiled, tilting his head down closer to hers. "Here, I don't know. A picnic, maybe. Or I'd ask you to take me to your favorite spot in the south, since you know the area better."

"The rooftop of a building a few streets down from mine," she said immediately.

"Yeah?"

"Yeah. It's a medical research building, so no one ever goes up there at night. It's quiet, and you can see practically the whole city."

"Sounds perfect."

He leaned in closer, until she could feel his breath against her lips. She squeezed the hand he still had tucked against his chest.

His head snapped to the screen suddenly, breaking the spell. "Did you see that? There's someone coming out of that building."

LENNON

LENNON WATCHED AS two men ran out the back door of a building on camera four.

"Do you recognize them?" he asked.

Maisie grimaced. "Yes."

He glanced at her. Her cheeks were a little pink, and he cursed himself for stopping before he'd kissed her. He should have ignored the movement on the screen.

He wanted to ignore everything. Forget the whole plan and kiss her until it was too late to go to the gate.

Quick footsteps sounded in the hallway suddenly, and they both froze. Maisie put a hand on her gun.

Ethan appeared at the door. "Hey, sorry—"

"They're already inside," Maisie said in a rush, cutting him off. She pointed at the screen. "Declan's men."

Ethan bolted across the room, frantically glancing between screens. "How? How did they get in? How did they—" He stopped abruptly, pulling his phone from his pocket. He pressed it to his ear, and then turned and took off running. "Come on!" he yelled over his shoulder.

Lennon followed behind Maisie as they raced out of the building and down the street. Ethan lowered his phone from his ear, cursing. He pressed a button and held it up again.

The compound loomed to their right, and Ethan led them across the street. They came to a stop in front of a tall metal-and-wood gate at the front of the compound.

"No one is answering!" Ethan lowered his phone again, and then typed frantically on the keypad. The gate slid open. "The one time I actually want them to talk to me! The *one* time!" He returned his attention to his phone, fingers flying at impressive speed. "I'm just mass-texting these jerks until someone realizes I'm trying to save their lives here."

They ran through the gate as Lennon was still processing Ethan calling his family *these jerks*.

Lennon glanced around as they headed down a street. The compound was made up of homes, almost certainly pre-zone. They were large two-story structures with garages and huge lawns, with wide streets built back when everyone drove a gas-powered car.

There were spots where he could tell the old homes had been torn down to make way for something new post-zone. He could see the rooftop of a large warehouse not far away, and it looked like a large swath of homes had been cleared to make way for a dirt parking lot, where several old cars sat.

Ethan skidded to a stop suddenly. He was out of breath, clearly not used to running. "You two need to go." He pointed toward the rear of the compound. "Straight back. Just climb the wall once you get back there; it's not hard."

"Are you sure?" Maisie asked. "We—"

An explosion rocked the earth, making them all jump. Lennon instinctively reached for Maisie's hand, but she was already pulling out her gun. Smoke rose from a building a street over. He could hear yelling nearby.

"Yes, *go*," Ethan said. "It's too late for you to help. Just get him out of here."

Maisie took a step back with a nod. Lennon pulled out his gun.

"Don't—" Ethan winced. "Try not to shoot anyone, okay? Or shoot them in the leg or something."

"Of course," Lennon said.

Another explosion. Ethan whirled around, and then took off. "Straight back!" he yelled, pointing.

"Thank you!" Lennon yelled after him. "For everything."

"Don't thank me yet, my dad might still kill you!" he called over his shoulder.

"Damn, he could have just said 'You're welcome.'"

"Come on. We're getting you to that gate," Maisie said.

Another explosion, this one on the other side of the compound. Lennon's chest squeezed, and not just because of the imminent danger.

He was leaving Maisie in this. He was about to waltz through that gate back to his life, and he'd have no idea what was going on inside the walls. She was headed straight back into battle. He was headed to a nice room at CDC quarantine.

"Lennon," Maisie said, clearly not for the first time. She was several steps in front of him.

"Sorry." He broke into a run.

They turned a corner, and Maisie came to a sudden stop.

Lennon bumped into her, putting a hand on her waist to keep from toppling them both. She pushed him back, so they were partially hidden behind a tree.

"I think that's . . ." She trailed off, nodding at something ahead.

It was Ethan, standing next to an older man almost as tall as him. Lennon recognized the man's angular, bearded face from photographs. Jonathan Spencer.

"It is," Lennon whispered.

Jonathan said something to Ethan, and then roughly grabbed him by the arm. They walked across the street, into the warehouse.

"What the *hell?*"

Lennon slowly turned at the sound of the familiar voice.

Declan stood in front of them, his gun pointed at their faces.

MAISIE

MAISIE LAUNCHED HERSELF at Declan before he could shoot Lennon. She'd seen the moment he decided, when he started to turn the gun toward him.

Given that Lennon hadn't raised his gun, he had missed it.

Declan yelled, and they both toppled to the ground.

"What the fuck? How did you—" Declan rolled away from Maisie, cutting himself off. He sprang to his feet. "How did you get here?"

"It's a long story, and we already know that the ending is basically that you're an asshole, so let's skip it."

"Dammit, Maisie, I—" He stopped himself again. He grabbed his gun from the ground.

And pointed it at Lennon.

Lennon darted away just as Declan fired, the shot ringing in her ears. Thank god he was fast.

Maisie tackled Declan again, grabbing a fistful of hair and yanking it hard.

"Ow! Maisie, I swear to god, I will shoot you, too!" He swung an arm out, knocking her away. He got to his knees.

A foot connected with his chest suddenly and he wheezed, toppling to the ground again. Lennon lowered his foot and stepped back.

Maisie scrambled to her feet.

"Drop it!" someone yelled. "Now!"

Maisie whirled around to see Jonathan Spencer and several others headed right for them. She heard running footsteps. Declan disappeared around the corner.

"Go after him!" Jonathan yelled. Two men peeled off from the group and sprinted past them.

Jonathan lifted his gun, meeting her gaze. "I said drop it!" The men behind him also had their guns pointed at them. She took a quick glance around for Ethan, but she didn't see him.

Maisie slowly knelt down, dropping her gun. Lennon did the same. "Jonathan—"

"Shut up," Jonathan snapped. He lowered his gun and turned to walk back toward the warehouse. "Bring them!" he yelled over his shoulder.

Jonathan's men scooped up their weapons, then grabbed Maisie and Lennon by the arms and hauled them to the warehouse. Maisie glanced over her shoulder at Lennon. They only had about thirty minutes left to get him to the gate.

There were several more men in the warehouse, and piles of boxes and other shipping supplies. It must have been used to get shipments out to the rest of the Q.

She looked up. Stairs led to a walkway on the second

level, and Ethan stood against the railing, his eyes wide as he watched Maisie and Lennon being marched in.

"Boss, I recognize them from the video," the man holding Maisie's arm said. He let it go, stepping back to point his gun at her. "Maisie Rojas." He jerked his gun at Lennon. "Lennon Pierce."

Jonathan turned, his gaze skipping between them. He paused for a moment.

"Kill her. We'll keep him."

"No, wait, I just want to talk—" Maisie started, but Jonathan had already turned around again. The men around them were lifting their guns.

"Actually, I think you should keep them alive," Ethan said in a rush, flying down the stairs. "It would be better if—"

"Ethan, shut up and go home."

"Dad, I—"

Jonathan grabbed his son roughly by the collar. Ethan's words cut off suddenly, only a squeak coming out as the fabric tightened around his neck.

Jonathan released him, and Ethan let out a breath, taking several quick steps back. He cast an apologetic look at Maisie.

She felt Lennon's shoulder brush against hers. The world seemed to tilt slightly as her brain refused to acknowledge that she was about to die. Lennon was saying something to the men, but all she could hear was the buzzing in her ears.

She wished she'd radioed Hadley one more time. She wished she'd told Beto that she thought Lopez was totally wrong to cut them off from the world. Maybe he would think of it on his own.

She was surprised to discover that she was actually really disappointed she wasn't going to get to lead the south. That possibility hadn't ever seemed real, but now that she was facing down a gun, she had to admit that she'd been excited about it.

And she would have been good at it. Declan and her dad caused chaos and called it leadership. She could have been different. Better.

A giant crash sounded from above their heads. The men all flinched at once, whirling around to find the source.

Something tumbled from the sky. She didn't care what it was. She took off, Lennon close behind.

She heard yelling from behind her, and then gunfire, but she didn't turn.

They ran for the door. The sun was rising high in the sky, casting a soft glow through the windows near the roof of the warehouse.

"Declan," Lennon panted suddenly.

She glanced over her shoulder. Declan and three of his men were in the warehouse. Ethan had his gun out, but he was rooted in one spot, wide-eyed.

She didn't care anymore. Let them all kill each other. She was just going to get Lennon to the gate and get the shipment south. She'd deal with whoever was still alive after.

They hit the door. She pressed both hands to it.

Tick-tick-tick-tick.

She stopped. She knew that warning *tick*.

She turned to find the source of the ticking.

"Is that—"

She didn't hear the rest of Lennon's words. She raced for

the bomb Declan had just thrown at Ethan's feet. He looked down at it.

"Ethan, run!" she yelled.

His head snapped up, her panic reflected in his eyes. He stumbled back, tripping over a body on the ground behind him. His butt hit the floor.

Tick-tickticktick.

She needed to run the other way. She needed to not be running straight toward a bomb that was about to explode, but here she was, like an idiot.

She grabbed the bomb and launched it at the window. The glass shattered.

The bomb exploded.

The Spencer guys all shrank back at once. Jonathan, standing next to a terrified Ethan, gaped at her.

Maisie sprinted to Lennon, who had a look on his face that was somewhere between bewilderment and fear.

Someone grabbed her shirt suddenly, pulling her away. She yelped as they dragged her away from the door.

Lennon lunged at them, and out of the corner of her eye, she saw her attacker raise a gun.

"No," Jonathan said. "Wait a minute." He strode closer to them, his expression full of suspicion. "How do you know my son?"

LENNON

LENNON TRIED TO grab Maisie's hand, but one of Jonathan's men grabbed him, holding him by the arm.

Ethan stood several yards behind his dad. He looked like he might puke.

"I don't," Maisie said.

"You called him *Ethan.*"

"*You* called him Ethan," she retorted. Lennon was impressed by how smoothly she was lying. "'Ethan, shut up and go home,'" she said, lowering her voice in an impression of him.

Jonathan regarded her suspiciously. "Why did you just do that?"

"What? Save his life? You're welcome, by the way."

"Thank you!" Ethan called.

Jonathan closed his eyes briefly, his jaw twitching like he was trying to control his temper.

"I didn't save just his life. I probably saved yours, too, and all these other dudes." She gestured at the men around them.

"We're not with Declan. I'm not trying to blow anyone up. I tried to get here earlier to stop this, but I didn't make it. I'm sorry. It's been a really busy few days."

Lennon almost laughed. That was an understatement.

Jonathan's confusion intensified.

"But, listen, I need for you to let us go, because we have to get to the gate in . . ." Maisie trailed off as she checked her watch. "Jesus. Less than fifteen minutes."

"No," Jonathan said.

"No?" Lennon repeated.

"No." He pointed at Maisie. "I'll let you go, as a thank-you for that stupid stunt you just pulled. The future president's son stays with me, however."

"Why?" she asked.

"Because I want him." He shrugged, like *obviously*. Lennon met Ethan's eyes briefly. He gave Ethan a sympathetic look, because while this might have been a real shit situation, the guy had a real shit father.

"He's no good to anyone on this side of the wall."

"Are you kidding? He's *gold*. No one will touch the Q while he's in here. And all I have to do is lightly threaten to do terrible things to him on occasion and I can get whatever I want."

"They don't negotiate with terrorists on the other side of the wall."

Jonathan waved his hand. "They just say that. I'm sure we'll be able to work something out."

Ethan was staring at Lennon in a weirdly intense way, and Lennon raised his eyebrows, silently asking what was going on. Ethan just barely nodded his head down, to where he was holding something in his hand.

It was one of Ivy's smoke bombs.

Lennon saw Ethan's thumb move.

He drove his elbow back into his attacker's stomach, as hard as he could.

Smoke filled the room.

MAISIE

THROUGH THE SMOKE, Maisie saw the outline of Lennon as he ran for her. She held out her hand, grabbing his and breaking into a sprint.

Gunfire echoed around her. She heard a man yell out in pain.

Jonathan Spencer was shooting despite his own men being in the line of fire.

She looked over her shoulder, but she couldn't see Ethan. She hoped he was okay. She hoped his father hadn't seen him throw that smoke bomb.

Light streamed across her face as they bolted outside. She let go of Lennon's hand as they picked up the pace.

"That way!" She pointed right, and they ducked around a building and onto another street.

Footsteps pounded the pavement behind her.

"Stop them! Someone stop them!" a voice yelled.

She pushed forward, flying down the street. They turned a corner. The back of the compound loomed ahead of them, a stone wall about fifteen feet high. They just had to manage to get over it and they'd be in the clear to the gate.

"Go!" she panted to Lennon. "Just run as fast as you can." She knew he was going slower for her.

"No!"

Someone fired a gun, and they both tensed. She ran as fast as her legs could take her.

"Dammit, Lennon," she wheezed. She zigzagged as she heard more gunfire, trying to make herself a difficult target. Lennon did the same.

They were at the wall. She skidded to a stop and grabbed the stone, ignoring the scream of pain from her left hand.

One, two, three steps and she was up. A bullet whizzed by her ear.

She heard the sound of Lennon hitting the other side.

She jumped.

Her feet hit the ground.

On the other side, someone cursed.

They'd made it.

"Jesus." Lennon took several quick steps away from the wall, breathing heavily. "What time is it?"

She checked her watch, letting out a sigh. "We made it with eight minutes to spare."

"Jesus," he said again, and then blew out a breath.

She looked past him. They were only a few yards from the gate. It was high—as high as the wall—and solid steel. Lights and cameras were mounted on top of it.

"Well," she said, her breathing beginning to slow. "I guess this is it."

He pushed a hand through his hair, and she watched with amusement as it fell awkwardly, one piece sticking up.

"What?" he asked.

"You have the most ridiculous hair, you know that?"

"I do. It's part of my charm."

She couldn't argue with that.

His smile faltered a little, and he cleared his throat. "Thank you. For getting me here. And just . . . for everything."

"Sure," she said quietly.

"Know that the only reason I'm not asking for you to come with me again is because I understand now how stupid it was to think you ever would," he said. His hand brushed hers, and she let her fingers slide between his. "Not because I don't desperately want you to."

She smiled. "I appreciate that." She squeezed his hand. "I don't want to leave the Q, but I do want to go with you, if you want to know the truth."

He nodded, a small smile crossing his face. "I . . ." He trailed off, and didn't finish whatever he was going to say.

She slipped her hand out of his and nodded at the gate. "You should go."

He didn't move for a moment, but then took a small step back, turning toward the gate.

Then he jumped back, grabbed her around the waist, and kissed her.

She looped her arms around his neck, letting the fingers of her good hand tangle in his hair. He pulled her closer, until her body was pressed to his.

She'd almost wanted him *not* to kiss her, because she didn't want to know how great it would be. It almost seemed better to just wonder, instead of knowing for sure exactly what she'd be missing when he was gone.

Now she knew. She knew the feel of his lips against hers, the warmth of his hand pressed against her back, the way he kissed her like it was the only thing in the world he'd ever wanted to do.

She wasn't sorry that she knew, but she was going to miss him so much more now. She was going to miss everything that could have been.

When he pulled away, she stepped back, because she might start kissing him again if she stayed too close.

"Go," she said.

"I . . ." He looked over his shoulder.

"Seriously, go," she said with a laugh. "You're making me nervous."

His lips curved into a sad half-smile. He nodded, and took a step back.

"Bye, Maisie."

He turned and walked to the gate.

LENNON

THE GATE OPENED as Lennon approached it. It slid open slowly, and his heart pounded as it did.

The first thing he saw was the man in the hazmat suit.

Behind him was the secondary gate, the chain-link fence in front of the Q gate.

Beyond that was wide-open space, and then a sea of reporters. Lights flashed furiously.

Farther back, a crowd of spectators were gathered behind yet another fence. They held signs of support. A giant countdown clock had been set up, like this was some kind of sporting event. He looked away, uncomfortable.

The man in the hazmat suit approached him with a swab. "Open your mouth," he ordered. Lennon did.

He swabbed his cheek, and then turned and walked to a cart with an open testing kit in it.

Lennon glanced over his shoulder. Maisie stood only a few paces back, looking out at the flashing lights.

"Mr. Pierce," the man in the hazmat suit said. Lennon

returned his attention to him. "Your results will just take a minute. In the meantime, let me explain what's going to happen."

Lennon nodded numbly.

"If you're negative for the virus, you will be getting into that SUV over there." The man pointed to the left of the reporters, where a black SUV waited.

Lennon squinted at the familiar figures. "Are those my parents?"

"Yes. Mr. Pierce, focus. If you don't do as I say, those men over there may shoot you."

Right. He snapped his attention back to the man.

"I have a hazmat suit for you. You cannot cross the fence until you put it on, do you understand me?"

Lennon nodded.

"You'll put on the hazmat suit, and once it's on, you may step foot outside the Q. Not before that. You got it?"

"I got it."

"The CDC has specified that we are not to open that fence if it's past eight a.m., *andddd . . .*" He peered at the screen on his kit, and then smiled at Lennon. "Looks like you're going to make it with four minutes to spare, Mr. Pierce. Negative."

Lennon blinked at him. He probably should have felt relieved. He didn't, really.

The man put the suit in his arms. Maisie still stood in the distance behind him. She lifted a hand in a hesitant wave.

The man began rolling his cart away. Lennon took a step toward the fence.

"Hazmat suit on before you cross!" the man yelled.

"I . . . I know." He turned. "Can I say something first? To the cameras?"

The man made an amused noise. "I'm sure they'd love that. As long as you don't cross the fence line without the suit on, you're fine."

Lennon looked back again at Maisie. She stood right where the gate had opened, watching him.

"He's gold. *No one will touch the Q while he's in here."* Jonathan Spencer's words echoed in his head. He was an asshole, but he wasn't wrong.

He approached the fence, still holding the hazmat suit. He put it down on the ground.

"Lennon, are you okay?"

"Lennon, what took so long? Why—"

"Lennon, can you tell us about your time—"

The reporters shouted questions. They stretched microphones on long poles over his head.

He turned to find his parents. They were behind the wall of soldiers, but he could see them both, holding hands, peering anxiously in his direction.

The cameras started flashing wildly, and he looked over his shoulder. Maisie had taken a couple of steps inside, closer to him. The man in the hazmat suit said something to her, pointing to the fence. She nodded.

He turned back to the reporters. They were still shouting questions. He took a breath.

"I—" He stopped. Everyone had gone immediately silent.

Thank you all so much for support! Everyone was so kind to me inside the Q, and I can't wait to tell you all about what it was like inside. I met the most wonderful people. In fact, there's one right there. Thank you so much to Maisie Rojas for making sure I got here in time!

The speech was right there. That's what he should say. He should say it, and smile, and put on the hazmat suit. They'd cheer, and clap for Maisie, and there'd be a picture of her at the top of every news site in an hour. That would go over very well with people, because she was pretty, and they'd like that nice, pretty picture of the Q.

His parents would be proud, and his sisters would tease him about how cheesy he'd been, but really, they'd be proud too. His dad's campaign—or "transition team" now—would be delighted. Cal would have him on every news show as soon as his quarantine period was over. Before then, actually. He'd do some virtual interviews as soon as possible.

Life would be hectic, but then his dad would be president in January, he'd go back to Yale next fall, and eventually people would stop asking about it so much. It would be that story he told at parties, about those wild three days he spent in the Q.

It was easy, that choice.

It was also wrong.

"When I was dropped in the Q, the only thing I wanted was to get out," he called. The reporters leaned forward. The spectators had gone still, lowering their signs.

"I wanted out, even though I knew that no one gets out. No one ever has. Until now, I guess."

Everyone cheered, misunderstanding.

"I'm allowed to leave. He just said my test is negative." He pointed at the man in the hazmat suit, who waved as the crowd cheered again.

The countdown clock showed less than two minutes.

Below it, his parents were both smiling.

"I thought that it was my responsibility to get out, and to

tell all of you what it's like inside. That it isn't what you think. That it isn't some scary hellhole full of criminals. And that's true. It's not." He paused. "But maybe that's not my responsibility here."

He glanced over his shoulder at Maisie. She was watching him, a tiny smile on her face.

She didn't look surprised.

A grin spread across his face as he turned back to the crowd. "No one leaves the Q, right? Those are the rules."

The crowd didn't cheer this time. The smiles fell from his parents' faces. His mom shook her head. He couldn't hear her, but her lips formed the words *Lennon, no.*

He laughed. He'd heard those words so many times, from both of his parents.

"For years, no one has left the Q. I'm not special. I'm just a guy who got here a little late. But I'm here now, and the rules apply to me, too. So, I'm staying."

Confused murmurs went through the crowd.

"Lennon, no!" He could actually hear his mom this time. He wished Caroline and Stella were here, so he could see their faces when he did this.

But he was pretty certain they'd be proud.

He took a step back from the fence. He pointed to the countdown clock, which now showed: 00:00:00. He lifted his arms in a shrug.

"Sorry," he said, smiling as cameras began flashing again. "Time's up."

He waved at his parents, who were gaping at him. "Congrats on winning the election, Dad! If you need me, I'll be in here!"

Laughter rippled through the crowd. A few people started cheering.

He turned. Maisie was grinning now. He ran to her.

"Gate closing!" someone yelled.

The cheers grew louder. Lennon grabbed Maisie around the waist, and they took a few quick steps backward together. The gate banged closed.

"Seriously?" she said, her eyes sparkling with amusement. "After I worked so hard to get you here on time?"

"Yeahhh." He put a hand on her cheek. "Sorry about that."

She rose up on her toes, pressing her lips to his. "I think I can forgive you."

He smiled, kissing her again.

"I do have bad news, though," she said.

"What's that?"

"Now we have to go all the way back down south."

WEEKLY UPDATE WITH MAISIE ROJAS

HEY THERE, FOLKS, Maisie Rojas here with your weekly Q update.

It's been a hell of a few weeks, but I'm pleased to report that things are finally running as usual over at the hospital. If you've been putting off your scans, please make sure to head on over there soon. They're ready for you.

In other news, I am supposed to tell you to stop shooting down drones from the US. They are not amused by it. To quote this dude I talked to yesterday, "Those cost more than your house!" He has never seen my house, so I guess he's just assuming.

On the other hand, I don't actually care, and the drones are sort of creepy, so do whatever. Just try to shoot them in areas where the debris won't hurt anyone.

Some good news—we finally got the food shipment from the north, so everyone who has been asking me about soda and those weird sour candies can stop bugging me now. We're also working on a deal with the US to get food dropped directly into the south, so I will keep you all updated on that.

For all you kids, we're starting a video exchange program with kids in the US. Far less creepy than drones. Sign up with our newest addition to the Q, Lennon Pierce.

And we're trying another joint broadcast with the US tomorrow, so get ready for that. This one will feature Hadley Lopez, joined by Lennon. Should be very exciting.

Lennon: Is *exciting* the word? What are we even talking about tomorrow?

Maisie: I don't know, it's your broadcast!

Lennon: I should probably figure that out, huh?

Maisie: Either figure it out or Hadley will start telling some stories that no one should hear, on either side of the wall.

Lennon: On it.

Well, that's it for me. Tune in tomorrow to find out if Lennon and Hadley know what they're doing.

Stay safe and healthy out there, Q. Until next week, Maisie Rojas, signing off.

ACKNOWLEDGMENTS

The road to *The Q* was a long, weird one, complicated by a real-life global pandemic that I thought would surely doom this book. Thank you to:

Emmanuelle Morgen, who believed in *The Q* when I didn't and wouldn't let me give up, even though I kept trying.

My editor, Emily Easton, and Claire Nist, for your excellent insight, which made this book so much better. I especially appreciate how you both wanted me to add more romance. Happy to oblige.

The whole team at Penguin Random House for working to get this book into the hands of readers.

My sister, Laura, and Emma and Daniel, who had to listen to me complain about my pandemic book during a global pandemic. You're all very patient.

My parents, for the support during a strange couple of years and not getting mad when I moved across the country (again).

And a huge thank-you to all the readers who have supported me through the years and who keep picking up my books. You're the best.